HOT WORDS

"Don't delude yourself into thinking that your being a Hunter will affect me the same way it seems to affect everyone else in Diablo."

Stiffening noticeably, Quince responded, "What's that supposed to mean?"

"It means I didn't appreciate your little act a few days ago."

Quince's light eyes grew cold. "What act was that?"

"Your pretense of being a saddle bum when we met."

"You made that assumption on your own."

"You didn't attempt to correct my assumption."

"I didn't feel the need."

"No, instead you waited for the opportunity to embarrass me."

"You're wrong."

"No, I'm not."

"Believe me, *ma'am*, you are. I wouldn't waste my time."

Her fair complexion coloring the exact shade of her hair, Glory snapped, "Unfortunately, I know better. But since that's your attitude, we have nothing else to discuss. I won't *waste your time* any longer."

RENEGADE MOON

ELAINE BARBIERI

LEISURE BOOKS NEW YORK CITY

A LEISURE BOOK®

July 2003

Published by

Dorchester Publishing Co., Inc.
276 Fifth Avenue
New York, NY 10001

ISBN 0-8439-5178-8

Visit us on the web at www.dorchesterpub.com.

To Michael Barbieri, Jr.,
the newest member of the Barbieri clan.
Much love to you, my little darling.

RENEGADE
MOON

Prologue

Arizona Territory, 1880

Heavy gunfire echoed against the sundrenched, mountainous slope, and bullets struck the earth. Quincy Hunter turned sharply at the sound of a gasp, in time to see Private Jeremy Sloan clutch his chest as he slipped slowly to the ground.

The young private's groans deepened Quince's silent resolution as he assessed the scene surrounding him. Too many more troopers would be wounded in a situation that appeared increasingly hopeless. His years of scouting for the army had taught him a hard truth that now rang foremost in his mind. The difficult Arizona Territory was home to the Apaches, affording them a distinct advantage in this particular location.

Dodging a new hail of bullets, Quince moved to

the side of the agitated commanding officer and grated, "Geronimo has us where he wants us, Major."

"We outnumber his band five to one. We're going to get him this time."

"He's too heavily entrenched up there behind those rocks. Your men are firing at an enemy they can't see while he's whittling down the patrol one by one."

"We've run him to ground. We just have to wait him out."

"I don't think so." Quince had scouted for Major Jonah Tremain for several months. A graduate of West Point and from a family that had distinguished itself in the service of its country, the major was young and serious, an officer who handled all aspects of his position conscientiously. Tremain's men liked him. Quince liked him. Close in age, Tremain and he had become friends.

Aware that Tremain relied on his experience with the Apaches, Quince pressed, "Geronimo has avoided capture for years. He knew we were right behind him. He wouldn't have led us here if he didn't have a way out."

"What are you saying?"

"I think it's a trap."

Dark brows furrowed, Tremain was about to respond when a mumbling among the troopers turned him toward the rocky slope above them.

Tremain squinted at the sun-bleached terrain. He scanned it silently, then cursed and turned to the soldier beside him. "They've stopped firing, Lieutenant. Send Sergeant Wiggins up there with a few men to see if he can find out what's going on."

Tremain's frown darkened when the men returned to make their report. "They're gone, damn it!" Tremain said. "Geronimo only stopped to regroup. He's going to get away."

Not waiting for Quince's reply, Tremain turned toward the officer awaiting his directive and ordered, "Assign some men to the wounded, then have the rest mount up. We're going after them."

"I'll take a look around first, just to be sure," Quince interjected, a warning knotting in his gut.

"We don't have time. If Geronimo gets too far ahead of us on this terrain, we'll lose him."

The warning knot in Quince's stomach twisted tighter as the troop mounted. He looked up, his strong features fixed as the major asked, "What's the matter? Aren't you coming with us?"

"I've got a bad feeling about this, Major."

Hesitating momentarily, the major shook his head. "I can't depend on feelings, and I can't chance letting Geronimo get away."

Quince watched as the major signaled his men forward, then turned abruptly toward his horse. He was in the saddle, his mount struggling up the rocky slope behind them, his gaze intent on the major's lead figure as the patrol's laboring horses reached the crest. Startled when a single shot initiated a frenzied barrage on the troop, he saw the men scatter for cover as the major fell motionless to the ground.

Digging his heels into his mount's sides, Quince pressed his horse upward. He dismounted on the run as he neared the crest of the rise, moving from boulder to boulder until he was afforded a clear view of the scene. Squinting in the glare of the unrelenting sun, he saw gunfire still coming from the Apaches' concealed positions. A few wounded soldiers had dragged themselves behind the protection of the rocks, while the major lay unmoving only a short distance from cover. Staring intently, Quince saw the major's chest rising and falling in shallow breaths.

He was alive.

His decision immediate, Quince slid toward the soldiers firing from behind a nearby boulder and grated, "I'm going out to get the major. Keep firing. Don't let those Apaches lift their heads from behind those rocks."

Cautiously making his way, Quince paused behind a rock only a few yards from the unconscious major. He glanced at the soldiers behind him, nodded, then took a deep breath and scrambled out into the open. With bullets picking at the ground around him, he dragged the major backward to safety with a supreme effort that left him gasping.

Still breathing heavily as Sergeant Pace hurried over to tend to the major's wounds, he rasped down into his friend's motionless face, "Damn it, you should've listened to me, Jonah."

"Damn it, I should've listened to you, Quince."

Standing beside the major's infirmary bed, Quince did not immediately respond. Jonah's speech was labored. He was as weak as a kitten, his eyes deeply sunken, and his naturally robust

4

color poor. His leg wound was severe, and he'd lost a dangerous amount of blood. He had barely survived the aborted attempt to capture Geronimo two days earlier—a mission that had ended when Geronimo had abruptly withdrawn his men and disappeared, leaving the troop to transport their wounded back to the fort. Jonah had barely cheated death, yet his first concern upon awakening had been for his men.

Frustration flashing across his pale face, Jonah grated, "So he got away again."

Shrugging, Quince replied, "Geronimo knows these mountains like the back of his hand. He's been eluding capture for twenty years."

"The bloodthirsty bastard."

"You'll get him next time."

"*We'll* get him next time."

"No, not *we*."

Appearing confused, Jonah replied, "What do you mean, 'not we'?"

"I only stayed around this long to say goodbye. I'm going home."

"Home . . ."

"To Texas."

"Why?"

"I've got business there."

Obviously surprised, Jonah responded, "This is sudden, isn't it?"

The letter tucked inside Quince's shirt seemed to burn his skin as he replied, "Not so sudden. It's been waiting five years."

Briefly silent, Jonah replied, "Is there any way I can change your mind?" His fleeting smile was weak. "I expected you'd be with us when we finally cleaned up these renegades."

His own smile going almost unseen behind his untended beard, Quince remembered Jonah's reaction upon their first meeting months earlier. A spit-and-polish officer, Jonah had surveyed Quince's stained buckskins, long hair, and bearded face and had actually winced at the sight of him. Intelligent and perceptive, however, Jonah had quickly changed his negative opinion of the man he now considered a friend.

Friend. Quince turned the word over. A friend was an uncommon commodity in a world where husbands turned against wives, and brothers turned against brothers.

With that thought in mind, Quince responded sincerely, "I wish I could be."

Jonah's color was turning gray. His strength was fading.

Stepping closer to the bed, Quince extended his hand and said with true remorse, "Goodbye, Jonah. Good luck. It's been a pleasure knowing you."

Quince closed the infirmary door behind him, then paused, reviewing in his mind the letter that had been waiting for him upon his return to the fort two days earlier. Months old, it had followed his travels and had finally found him.

There had been no question what he would do after he read the letter. It was from Abby. She needed him, and he was going home.

Chapter One

The mid-morning sun burned hotly into his back as Quince guided his mount carefully along the narrow trail. He surveyed the familiar terrain with bittersweet feelings. The last of the season's bluebonnets still tinted the ground with a haze of color, but the bright green of spring had all but faded. The knowledge that summer would soon bleach the landscape a paler hue as long, dry days settled in brought memories of the many times he had used this particular shortcut on his way home while growing up. He knew the advantage as well as the danger in taking it. It hadn't mattered to him when he was younger that he was crossing Old Man Potter's land, or that the crabby old coot

7

would be riled if he knew. The truth was, it didn't matter to him now, either.

The thought flashed across his mind that he hadn't changed much, but Quince revised it instantly. He *had* changed. At three inches over the mark of six feet, he had always been tall, but five years on the Arizona frontier had added a formidable breadth of muscle and sinew to his formerly lanky frame. Still wearing buckskins, fully bearded, with his dark hair having gone uncut longer than it should, he bore little resemblance to the youthful, clean-shaven wrangler he had once been. Yet the greatest change in him wasn't physical. It was reflected in startling green eyes that were now coldly assessing, in an intimidating demeanor that discouraged all challengers, and in a silent, occasionally dangerous resolve that was conveyed without words. Having had no recourse but to leave the family ranch five years earlier, he had ridden away an angry, frustrated young man. He was returning now, mature, ready to face all problems squarely, and determined that no one would ever drive him away again.

Quince's jaw hardened.

No one.

Abby's letter flashed to mind again. He had read it many times during the endless journey home. He had felt the deep emotion and panic in her words when she had written:

Dear Quince,
   I haven't received a letter from you in a long time, but I know you think about me like

8

I always think about you. I know you wouldn't have left the Half-Moon if you didn't have to, and I know you wish you could be here right now. In my last letter I said things had settled down and were going all right, but everything's changed now.

Papa's coming home.

I don't know what to do, Quince. Brent still won't talk to me about what really happened that day, and Matt and Brent did nothing but argue about Papa the last time Matt came home. All I know is that Brent's determined to meet Papa at the prison and bring him here.

I'm not sure what Matt will do when he finds out.

I'm not sure what I should do.

I need you here, Quince. Please come home.

Your loving sister,
Abby

Matt and Brent arguing.

Nothing had changed there.

Quince frowned. For as long as he could remember, he had been at odds with Brent, too. Only a year older than he, Brent had taken the role of elder more seriously than Quince felt he had any right to. Conservative and serious, Brent had disapproved of him, of his humor and spirit of adventure, and of his willingness to take risks to achieve his goals. Brent had been unable to comprehend the special bond that existed between their mother and her second son—a son whose rough, masculine features and strong-willed personality so resembled the father she had adored.

Sadness stirred when he thought of Elizabeth Quincy Hunter—beautiful, gentle, soft-spoken, loving, and so undeserving of her violent, premature, and meaningless death.

A familiar resentment brought back thoughts of Quince's younger brother, Matt. Always wild and rebellious, Matt had been a source of constant grief to Beth Hunter. Yet Quince knew that same quality in Matt had somehow earned him a unique place in their mother's heart—making even more painful Quince's conviction that Beth Hunter might still have been alive if not for her youngest son.

The image of a slight, dark-haired sprite appeared suddenly before Quince's mind, ejecting all negative thoughts. Her skin tanned a golden hue and her green eyes dancing, Abby had always made him smile. Eleven years younger than he and determined not to let him leave her behind, she had trailed at his heels from the time she took her first step. She had imitated his every move and had been on her way to becoming as skillful a wrangler as any man. He had been proud of her. Left motherless at the age of eight, Abby had turned to him when the resulting turmoil at the ranch became too hard. Leaving her behind had been the hardest thing he had ever done.

As for Pa—

His thoughts were interrupted by a screeching whinny in the distance, and Quince was suddenly alert. The whinnying grew louder, more strained as Quince nudged his mount to a faster pace along the trail. He arrived at a familiar section of trail bordered by thick brush and heard a soft cursing join the frantic whinnies. Proceeding cautiously, he nudged his mount into an area where a stream fed into a depression in the terrain, creating a swampy expanse that was both unexpected and treacherous. Almost thirty feet in circumference, the quicksand had grown larger during his five-year absence. Caught in the middle of the sucking mud, fighting frantically to escape its relentless downward tow, was a panicked mare with a furious young woman mounted on its back.

Annoyed by the rider's lack of control over the frenzied animal, Quince ordered abruptly, "Hold that mare still, damn it! All that thrashing about is only making matters worse."

Her head jerking up toward him, the rider revealed a small-featured face flushed with frustration and angry dark eyes that burned as she spat back, "Don't you curse at me!"

"Use your head, then." Quince's reply was curt. "The more that animal struggles, the faster it's going to sink."

"You're not telling me anything I don't know!" Fiery tendrils of hair protruded from underneath the brim of her hat, as she glared at him. "Well, are you going to get us out of here or not?"

"I don't know." Goaded by her arrogance, Quince said coldly, "Maybe not."

The woman muttered under her breath as Quince dismounted to assess the situation more closely. The mare was still out of control. At the rate she was sinking, her legs would soon be totally engulfed.

He stated flatly, "You're going to have to calm your horse down. If you don't, there's no way I'll be able to get her out."

The young woman grew livid. "Just stop preaching and get us out of here!"

Right.

Ignoring his inclination to leave the red-haired witch exactly where he had found her, Quince reached for the rope on his saddle, then said, "Grab the line when I toss it to you. I'll pull you out first."

"No. I can do a better job of controlling the situation if I stay where I am."

Quince's jaw hardened. "You mean like you're doing now?"

"Look . . ." The young woman seethed. "I don't have time for your macho attitude."

"Look . . ." Quince retorted, "It's my way or no way. *Comprende?*"

"*Comprendo*. Now get us out of here, damn it, or I warn you, you'll be sorry!"

"Really?" Quince's gaze turned to ice. "There isn't too much you'd be able to do from underneath a few yards of mud, *ma'am*."

Allowing the witch to stew over that thought for a few seconds, Quince then ordered, "Grab the rope when I throw it to you and I'll drag you out."

"My horse—"

"Grab the rope."

"All right!"

Throwing his loop with a practiced eye, Quince grunted with satisfaction when it settled around the stiff-faced female's shoulders. He waited until she adjusted it around her waist and gripped it firmly, then said, "All right, now let yourself slip down onto the mud, lying flat on your stomach so I can pull you out."

"That isn't necessary. I can walk out if you have a rope on me."

"I said—"

"All right!"

With a quick twist, Quince secured the rope over his saddle horn, gave his mount a few swift commands, and guided the line as the woman slipped belly down onto the mud and was towed gradually nearer. Grasping her arms when she reached him, he pulled her to her feet.

The young woman turned on him, ignoring the slimy grit that plastered her riding clothes to her body, and said without a word of thanks, "My horse is still sinking."

"I don't know if I'll be able to get her out."

The woman went momentarily still, then said, "You don't mean that."

"Look at her." Sober and hard-eyed, Quince indicated the frenzied animal, which had sunk to its belly into the mud, "I can loop her around the neck and try having my horse pull her out, but—"

"No buts! Let's do it!"

Gritting his teeth, Quince looped the mare with the first throw. He clenched his jaw tighter as his horse attempted to tow the mired animal out. He lent his own weight to the effort, making no comment when the woman joined in.

The woman released the rope without a word when the mare, still whinnying frantically, was engulfed to her shoulders. She muttered, "We're not going to get Cinnamon out." Turning on him abruptly, dark eyes direct, she pressed, "Are we?"

"No."

Her voice devoid of emotion, she said, "My rifle is on the saddle."

Which was rapidly sinking out of sight.

Quince reached for his own gun. Out of the corner of his eye he saw the woman take off her muddied hat and slap it down onto the ground with disgust before she turned and walked away. She did not react when a single gunshot shattered the silence and the mare's struggles ceased. Instead, she continued walking directly toward the sun, which was rapidly rising toward its zenith.

Moving with slow deliberation, Quince retrieved his rope and secured it on his saddle. He stared for long moments at the slight figure silhouetted against the brilliant sunlight as the young woman continued trudging eastward. Narrow shoulders held painfully erect, her fiery hair blazing in the sun, she did not look back as she walked with silent resolution, ignoring him as easily as she did the mud already baking hard on her skin in the heat of the day.

She was as tough as they came.

Studying her more closely, Quince frowned. Yet for an instant he thought he had seen—

Quince mounted abruptly. Silently cursing, he

took off after her, then rode at her side for a few moments before asking, "Where are you going?"

After ignoring him briefly, the young woman replied with a touch of belligerence, "Home."

"Where's that?"

"The Diamond C ranch house."

"The Diamond C?"

She glanced up at him with disdain. "You're on Diamond C land."

"This is Old Man Potter's land."

"He's dead. It's the Diamond C now."

Quince nodded. Old Man Potter's ranch house was approximately three rough, desolate miles from where they were.

He said, "I'll take you there."

"I can walk."

Right.

He should let her do it, too.

But there was something about the little witch's determination, the set of her chin . . . and the vulnerability he had glimpsed in the almost imperceptible twitch of her cheek a moment earlier.

Ignoring her protest as well as her muddied state, he reached down, scooped her up, and set her down across the saddle in front of him.

"I said—"

"I heard you."

The silence between them deepened as Quince's arm closed securely around her waist and he nudged his mount into motion.

Things just went from bad to worse.

Sitting rigidly, intensely aware of the strong

15

chest supporting her and the brawny arm draped loosely across her waist as the stranger's mount plodded forward, Glory Townsend closed her eyes in pure despair. She snapped them open again when the image of her mare's fear-crazed eyes flashed before her. Cinnamon had been prized by her father and her since the first day they arrived at the Diamond C four years earlier. Pa and she had been stunned to see so valuable a young horse in one of the dilapidated stable stalls, almost as stunned as they had been a few months earlier when they received a letter informing them that Mr. Elijah Potter had deeded his Texas horse ranch to Pa in his will.

Mr. Elijah Potter.

It had taken Pa a few minutes to remember the name. When he did, his eyes had filled. Will and Henry Potter, Elijah's only sons, had been in her father's company during the war. Pa had told her they were good men—boys, really—who had fought valiantly for the Confederacy. He had grown close to them, and when they were both killed only minutes apart, he had suffered their deaths keenly. He had not realized, however, that the simple act of writing their father a letter when the war ended, telling of his personal, affectionate regard for the old man's sons and describing in detail their bravery in battle, would bring him such a reward.

It had taken the letter detailing his inheritance several months to trace their travels, but it couldn't have arrived at a better time. His plantation devastated by the war and the land usurped by carpetbaggers years earlier, Byron Nathaniel Townsend had piled his wife, six-year-old daughter, and their remaining belongings into a wagon and had driven west, vowing to restore to his family everything they had lost.

It hadn't happened. Instead, nine years of failure had left her father more frustrated with each passing day. Her dear mother, Evangeline Parks Townsend, had died in the interim, still believing in her husband. That belief had been passed on to Glory, and when her father and she reached the Diamond C and saw its potential, she had believed her faith would prove justified.

The story did not have the happy ending she had anticipated. Elijah Potter's ranch had been mortgaged to the hilt, and foreclosure had been imminent. The last of her father's savings had halted the process, but they had been struggling ever since.

Nor had Glory anticipated that her father would be thrown from his horse in a freak accident two years later—never to walk again.

Having assumed her father's responsibilities on the ranch, Glory had sworn to restore the Diamond C to financial stability, but that wasn't happening, either. Instead, costly mishaps had become a common occurrence over the past years. Now, in another freak accident for which she could not account, Cinnamon had bolted unexpectedly when they neared the bog that morning and had plunged deeply into the deadly mud before Glory was able to regain control—bringing a heartbreaking end to dreams of breeding the most valuable mare on the ranch.

Glory needed no one to tell her that her father's health had deteriorated badly in the past year, that he was facing his last chance to see his dream realized—or that she had failed him miserably. That fact would be only too evident to everyone on the ranch, too, when she returned covered with mud, seated across the saddle of a shabby, arrogant, itinerant wrangler who did not bother to conceal his assessment of her ineptitude.

Glory silently seethed.

She was angry at herself for not having controlled Cinnamon when the mare bolted.

She was irate that fate seemed somehow set against her.

She was incensed at being made to appear less than she was, when she knew in her heart she was as capable as any man.

But most of all, she was furious with the obnoxious, cold-eyed stranger who had had no qualms about letting her know he had done everything right—while she seemed to have done everything wrong.

Her back stiffened as the Diamond C ranch house came into view in the distance, and Glory felt a familiar determination rise. She had worked hard to convince the Diamond C wranglers that she was worthy of their confidence after her father's accident. To arrive back at the ranch now and have an egotistical saddle bum describe in mortifying detail the story of her costly mishap was a defeat and a humiliation she could not allow.

"Stop this horse," Glory ordered sharply.

The arm across her waist tensed, but the horse plodded on.

Infuriated, Glory demanded, "I said, stop this horse!"

The stranger reined his mount to a sudden halt. Turning toward him when his grip across her waist inexplicably tightened, she met his gaze and said, "Let me down. I'll walk the rest of the way."

No reaction.

She grated, "Did you hear me?"

The stranger searched her face with his penetrating, green-eyed stare, then replied unexpectedly, "Accidents happen. There's no shame in it."

Did he read minds, too?

Glory snapped, "I don't owe you any explanations for my behavior. Just do what I said!"

The stranger's gaze went frigid. "No, you don't owe me anything at all."

The fine line of Glory's lips twitched, "I could've gotten out of that quicksand any time I wanted to."

His silence spoke volumes.

"You give yourself too much credit."

"I was thinking the same thing about you."

"I said, let me dow—"

Releasing her abruptly, the stranger did not react when Glory slipped from the saddle and hit the ground with a thump. Standing up, refusing to rub her throbbing backside, she said, "I should've expected that from you."

"No, but I'd say you earned it."

A movement in the distance caught her eye, and

Glory recognized her foreman's distinctive Appaloosa starting out from behind the ranch house. Suddenly desperate to be rid of the arrogant stranger, Glory relented. "All right, I suppose I do owe you something for your help. You'll probably be in town for a few days. If you're there this weekend, I'll come in and see to it that you receive some compensation."

The silence between them grew deafening.

She knew what he was waiting for. Somehow unable to say the words, Glory turned and started toward the ranch house. She felt his gaze burning into her back but she kept walking. She refused to react when his deep voice sounded coldly behind her.

"You're welcome, *ma'am*."

Bastard.

Relieved when she heard his horse turn, when the sound of the animal's hoofbeats gradually faded, Glory realized belatedly that she hadn't even asked the stranger's name.

Chapter Two

He was tired. He was hungry. He was more than a little annoyed.

Holding his mount to a steady pace down the main street of Diablo, Texas, Quince glanced at the sun as it made its slow, downward descent in the western sky. The image of a slender, mud-covered, fiery-haired female butted into his thoughts, and his annoyance increased. He had wasted too much time helping someone who hadn't really wanted to be helped. Because he'd played Good Samaritan, he was going to lose another day before getting home.

The hotheaded female's attitude that morning rankled even in retrospect. It hadn't seemed to occur to her that she might not have made it out of that bog if not for him. He must have been crazy to think even for a moment that he had seen a spark of vulnerability in those scorching dark eyes. He should have known better. He had become familiar with that redhead's type over the years—all female on the outside, but with a heart as tough as a mule skinner's hide. He had made a mistake, and he was now paying the price. His buckskins were caked with mud, and it was too late to reach the Half-Moon before dark.

Telling himself another day would be of little consequence after an absence of five years, Quince forced his attention back to the rutted main street of the town that had been the center of his social life while growing up. It didn't surprise him that nothing seemed to have changed very much. The main thoroughfare—still appearing to be the only thoroughfare—was still deeply rutted and susceptible to cavernous puddles with the first good rain. An effort had obviously been made to combat that problem by the construction of a board crosswalk spanning the street, but the walk was presently dilapidated and all but useless.

Quince rode slowly in the lull of pedestrian traffic that preceded the arrival of nighttime revelers. He noticed the new hotel that had been built in his absence. He passed the stagecoach office on the right, noting the faded paint and wondering if Jake Howard still manned the desk with quiet authority; the blacksmith shop on the left, unconsciously seeking Bill Weatherby's sober, red face; the sheriff's office, remembering the many mornings he had gone there to find Matt in the attached jail, sleeping off a night on the town. His brow knotting, he remembered his last visit there, when it had been Pa behind those bars, but he forced that thought from his mind.

Relieved when the familiar red-and-white-striped pole of the barbershop came into view, Quince urged his mount toward the hitching post and dismounted. He paused briefly in the doorway of the small establishment, silently grateful to find it free of customers so he might briefly avoid the inevitable, inquisitive stares.

"Quincy Hunter!" Charlie Herbert, barber, dentist, undertaker, bathhouse operator, and jack-of-all-miscellaneous-trades, stepped out from the curtained back room and walked toward him. His hand extended in greeting, he said with a laugh, "That *is* you underneath all that hair and buckskin, ain't it, boy?"

Short and wiry, with a little less hair than the last time Quince had seen him, Charlie shook his hand warmly. "Where've you been, boy?" Not waiting for Quince's response, he continued, "Wherever it was, I got to say you look a little the worse for wear."

"You might say that's true, Charlie." Quince could not help smiling. Charlie had never been one to mince words, but he was honest and one of the few in town whose attitude toward Quince hadn't changed after his father was sent to prison.

Quince continued, "I figure I could use a couple of your establishment's services before I go home."

"There's truth in that, too!" Charlie laughed, guided him to the nearest barber chair, then waited for him to sit down before adding, "You ain't been home to the Half-Moon yet, then, huh?"

Charlie's smile faded. "There's been a peck of changes at the ranch in the past couple of months." His scissors were clipping away when he added after a brief hesitation, "Your pa's home, you know."

Quince's expression went cold. "I thought he would be by now."

"Brent brought him home—met him at the prison door with a horse when he was released—but it's my feeling there's no love lost between them."

"That seems about right."

"As a matter of fact, talk is they ain't getting along at all well, your pa and Brent."

"That wouldn't be anything new."

"It kind of surprised me, too, since your pa and Brent's wife seemed to hit it off pretty good."

"Brent's wife!" Quince's shocked response was spontaneous. Brent, always so sober, never having time for a serious relationship with a woman—married!

Charlie paused, scissors held high. "You didn't know he got himself a wife? Hell, I'd have thought somebody would've let you know."

Quince did not respond.

"Anyways, Crystal and Abby seem to get along all right. At least it looks that way when they come into town. That's good, I guess, even if some people in town—Reverend Crawford, for one—thought Crystal might not be the best influence on a girl as young as Abby."

Quince knew he wouldn't have to wait long for an explanation of Charlie's last statement.

"Crystal was a singer in the Lone Star, you know—the best singer that saloon ever had, I might add."

Quince fought to swallow his amazement. Brent married to a dance-hall singer?

"I'm thinking that sweet voice of hers is going to come in handy singing lullabies for the baby she's carrying."

Hell, what was next?

"I hope you ain't expecting to see Matt when you get to the ranch, because he ain't going to be there." Charlie shrugged. "I'm thinking your kid brother took a trip to England to get that champion stud horse he was always talking about so's he wouldn't have to be here when your pa came home."

"Champion stud horse?"

"Didn't know that either, huh, about Matt wanting to get into raising race horses on the ranch like his pa wanted to do? Of course, Matt don't like to hear nobody say he's anything like his pa. He's still holding a mighty big grudge against the old man for what he did."

Quince's jaw tightened.

"Now, Quince"—Charlie glanced cautiously around the empty shop, then added in a softer voice—"you ain't going to hold a grudge against your pa, too, are you? I'm thinking he was so drunk he didn't know what he was doing. I'm thinking he spent those ten years in prison regretting with all his heart that he killed your ma."

. . . *that he killed your ma.*

Quince went still as the events of that unforgettable day returned in a grisly flash:

Brent leaving him and the ranch hands in the west pasture while he returned to the house with Hank to pick up some wire.

The eerie feeling that crept down his spine when Brent didn't return.

His strange sense of dread as he rode home to find Brent.

The sight of Ma lying dead on the kitchen floor, a gunshot wound in her chest.

He remembered that Brent's voice shook with fury when he related how he and Hank had heard a shot in the distance when they approached the ranch house, how he had galloped home to find Pa still standing over Ma's body with gun in hand—so drunk that he was reeling.

He remembered the chaos that had reigned afterward, when Ma was buried while Pa sat in the jail cell, refusing to speak. The trial that ensued was a continuation of the nightmare, with Pa's ten-year jail sentence followed by the discovery that the ranch was deeply in debt because of Pa's gambling.

Certain that his way was the only way, Brent then took over control of the ranch with an iron hand, and the dissension between Brent and himself started up in earnest.

Unable to make sense of what had happened, begging her brothers to explain the unexplainable, eight-year-old Abby was confused and lost.

Matt, the cause of constant conflict between his mother and father, left the Half-Moon immediately after their mother's funeral to return only occasionally—increasing Quince's resentment at the belief that their mother might still be alive if Matt had come home when he should have instead of staying out whoring and drinking.

A family at odds, they had been joined only in their crushing grief at the loss of the mother they had loved, and by their disgust for the father who seemed unable to explain how or why he had killed her.

Quince took a heavy breath. Disagreements between Brent and him about the handling of ranch affairs grew fiercer and more frequent as time passed. They exploded into violence five years after their father was sent to prison, when Brent gave him an ultimatum and Quince realized with sudden, painful clarity that he needed to leave the Half-Moon before Brent or he did something they would forever regret.

"And he ain't had much of a welcome home from this town, either."

Snapped back to the present by Charlie's statement, Quince questioned, "What do you mean?"

"I'm saying everybody in town has been keeping their distance from your pa, except for Edmund Montgomery, who showed everybody how he did his Christian duty by welcoming him home."

His Christian duty . . .

At Quince's silence, Charlie added, "Edmund is your pa's oldest friend, after all."

Right.

Quince's sense of distaste at the mention of Edmund Montgomery was familiar. It remained as

Charlie continued, "But I ain't sure how Edmund's help has been affecting your pa. He—"

Looking up as a bearded wrangler entered the shop, Charlie gave a snort of disgust which ended their conversation abruptly.

But Quince had heard enough.

Yes, Abby was right. It was time for him to come home.

Edmund Montgomery stood up slowly behind his massive mahogany desk at the Diablo State Bank. He paused to adjust the jacket of his custom-tailored suit, aware that the expensive fabric and expert fit of the garment clearly declared his position as the town's wealthiest citizen. He was keenly aware that at the age of fifty-one, he was still a handsome man. The blond hair of his youth was only touched with gray, his skin was not leathery like that of most ranchers his age, and his carefully tended physique was still tight and muscular. He knew people envied him, and that thought pleased him more than anyone knew. Wealth and success were dominant factors in his life, yet they were secondary to the prestige which naturally followed.

Edmund smiled inwardly. Everyone knew his name. Everyone deferred to him, and he had seen to it that his establishment as deacon in Diablo's only church left no doubt as to his "high moral caliber."

Standing motionless, Edmund assessed his two tellers as they worked. He had had the tellers' cages situated where he could easily watch all daily transactions from his office. That advantage had served him well. His senior teller, Wilfred Marks, had worked for him for fifteen years. Marks had proved early on to be a timid mouse of a man who lived in fear of losing his boss's favor—the perfect employee. Then there was Gilbert Tolley, the junior teller, whom Edmund had hired three months earlier.

Edmund's pale eyes narrowed. He didn't like Tolley. Tolley was too friendly, too likable, too gracious with the bank's customers. Despite Tolley's short duration of employment, longtime patrons of the bank had begun approaching Tolley instead of him with their problems—a transference of customer confidence that Edmund would not tolerate. The Diablo State Bank was *his* bank. He held all the mortgages in the area—the power of life and death over most of the major ranches. His authority in the community was unmatched, and he would not allow it to be breached in any way.

Edmund made an abrupt decision. He would fire Tolley as soon as he found a replacement.

Pausing on his way toward the street door as the two tellers tallied up for the night, Edmund inquired, "Will you be done soon? I want to get home on time tonight. Mrs. Montgomery"—he hesitated briefly for effect—"is *unwell* today."

The two men exchanged knowing glances before Tolley replied, "It won't take us longer than twenty minutes to finish up here, sir."

Distaste rose in Edmund's throat as Marks nodded dutifully, consigning authority for his response to the junior employee. Concealing his reaction with practiced ease, Edmund answered, "I'll be back to lock up in twenty minutes, then." Looking directly at Tolley, he added, "Good work, Gilbert. You've distinguished yourself in this bank during your short term of employment. You'll go far."

A smile picked at Edmund's lips as he walked onto the street. Yes, Tolley would go far—right out the door.

That thought amusing him, Edmund turned toward the general store. He needed to stop to see if his package had arrived on the afternoon stage before he went home. His dear wife, Iona, was waiting for it.

Two steps into the general store and the storekeeper approached him eagerly, his nasal tone turning customers' heads toward them as he said, "You'll be pleased to know your package arrived this afternoon, Mr. Montgomery."

Beaming as if the arrival of the package was his personal accomplishment, the small, ferret-like fellow continued, "I put it aside for you. I got in two bottles of that perfume your missus likes, too—just in case you wanted to know."

"Oh? Did you put a bottle of the perfume aside for me, too?"

"No, sir, but I'll be glad to do that if you like."

The perfume was expensive—the price of a full day's groceries for the average family. Edmund smiled benevolently. "I'll take both of them. Iona does love that fragrance."

His packages in hand, Edmund glanced up at the sky as he stepped back out onto the street. The sun was setting. Iona would be waiting for him. She—

"What's your hurry? You going somewhere?"

Edmund turned at the sound of the familiar gravelly voice. His smile was forced as he replied in a subdued tone to the swarthy fellow who stepped out of the shadows, "This is not wise, Kane."

Kane shrugged. "I'm just passing the time of day. There's nothing wrong with that, is there?"

Lowering his voice, Edmund snapped, "This is neither the time nor the place for small talk. Just tell me—did you accomplish that job we discussed?"

"Oh, yeah . . . one more nail in the coffin."

"Meaning?"

"Meaning that little spitfire don't have that mare she was so proud of anymore. Matter of fact, she would've had to walk all the way back to the ranch house if some saddle bum hadn't showed up."

"Did either of them see you there?"

Kane sneered. "I ain't no amateur."

"All right." Nodding benignly to a passing matron, Edmund then extended his hand toward Kane as he raised his voice and said for her benefit, "Come into the bank anytime, Mr. Kane. I'll be happy to open an account for you."

Kane smiled as he shook his hand. "Sure, I just might do that."

Relieved to have left Kane behind him, Edmund turned back toward the bank, silently cursing. It was all a game to that damned fool. He was going to have to see to it personally that Kane would be sorry if he pulled that stunt again.

Still seething, Edmund was at the bank's door when he spotted a tall figure emerging from the barbershop. He stepped into the shadows of the doorway as the fellow crossed the sidestreet and continued walking toward the far end of town. The fellow was bigger, broader, and more muscular, but the set of his shoulders, his powerful stride—

The man turned briefly in his direction, and Edmund glimpsed startlingly light eyes visible under the brim of a hat worn low on his forehead.

There was no mistaking him.

Quince Hunter had come home.

Edmund cursed under his breath. Quince had never liked him, even as a boy. He recalled thinking at one time that if Beth Quincy had married him instead of Jack Hunter, Quince might have been *his* son—but he had immediately cancelled that thought. His sons would not have been anything like Quince or any of Jack Hunter's other sons, because he would not have allowed it.

He would have made sure *his* sons toed the line—or paid a heavy price if they did not. He would have eliminated any lingering resistance to his demands by keeping them under strict rein until he personally determined the right paths for their futures. He would have made sure they kept foremost in mind the fact that Montgomery blood made them better than the uneducated trash that inhabited this small town. When it came time for marriage, he would have found women for his sons who were as wealthy as the boys would some-day have been, women of spotless reputation, un-like the former dance-hall singer whom Brent had chosen—a woman who would forever mark his children as common.

No, Quince and his brothers were Jack's sons—and he despised them as much as he despised their father.

Edmund knew that *his* progeny would have been worthy of inheriting the empire he was cre-ating—an empire that now only partially compen-sated him for the one great failure of his life.

A familiar agitation returned. He had lusted for the beautiful Beth Quincy from the moment he first met her in New Orleans as a young man; he had been determined to have her. Aware that her family was on the outer fringes of society, while his family was prominent, he had intended no more than a temporary liaison to satisfy his carnal desires—a liaison that would not interfere with a more socially acceptable marriage when he was ready to end his bachelorhood. That plan went awry, however, when his boyhood rival, Jack Hunter, returned from a prolonged absence from New Orleans.

Jack surprised Edmund by renewing an old ac-quaintance with Beth, and by then pursuing her with the reckless enthusiasm that was so strong a part of his personality. Infuriated by Jack's inter-ference in his plans, and determined not to allow his adversary another of the frequent victories that typified their youth, he became obsessed with win-ning Beth.

Forced to abandon his matrimonial ambitions in order to accomplish that end, he had pursued Beth openly and avidly. Stunned when Jack unexpectedly proposed marriage to her, he realized he had no choice but to do the same, or lose her.

He had struggled with that choice. Knowing he was the better candidate, he had been certain that both Beth and her family would immediately accept his proposal should he offer it. He was wealthier and more handsome than Jack. His family was a longstanding force in New Orleans society, while Jack came from a long line of itinerant gamblers. His future was brighter than Jack's, his circle of friends larger and more socially acceptable, and where all of Jack's vices were public knowledge, his own self-indulgence in houses of ill repute that tolerated the sexual deviancies he enjoyed was a well-kept secret.

His decision made, he proposed to Beth, confidently anticipating her acceptance. He remembered his shock when he learned Beth had defied her family by running away with Jack. He had been humiliated—while vivid images of Beth and Jack together only increased his bounding lust.

Obsessed by the determination to hear Beth admit she had married the wrong man, to have her grovel for his forgiveness, he had deliberately cultivated the newlyweds' friendship. With a smile on his face, he had silently seethed and indulged fantasies of the ways he would make Beth pay for the indignities she had caused him.

He recalled the day a year after their marriage when he learned Jack had won a Texas horse ranch in a card game. He was stunned, unable to immediately react when Jack moved his wife and infant son away from New Orleans to live there.

Refusing to admit failure, certain that Beth would come to her senses before too much more time elapsed, and determined to be there when she did, he followed them to Diablo. He renewed his friendship with the Hunters and set up his bank, professing a need to prove himself as his father had done before him.

As he had foreseen, his bank had flourished while Jack's fortunes faltered; and Beth had borne Jack three more children while growing more beautiful with each passing year. His satisfaction grew with each setback Jack's ranch suffered, and he willingly advanced Jack credit until the Half-Moon was heavily mortgaged. And as Jack's debt grew, his drinking and gambling increased.

Pretending an affection for her children in order to win Beth's approval, Edmund had waited, certain she would soon turn to him.

Edmund frowned. The waiting had been more difficult than he'd ever imagined it could be. During a period of infuriating frustration—hoping to make Beth realize what she had lost—he made an uncharacteristic error in judgment. He married Iona, a wealthy widow—only to realize belatedly that not only did his obsession for Beth still consume him, but he also had a wife whom he abhorred.

Remorse tightened Edmund's throat.

Beautiful Beth.

Captivating Beth.

Enticing Beth.

Foolish Beth!

Sudden rage flushed Edmund with heat. Beth would be alive today if she hadn't married Jack Hunter! Instead, she was lying in a solitary grave.

Edmund's rage deepened as Jack Hunter's image flashed in his mind. The ten years that Jack had spent in prison had not diminished Beth's loss, but they had allowed Edmund time to conceive the perfect plan for revenge—a plan that was progressing flawlessly.

It had not been difficult to gain Jack's confidence after his release from prison. Jack was a fool. Jack believed in the friendship Edmund professed. At odds with Brent and angry at Matt and Quince for not being at the Half-Moon when he returned, Jack had been easy to lead astray.

Revenge would soon be a reality. Jack would lose the ranch and emerge a penniless drunk; his sons would be ruined as well and would shun their father for having lost their inheritance. The Hunter family would be destroyed, and the Half-Moon would belong to him. His need for revenge would be sated, and he would emerge victorious at last, with a growing empire to prove his worth.

Hatred burning in his gaze, Edmund watched Quince walk through the swinging doors of the Lone Star Saloon at the far end of the street.

Like father, like son.

That thought fixed in his mind, Edmund turned to his startled tellers and snapped, "Are you done yet?"

Marks blinked as Tolley responded tentatively,

"Almost. A few more minutes and we'll—"

"Almost isn't good enough. Get out! Go home, both of you! I'm going to lock up."

"But—"

Ignoring Tolley's attempted reply, Edmund withdrew the keys from his pocket. He'd lock the damned fools in if they didn't move fast enough.

Grunting with satisfaction as the two men hurried out the doorway, Edmund slammed the door shut behind him with one thought uppermost in his mind.

Revenge would be sweet indeed.

Chapter Three

Glory took a deep breath, forced her shoulders back, and started down the hallway toward the dining room. The aroma of Pete's cooking had penetrated her bedroom as she prepared to meet the new day, but she had little appetite. Her muddied riding clothes from the previous day's fiasco were still soaking in a washtub outside the kitchen, and the accident still weighed heavily on her mind. Exhausted from the ordeal, she had passed the hours after arriving back at the ranch in her room, attempting to wash the nightmarish incident from her body and mind, but the memory haunted her. She did not relish meeting the glances of the hired hands sitting at the long, plank breakfast table—men who had worked as hard as she to get the Diamond C back on its feet during the past few years.

Her father would also be waiting, sitting at the head of the table in the makeshift wheelchair that Pete had assembled from a kitchen chair and spare dogcart wheels, his Southern roots apparent in an aristocratic bearing that was unaffected and in-born. He had sat silent and still in the same way while she had described the incident in devastating detail the previous day, but the lines in his pale face had deepened revealingly. The twitch of his lips had torn at her heart when he said to her with a forced smile, "You're all right. That's all that matters, darlin'." Then, "Accidents happen. There's no shame in it."

Those last words, coincidentally identical to the arrogant saddle bum's unexpected comment, had shaken her, but she had wasted no time on regrets for her behavior toward the obnoxious fellow. His imperious, condescending manner—as if she were "only a woman"—was too familiar, and she had resented it.

Yet those same words spoken by her father had touched her deeply. In the privacy of her room, the tears she had so stringently withheld had finally fallen. The truth was, she had loved that mare. The memory of the animal's frantic last moments were burned into her mind. It would be a long time before she would be able to forget them. Nor could she easily dismiss the realization that she had let her father down.

The rumble of conversation at the breakfast table halted abruptly as she turned the corner into the room, and Glory raised her chin a notch higher. Taking her seat at her father's right, she was saved from the awkwardness of the moment by Pete's entrance from the kitchen with a plate of steaming biscuits.

"We all heard about Miss Glory's accident yesterday," he said bluntly. "She ain't no happier than any one of us are about it, but it's over and done—and since she came out of it all right, I'm expecting nobody's going to say nothing that might spoil her appetite this morning."

That warning given with a stern glance, Pete disappeared back into the kitchen, and Glory was tempted to smile. Pete, the whiskered, bald-headed master of the kitchen, had always been her champion. She loved the old coot.

Jan Williams, their sober, ruddy-skinned foreman, who had worked for the Diamond C since its inception, broke the silence by addressing her directly. "I figure I'm speaking for the other boys when I say we're sorry to hear how you lost the mare, Miss Glory, but we're real glad to see you're all right."

Heads nodded all around the table as Robbie Lang, the youngest member of the crew, spoke up. "We was all just wishing one of us had been nearby so we might've done something to help you out."

"That quicksand bog is a nuisance." Slim Howe, a soft-spoken fellow who normally said little and appeared to think much, continued with a frown, "There's no tellin' how many animals have gone down in it over the years."

Glory's face whitened.

"Now see what you done! You got her upset."

40

Robbie's boyish face flushed as he leaned toward Glory and said consolingly, "Don't you listen to him, Miss Glory. Like I said, you're all right, and that's all that matters."

The knot inside Glory tightened. They were good men. All of them felt her discomfort. She needed to put an end to it. Forcing a smile to match a brisk tone that was equally affected, Glory said, "Thanks, boys, but Slim is right. There's no telling how many animals have been lost in that bog over the years. Pa and I were saying last night that it might be best if we fenced it off to avoid trouble in the future."

"Good idea."

"That's right."

"We'll get it done right fast, too."

Heads again bobbed all around when Jan added, "We'll start this morning, Miss Glory."

Interrupting, the purr of his Southern accent carrying clearly in the small room despite his weakness, Byron Townsend said, "Glory and I appreciate your concern, but that fence can wait another few days, fellas. You all had better finish up your present chores first."

"Yes, sir."

"All right."

"Whatever you say, boss."

The innate respect that rang in the men's response to her father was somehow comforting. Glory picked up her fork and forced herself to eat. Yes, they were good men—all of them.

Nevertheless, she was grateful when the last of the hands had left the table. Glory looked at her father, then hesitated briefly. Pa looked bad. She didn't need anyone to tell her that his health was rapidly declining, or that this latest blow had taken a heavy toll on him.

Glory said softly, "I'm sorry, Pa. I went over the accident a hundred times in my mind during the night, and I still can't figure how it happened. I took the same trail every day when I exercised Cinnamon and never had a problem. I knew about the quicksand. I thought I was a safe distance from it. I still can't figure what made Cinnamon rear up like that, or what made her bolt out of control."

"A rattler maybe. She could've stepped on one and gotten bitten."

"I suppose." Glory shook her head, unconvinced.

Her father's bony hand covered hers. "Don't bother your head about it anymore, darlin'. It's just more of the bad luck that's been plaguing us. It wasn't your fault."

Holding his gaze a moment longer, Glory said, "I was supposed to deliver Cinnamon to be bred at the end of the week."

Her father did not respond.

"I'll ride over this morning and let them know she won't be coming."

"You don't need to. Jan can do it."

"No. It's my responsibility."

Pa frowned. He did not attempt to dispute her decision. Instead, he said, "Take Shorty with you."

Shorty—the biggest wrangler on the Diamond C. He was as tall as a tree, had a neck like a bull, shoulders wider than the Texas plains, and hands as big as hams.

Glory smiled. "I'm all right. I don't need a nursemaid, Pa."

"Take him with you," he directed. "Come straight back when you're done. I have some paperwork to do in the meantime that we'll need to go over together."

Glory's stomach knotted tight. She knew what that meant.

Her heart heavy, she started for the door.

It was mid-morning when Quince rode into view of the Half-Moon ranch house at last. Awake most of the night, he had risen early and dressed in the clothing he had purchased in Diablo the previous day. He hardly gave his discarded buckskins or the clean-shaven fellow staring back at him in the washstand mirror a second thought before fastening his gun belt around his hips and turning toward the hotel room door.

He had realized he'd made a mistake the moment he walked into the Lone Star Saloon the previous evening. He had entered with the intention of passing an hour with a drink in his hand while sorting out his thoughts, only to be approached time and again by familiar townsfolk less bent on welcoming him back than on discussing the details of his mother's death and his father's recent release from prison. Hardly in the mood for small talk, he had not bothered to spare their feelings. Nor in the mood for distracting dalliances, he had rejected the approach of a young, unusually determined saloon girl named Blanche and had left before the hour was done, only to lie awake until dawn, haunted by memories.

Anxious to face his demons, he had retrieved his horse from the livery stable and started out for the Half-Moon, but he had not anticipated the ambivalent emotion that the first sight of the ranch house would stir.

Hardly aware of his mount's steady forward progress, Quince stared at the low-lying wooden structure and assessed it keenly. It appeared well kept, as did the outbuildings a distance away. His throat tight, he noted that the old rocker where his mother had sat in the twilight hours—her one self-indulgence in her day—still occupied the corner of the porch. But the patch of green which had been an herb garden, visible even from a distance under his mother's careful tending, was a somber brown indistinguishable from the surrounding, heavily trampled soil.

He saw horses moving in the corral, a few heads of beef cattle in the field beyond, chickens picking at the ground between the buildings, a cat scampering into the barn. It was a deceivingly peaceful midday scene that he knew instinctively would soon be compromised by the tall male figure who walked out onto the porch to stare in his direction.

Quince's jaw hardened. He could see Brent's scowl even from this distance. It was just his luck that his brother would be home at a time of day when he should be out working on the range. He had hoped—

The emergence from the house of a smaller,

more delicate figure in male clothing stopped Quince's thoughts cold. He saw the long dark braid that flapped against Abby's back as she turned to respond to Brent with a clipped reply, then stepped down off the porch into clearer view. Her broad smile and quick wave were somehow the signal he had been waiting for. Quince nudged his horse into a canter.

Dismounting, Quince grinned with true warmth as Abby ran forward and threw her arms around him. The tug in the pit of his stomach was unexpected when she drew back at last, then looked up at him with their mother's eyes and whispered, "Welcome home, Quince."

The poignant moment was abruptly dispelled by Brent's cold voice. "What brought you home, Quince?"

"I did." Responding in his stead, Abby announced boldly, "I wrote Quince a letter and asked him to come."

His gaze remaining on Quince's face, Brent pressed, "That doesn't answer my question."

Quince eyed his brother in return. Unlike Quince, both Brent and Matt had always borne a distinct physical resemblance to their handsome father. Brent's resemblance had grown pronounced during his absence. Sensing from his brother's reception that Brent's resentment toward him had grown pronounced as well, Quince replied, "I figured it was time."

"Really? Why the sudden flash of conscience?"

"Brent!"

Looking briefly at Abby, Brent responded, "It's a reasonable question."

"Is it?" Quince snapped.

"Stop this, will you!" Abby's light eyes blazed. "Quince came home because I asked him to, Brent—because Papa was coming home, and he belongs here with the rest of the family."

"Too bad he didn't feel that way five years ago when he left us with the mess Pa made."

"Brent—"

Halting Abby's objection with a touch, Quince replied, "Don't waste your time, Abby. This is between Brent and me, just like it's always been."

"That's where you're wrong!" Jack Hunter stepped forward out of the shadows unexpectedly, and Quince was momentarily stunned. His father— the handsome man who had once stood tall and proud—had aged to a shocking degree. His hair, once dark and thick, was now lusterless and gray; features once clearly defined were now altered by deep, downward lines that marked the passage of ten hard years. Most striking of all, however, was the lifelessness in his eyes as he continued flatly, "Both of you seem to forget—*my* name's on the deed to the Half-Moon. *I'm* the one who makes the final decisions about who goes or stays around here."

"That's right." Bitterness sounded in Brent's voice as he grated, "Just like you made all the final decisions here during the past ten years."

"Ten years . . ." Jack's jaw tightened. "Let's get one thing straight between us all right now. Those ten years I spent in prison are in the past. I've put them behind me, and I expect everybody else on this ranch to put them in the past, too." Turning toward Quince, he continued, "You've been gone for five years. I don't know why you left and I don't care. You're back now, and as far as I'm concerned, you've got as much right here as your brothers. You can stay as long as you understand I mean what I say when I tell you that I'm home now, and we'll be doing things *my* way."

Unable to ignore the challenge in his father's voice, Quince replied, "You and Brent have put your cards on the table, so it's time for me to do the same." Taking a step forward, he continued in a resolute tone uncompromised by its softness, "Abby asked me to come home, but that isn't the only reason I came." Sweeping his father and brother with an unrelenting glance, he continued, "Pa's name might be on the deed to this place, but this ranch belonged to Ma, too—and I know she would want me to be here. It may have taken me five years to come to that realization, but now that I have, nobody is going to push me into leaving again until I'm ready."

"You don't have to make explanations to either one of them, Quince." Her expression tense, Abby pulled him toward the house. "Come on, let's go inside."

"Wait a minute, Abby. I haven't finished." Turning back to the two men who stared at him in silence, Quince continued, "I want you to know something else, too. It isn't my intention to be dependent on anybody's charity here. I'll pull my own weight on this ranch. I'll work as hard as everybody else does, but I'll do it as a member of the family whose opinion counts as much as anyone else's. I want that to be understood."

Quince waited. He saw Jack's eyes narrow, then the almost imperceptible nod of his head before he walked unsteadily back into the shadows and disappeared from sight. Allowing his frigid silence to speak for itself, Brent turned and started toward the barn.

The hush that followed seemed interminable before Quince looked down at Abby.

"Quince," she whispered with solemn sincerity, "I'm so glad you're home."

I'm so glad you're home, dear.

Recalling Iona's greeting upon his return home the previous day, Edmund watched his wife's unsteady progress toward the dining room table. His stomach turned with revulsion. Always small and thin, Iona was fast approaching emaciation. Her halfhearted attempts at a toilette did not conceal the unnatural color of her skin or the dark circles under her eyes. Nor had it altered the casual disarray of thinning hair that was dull and streaked with gray. Looking at her now, he found it hard to comprehend how he could have been foolish enough to marry her for *any* reason.

Edmund's lips moved into a contemptuous smile. Winning her hand had been no true victory, of course. A lonely, wealthy widow with a nine-year-old daughter, Iona had been totally overwhelmed by his attentions and charm. As he recalled, the only problem he had briefly encountered had been with her daughter, Juliana, who unlike her mother, had been immune to his appeal. But Iona had been *in love*. She had been deaf to her daughter's protests and had docilely accepted the girl's decision to move in with her grandparents when Edmund pressed his suit. Within a matter of weeks, he had wooed Iona, swept her off her feet, and brought her home to Diablo with the thought that Beth Hunter would finally realize what she had lost.

How he could have ever believed that beautiful, inherently seductive Beth Hunter could envy this pathetic shell of a woman, even for a moment, was presently unfathomable to him.

Edmund paused at that thought. Of course, there had been Iona's fortune to consider at the time—a fortune left to her by her late husband. He now controlled all of it, with the exception of a small trust left for Juliana, which was in the town lawyer's hands. Yet he had learned the hard way that Iona's money was poor compensation for the daily hardship of enduring her presence.

Iona stumbled as she attempted to seat herself. Swallowing the bitter bile of contempt, Edmund hastened to her side and eased her into her chair. Breakfast when it was nearly noon had become a daily ritual for Iona, who spent the night drinking in her lonely room—an arrangement which had begun shortly after he claimed difficulty in sleeping and suggested they occupy separate bedrooms. Knowing that Iona would not have the courage to object, he had used the situation to relieve himself of marital duties, which had become repulsive to him, and to indulge his increasingly compelling sexual fantasies a distance from Diablo, where no one was the wiser.

Edmund picked up the small silver bell on the elaborately prepared table and shook it gently. Hilda hurried into the room and placed a plate in front of Iona. The housekeeper's disapproval of Iona's appearance was obvious in the pursing of her lips and the slight shake of her head, and in the sympathetic glance she cast in his direction before heading back into the kitchen.

Edmund smiled inwardly. All of Diablo would hear about Iona's morning intoxication in vivid detail before the day was over. He would be extolled as the long-suffering husband who tolerated his wife's vice with Christian forbearance.

Edmund's inner smile faded. Nothing could be further from the truth.

I'm so glad you're home, dear.

Yes, Iona had been glad to see him when he came home the previous day, especially when she had seen the package he had received in the mail.

Her medicine.

He remembered how Iona's hands had trembled when she accepted it from him, how she'd made some inane excuse and then hurried to her room, clutching the bulky package tightly. Listening at the door, he had heard her tearing frantically at the wrapping paper. Within minutes—far too long to satisfy him—total silence had reigned.

He had entered her room and stood staring at Iona where she lay sleeping, her scrawny body stretched out awkwardly on her bed and an un-capped bottle of laudanum lying on the nightstand beside her. He had felt a surge of triumph, know-ing she would sleep for hours and be out of his way. He remembered thinking that with any luck, he wouldn't have to see her again until the follow-ing day when he came home for his midday meal to assume the role of loving husband that he was presently playing.

"Edmund, dear . . ."

Iona's pathetic attempt at conversation began hesitantly. He waited as she brushed back a loose strand of hair with a shaky hand, then continued, "I want to thank you for getting my medicine for me. I really slept quite well last night."

Edmund smiled. "I can see that, dear."

"If I'm able to sleep well the rest of the week, I'm sure I'll be well enough to ride out to visit friends soon—if you'll agree to take me."

"Of course, Iona. Where would you like to go?"

"I thought I'd visit Abby at the Half-Moon."

"Oh . . . that might not be such a good idea. The situation on the ranch hasn't been too stable since Jack came home." Pausing for effect, Ed-mund leaned toward her to whisper, "Jack's started drinking again. You know how it is with drunks. It's humiliating for the family. I really wouldn't like you to be a part of it."

Iona's small eyes blinked. A weak smile quivered briefly on her lips before she removed her napkin from her lap and stood up unsteadily.

"I . . . I'm not feeling too well, Edmund. I think I'd like to lie down for a while."

"Your breakfast, dear . . ." Edmund stood politely, his expression solicitous. "Aren't you going to finish it?"

"I'm not hungry. You can tell Hilda to take it away."

"Of course. If you say so."

His concerned expression faded when Iona disappeared around the corner of the hallway. Edmund rang the silver bell, bringing Hilda into the room with obvious haste. To the housekeeper's inquisitive glance, he responded, "Mrs. Montgomery wasn't . . . feeling well. She went to lie down."

"Oh, I'm sorry, sir."

"I have to leave now, but if you could look in on her later, I'd appreciate it."

"I'll be happy to, sir."

"She is a dear woman, you know."

Hilda's florid complexion reddened. "Yes, of course, Mr. Montgomery."

Snatching up his hat as he walked out the doorway, Edmund smiled. Hilda was such a fool.

"Pa's drinking again, isn't he?"

The familiar barn scents were keen in Quince's nostrils as he posed his question to Abby abruptly. The silence between them that followed was underscored by sounds of impatient whinnies and the rustling of hooves in nearby stalls as he waited for her reply.

In the time since his brief encounter with Brent and Pa earlier, Abby had taken him into the house and proudly introduced him to the housekeeper, Frances Reilly, a stocky, middle-aged woman with faded blue eyes and an attitude that had raised his brows. She had installed him in his old bedroom and then brought him to the barn where she had introduced him to Navidad. The Mexican's warm handshake made it easy to believe Abby's claim that his unusual way with horses had made him invaluable to the Half-Moon.

Abby turned toward him with a frown as he waited for her reply, and Quince was momentarily taken aback by her startling resemblance to their beautiful mother. He knew instinctively that his little sister was neither aware of her budding beauty, nor would give it a second thought, so great had been the loss that had changed her life ten years earlier.

That loss had changed all their lives. Brent had ridden off in obvious anger shortly after their reunion this morning, Pa had not shown his face in the time since, and Matt wasn't even present on the ranch. Thankful that at least the special bond between Abby and him had been fully restored, Quince pressed gently, "Abby . . . ?"

Sighing, Abby responded, "Papa doesn't drink *all* the time. He just drinks when he's unhappy, or when things start going wrong on the ranch again."

"What do you mean?"

"The people in town are keeping their distance from him, and Papa doesn't take kindly to being ignored by people he used to think were his friends."

"And?"

"Papa and Brent haven't been getting along too

well. Papa's got this idea about changing things around here."

"Like?"

"Well, after you left, Brent got more determined than ever to make things work out. He had just about finished clearing up Papa's debts when Papa got out of prison."

"So?"

"Papa's got it into his head to do things his own way. He's been buying horses that Brent says we can't afford."

"Horses . . ."

"And property that Brent says we don't need and can't afford, either."

"Pa just got out of prison. Where's he getting the money to do all this?"

Abby paused. Her frown darkened. "Edmund's been making him loans against the ranch."

Quince's response was instinctive. "And Pa's been trying to pay the loans off by gambling like he always did—only he's getting himself in deeper every time."

Abby nodded. "Brent is furious because Papa's putting us deeper and deeper into debt, but Papa won't listen to him. He thinks Edmund's the only one who believes in him."

He should have known. Edmund, always Pa's *friend*.

Another nagging question needed to be answered. Quince pressed reluctantly, "What about Matt?" He paused. "Is he coming back?"

Abby shrugged, her gaze dropping toward the ground. "Papa doesn't seem to think so."

Quince went still. Matt—who had withdrawn from all of them after their mother's death, who had left the ranch and returned only occasionally to contribute financial support. Matt—whose negligence Quince still believed had played a part in the tragedy that ended their mother's life. Yet Quince had never truly believed Matt would desert the family for good.

"You haven't heard from him since he left for England?"

"No."

Abby's eyes grew suspiciously bright, and Quince felt anger stir. Abby had suffered enough because of something that was not her fault. He was home now, and he was going to see to it that things changed for the better, at least for her.

That resolve firmly set, Quince slid an arm around Abby's shoulders and said, "Well, are you going to tell me why you brought me into the barn?"

A smile breaking through, Abby said, "I've been busy on the ranch, you know. The hired hands tell me I'm one of the best wranglers on the place when it comes to training cutting horses." Her enthusiasm momentarily dimming, she added, "Of course, Brent thinks I'm getting too old for that kind of work—that I should put on a dress and high-buttoned shoes and start 'acting like a lady.'" Abby grimaced. "I told him I'm more comfortable on the back of a horse than I am in a dress, and I make a real contribution to this ranch doing what I do."

"What did he say to that?"

The bright sheen in Abby's eyes returned. "He said I'd never get a husband acting like I do. So I told him I don't want a husband if the only way I can get one is to get all gussied up and go simpering after a man like the girls in town—or if I have to hang out in a kitchen all day while my heart is out riding on the back of a horse!"

"And Brent said . . . ?"

"He said I might as well get used to these pants I'm wearing, because it looked like I'd be getting my wish."

Damn that Brent!

Quince forced a smile, then added with a wink, "Brent and I never did agree on much, and it looks like that hasn't changed."

Grateful that Abby appeared to brighten again at his response, Quince said, "So, what do you want to show me?"

Quince's arm dropped from Abby's shoulders as she turned abruptly and signaled for him to follow her to the rear stall. Unprepared despite Abby's obvious pride as she turned to watch his expression, Quince stared at the stallion snorting excitedly at their appearance. The velvet red roan stood approximately sixteen hands high. With white stockings, a white blaze on its forehead, and keen intelligence in its eyes, the stallion was the most magnificent animal Quince could ever recall seeing.

He looked at Abby and said sincerely, "Moon Racer didn't look like much when Brent gave him to you as a foal, but he's matured into a stallion that any man—or woman—would be proud of."

56

"He's a beauty, all right." Abby's throat worked tightly before she continued, "He's a handful, too, when I take him out for some exercise, but he's earned the Half-Moon a lot of money. I'm thinking he knows that—but the best is yet to come for him. Pretty soon he'll be put out to breed with one of the finest mares in this part of Texas. We've all been waiting a long time for Cinnamon to be ready for Moon Racer, and there's not a one of us here at the Half-Moon who isn't anxious to see the foal that'll come out of that matchup."

Cinnamon . . .

Quince frowned. He was about to speak when the sound of approaching hoofbeats turned Abby toward the barn doors. Quince remained behind when she walked out into the yard, then shouted out a welcoming hello.

He heard the horses approach and the sound of horsemen dismounting. Abby was the first to speak.

"What are you all doing here today? We weren't expecting you until the end of the week."

A brief silence followed before a woman answered, "That's what I came here to tell you, Abby."

Quince stilled. He knew that voice.

This was harder than she had ever thought it would be.

Glory could not manage a smile in response to Abby Hunter's broad grin. She knew Abby. Abby was young, a few years her junior, but she was a horsewoman through and through, and the thought of breeding her magnificent stallion to Cinnamon and seeing the foal that the pair would produce had excited Abby almost as much as it had excited her. Glory had hoped that match would mean the beginning of a bloodline for the Diamond C that would become renowned throughout Texas. Abby had been content simply to have Moon Racer play his part in an event that would make her proud.

Her throat thick as she faced the end of both their dreams, Glory said softly, "I won't be delivering Cinnamon for Moon Racer at the end of the week."

Her smile freezing, Abby shook her head. "Why? What happened?"

"Cinnamon's dead."

Abby's eyes widened—green eyes that struck a familiar chord somewhere in the back of Glory's mind as Abby gasped, then said, "But . . . but she looked wonderful the last time I saw her—healthy and ready to go into season."

"It was an accident."

"An accident?"

"When I took her out for some exercise. She had to be shot to be put out of her misery."

Abby's face reflected true distress as she rasped, "I'm so sorry, Glory. For you to have to shoot such a beautiful animal . . ."

Glory did not reply.

Behind her, Shorty shifted uncomfortably and Abby offered abruptly, "Frances has had a couple of fresh apple pies sitting on the windowsill for a few hours. I know she'll be glad to cut a piece for you if you're feeling hungry."

"Thank you, Miss Abby."

Smiling broadly, Shorty turned toward the main house, and Glory said sincerely, "Thanks for that. I don't think Shorty enjoyed playing nursemaid to me on this trip, but my father insisted, and he does what my father says." She paused, then continued, "I know you're almost as disappointed as I am that I won't be bringing Cinnamon . . ."

Glory's words trailed away as a tall man walked out of the barn and started toward them. There was something familiar about the way he carried himself, with an air of confidence and silent resolution; his stride; the way he wore his gun belt low on his hips and his hat pulled down onto his forehead to deeply shade his eyes.

He drew closer. His clothes were different and he was clean-shaven, but those light eyes, so green and penetrating . . .

It couldn't be.

Following Glory's gaze, Abby turned to look behind her.

Glory's heart pounded as Abby rewarded the fellow with a smile. Glancing between them, Glory felt the weight of identical light-eyed gazes fixed on her as Abby said, "I don't think you know my brother Quince. He's been away. He just got home today." Almost as an afterthought, Abby added, "This is Glory Townsend, Quince. Her father and she own the Diamond C—Old Man Potter's place."

Somehow unable to reply, Glory waited as his

penetrating green eyes raked her. Her lips tightened when he said with a polite tip of his hat, "Nice to see you again, *ma'am*."

The bastard!

Abby appeared surprised. "You've already met?"

Responding in that deep voice Glory remembered so well, Quince Hunter replied, "Yes, we met yesterday when I was on the way home. We didn't have much of a conversation, but Miss Townsend did say she'd most likely be seeing me again before the end of the week."

Abby said, "Glory's mare—the mare I was telling you about that was supposed to be bred to Moon Racer this week—was injured in an accident. It had to be destroyed."

Glory prepared herself for Quince Hunter's reply—his condescending description of the disastrous incident in all its sadly humiliating detail. She frowned when he said simply, "That's a pity."

He was a bastard, all right—and he wasn't fooling her with his pretense of sympathy.

Unwilling to play his game, Glory said abruptly, "I have to leave, Abby. My father's expecting me back." Meeting Quince Hunter's gaze coldly, she said, "Goodbye, Mr. Hunter."

She felt heat transfuse her face when the bastard replied, "Please call me Quince, *ma'am*. Everybody does."

Tempted to reply that she had no doubt he was referred to by other, more colorful names as well, Glory mounted up. Her clipped summons brought Shorty out of the house on the run as she rode out of the yard without a backward glance.

Chapter Four

His first two days back at the Half-Moon had not gone well.

That thought weighed heavily on Quince's mind as he entered the barn, picked up his saddle, and swung it up onto his horse. Glory Townsend's angry image flashed before him as it had countless times since their last meeting, but he cast it aside. He had already determined that the little snip wasn't worth the time he had spent thinking about her. He had more important issues to settle.

Quince glanced at the ranch hands saddling up around him. The sun had barely risen, but breakfast had already been eaten and the men were preparing to ride out for the day's work. Buck, Red, Curly, Hank—all were wranglers with whom he had worked side by side before leaving the ranch five years earlier. They had welcomed him home with an enthusiasm that did not betray their loyalty to Brent. Their comments about Jack Hunter's return had been limited; and, strangely, Quince had been somehow grateful. He had preferred instead to learn the details about the ranch's situation directly from the family.

Unfortunately, that wasn't happening. Abby had done her best to answer his questions, but her knowledge of ranch finances was limited. Pa seemed determined not to get involved in any private conversation. Instead, he was spending more time in Diablo than appeared wise.

Then there was Brent. It had surprised Quince that his older brother had chosen to live in the cabin by the creek with his new bride, Crystal. He had expected that nothing short of an earthquake would move Brent out of the family homestead after Pa came home. It appeared, however, that he had underestimated Brent's determination to keep his personal life separate from the apparent downward spiral of ranch affairs. Quince had yet to meet his new sister-in-law, although he was certain that despite his brother's apparent reluctance, he would meet her in good time.

Quince frowned. He supposed he should have realized, that Brent had no intention of discussing ranch affairs with him. It was that same unrelenting, autocratic attitude which had almost led to violence between them five years earlier, but he was determined not to let the same conflict build again. His need to see the Half-Moon on stable ground wasn't fostered by a desire to control the ranch, or by some misdirected loyalty to the father who seemed determined to compound his mistakes on a daily basis. He had returned for one reason only, to make certain that the dream Ma had confided to him would come true—that the Half-Moon would always remain "home" to the family she loved.

With the knowledge that he had no other recourse, Quince turned to address Buck as the mustached wrangler prepared to mount.

"You'll be meeting Brent in the west pasture this morning to finish up your work there." At Buck's nod, Quince continued, "I won't be coming with you. I have some business to take care of in town."

Mounting, Quince did not wait for Buck's reply.

Glory fought to control her irritation. Breakfast had been completed and the men had dispersed for their morning chores. She had already saddled up and was ready to ride out when she turned to see Shorty also saddled up and waiting behind her.

Her jaw clenching tight, Glory dismounted and approached the ranch house, where Pa sat watching the morning departures. Stepping up onto the porch, Glory faced her father squarely and said, "This has gone far enough, Pa. I don't need a nursemaid, and I won't have Shorty following me wherever I go. I'm not a child, and I won't be treated like one."

"I know you're not, darlin'." Byron Townsend seemed momentarily amused by his daughter's indignation, but the smile on his pale face faded as he continued, "But you're a young woman, and this is wild country."

"I've been riding alone in 'wild country' since I was fourteen years old!" Taking a calming breath, Glory continued more softly, "Pa, I know the accident I had with Cinnamon could have turned out far worse than it did—but it didn't. I made it back with no problems other than a thick coating of mud that I had trouble washing off. I'm fine."

"If that saddle bum hadn't shown up in time—"

Saddle bum.

Glory winced. She'd been so angry over Quince Hunter's deliberate deception, over his attempt to embarrass her by showing up to flaunt his identity, that she'd been unable even to discuss the situation with her father.

Feeling distinctly uncomfortable over her omission, she continued, "But he did show up! And even if he hadn't, I'd have gotten out of that quicksand without a problem."

When her father did not reply, she insisted, "I would have, Pa!"

"Don't you see, darlin'?" Byron responded softly, "I'm not willing to take that chance again—not when Shorty's available to accompany you."

"I have important things to take care of today, Pa, and I don't want Shorty following me around when I do them. He should be out doing his job on the ranch, not dogging my heels like a reluctant puppy."

"I can spare Shorty on the job, Glory . . . but I can't spare you."

"Oh, Pa." Glory shook her head. "I can't let this go on, no matter how you feel. The men will lose respect for me. Can't you see that? I've worked too hard to gain their acceptance to lose it now because of the remote possibility that something could happen again."

"Glory—"

"Pa, I'm asking you to believe I can take care of myself."

"That's not the point, darlin'."

"Yes, it is. What happened with Cinnamon was a freak accident. I know this territory as well as anyone else on this ranch. I have a rifle on my saddle in case of an emergency, and you know I know how to use it, because you taught me. So, you either believe I can take care of myself or you don't."

Searching her father's expression, Glory paused. "Just remember, Pa, if you don't believe in me, the men won't, either."

A responsive color rose to Byron Townsend's face, and Glory's stomach twisted with discomfort. If it wasn't so necessary to set things straight now, as much for the sake of her own confidence as for the sake of the men—

Interrupting her thoughts, Byron turned to address the massive wrangler who had remained mounted a distance away. Raising his voice so he might be clearly heard, he instructed levelly, "There won't be any need for you to accompany Miss Glory anymore, Shorty. You may return to your work."

Hardly able to speak past the sudden lump in her throat, Glory whispered, "Thank you, Pa."

With a swift kiss on his cheek, she turned toward her horse.

*   *   *

"I didn't mean nothing by it, Lobo!"

Blanche's anxious voice disturbed the afternoon lull in the Lone Star Saloon as she attempted to pull her arm free of Lobo's painful grip. When the glowering cowboy tightened his hold, Blanche continued, brown eyes wide with innocence, "You know the boss has been after me for spending too much time with you when you're here. I figured that Hunter fella was new in town when he came in a couple of nights ago. I was just trying to do my job when he walked up to the bar, but he wasn't one bit sociable."

"Yeah? That ain't what I hear." Lobo's lips tightened. "The boys tell me you stuck to him like glue, that you was hanging all over him and enjoying yourself too much for it to be strictly business."

Blanche glanced at the men seated at a table a distance away. They were smiling, laughing at her!

Blanche corrected that thought. No, they were laughing at Lobo. They were sick of all the bragging he did when he came in—about how he'd just made himself some big money doing this or that. They liked to see him get riled, and if they succeeded by putting her in the middle, that was fine with them. They didn't know that the only "big money" Lobo ever made was by taking most of whatever *she* earned, leaving her only enough money to barely scrape by.

Blanche stared at Lobo's vicious grimace. Alone and out on her own for the first time after the death of a father who had left her with nothing more than an old horse and rusty digging tools, she had arrived at the Lone Star Saloon a year earlier—scared, hungry, and green as grass. Young and pretty, she had also been desperate enough to do anything she needed to do in order to survive. She had taken a job as "one of the girls," and had been so ignorant that she'd actually been attracted to Lobo with his long, sandy-colored hair and wide smile. She'd thought that he was the kind of man who could protect her in ways she had been unable to protect herself.

She had never been more wrong. Lobo had stopped smiling, and she had been paying for her mistake ever since.

Lobo's hand bit more cruelly into her arm, and Blanche forced back tears. It was useless to tell him he was hurting her, because he enjoyed it. She had learned the hard way that it gave him a sense of power over her to cause her pain, and letting him see her distress only made things worse.

Refusing to flinch, Blanche wished she could tell Lobo the truth, that everything the "boys" had said was true. She had noticed Quince Hunter the minute he'd walked through the door that evening two days earlier, but it hadn't been until she'd heard someone say his name was Hunter that she'd turned her full attention on him. She'd heard about the Hunters. They'd had a lot of trouble in their family, and they weren't afraid to face it down. She had worked with Crystal in the Lone Star before Brent Hunter rescued her by making her his wife, and from what people were saying,

Quince Hunter was all that his older brother was, *and more*.

She had studied Quince Hunter more closely then. She had watched the way he handled the men who approached him—backing them down with a few chosen words, or looking at them with a glance that stopped them in their tracks. She had thought that if any man could help her get away from Lobo, Quince Hunter would be the one to do it.

But it hadn't worked out. She had tried her best to interest him with unspoken promises she would have kept willingly, but Quince Hunter's mind had been occupied with thoughts that left no room for anything she had to offer.

"Well, what have you got to say for yourself?"

Aware that no help was forthcoming from a bartender who had seen it all before, from male customers who figured she should have known better than to get involved with Lobo, or from the other saloon girls who were as scared of Lobo as she was, Blanche replied softly, "The boys were wrong, Lobo. I was only doing my job. Quince Hunter don't mean nothing to me."

"Liar!" Twisting her arm more harshly, Lobo hissed, "You're coming upstairs with me now. You'll tell me the truth before I'm finished with you."

"You're going too far this time, Lobo." Speaking up unexpectedly from behind the bar, Ken O'Malley caught Lobo's attention with his comment. Level-eyed and sober, the rotund barkeep continued, "I think you'd better leave for a while until you cool off."

Refusing to release her, Lobo replied, "I ain't going nowhere."

Blanche shared Lobo's surprise when O'Malley raised his shotgun into sight from behind the bar and said, "I'm not going to tell you again. Get moving, and don't come back until you've changed your attitude."

All activity in the saloon came to a halt at O'Malley's directive. Blanche held her breath as the silence stretched out painfully. She released it with relief when Lobo's hand dropped from her arm and he turned toward the door without replying.

Unable to move until the doors swung shut behind her tormentor, Blanche turned gratefully toward O'Malley, only to hear him grate, "This is your own fault, you know. If we wasn't short of girls, I'd tell you to get out of here now. I'm warning you, either you set Lobo straight about making trouble in here, or you find yourself another job."

Turning unexpectedly toward the table where Lobo's "friends" still sat, O'Malley ordered unexpectedly, "Get out, all three of you! And don't bother coming back if you intend to start trouble in here again." When the men stared back at him in astonishment, he waved his gun and spat, "Move!"

Motionless, robbed of speech, Blanche stared after them as they walked out the door.

* * *

Having arrived in town a few minutes earlier with one purpose in mind, Glory walked resolutely across the outer office of the Diablo State Bank. Edmund Montgomery sat at his desk, watching her approach, just as he watched every transaction that took place at the tellers' cages throughout the day. She wondered how many of the bank's customers realized that the loans Edmund held on most of the major ranches allowed him control not only over the ranches but over the ranchers' lives as well—a control that was gradually increasing.

Never more conscious of that situation, Glory reached Edmund's office door. There was no need to knock when Edmund stood up politely and said, "Come in, Glory. It's always a happy occasion when you come to see me."

Yes, she supposed it was—for him.

Waiting until she had entered and was seated on the chair in front of his desk, Edmund walked around her and closed the door. He seated himself again and focused his attention on her, sparking her antagonism. She had never liked Edmund Montgomery. She didn't like the way she caught him looking at her when he thought she was unaware. She had seen him looking at Abby Hunter that same way—Abby, who was devoted to Iona, Edmund's "beloved wife."

"What brings you here to see me today?"

Somehow, Glory had the feeling he already knew. Diablo was a small town and gossip traveled fast. The news about her accident with Cinnamon would have made the rounds quickly.

Proceeding as if those thoughts had not entered

her mind, Glory said, "We've had a serious set-back on the Diamond C, Edmund. Our prize mare was killed in an accident two days ago."

"Oh, I'm sorry to hear that." Edmund's handsome face drew into serious lines of concern.

"Pa and I were counting on Cinnamon. We had already made arrangements to have her bred to Moon Racer."

"Abby Hunter's stallion. Yes, he is a beauty."

"We've canceled those plans, of course, but Pa and I were going over the books. Cinnamon's foal was an important part of our long-range plan for the Diamond C. We don't have any other mares on the ranch that compare with her, and if the Diamond C is to remain a horse ranch with a viable future, we'll need to buy another mare of the same caliber, and do it soon."

Edmund nodded his head thoughtfully. "That makes good sense. The passage of large trail herds traveling north is drawing to a halt. That eliminates the income potential of supplying trail horses for the remudas that so many of the ranchers in the area have been depending on. You'll certainly need to plan for an alternate source of revenue."

"We have no immediate money problems." Aware that she was speaking a deliberate untruth, but feeling pressed to conceal the delicacy of the Diamond C's financial situation, Glory continued, "But Pa does want to replace Cinnamon."

"So, what can I do for you, dear?"

Her antagonism was sparked again as she responded, "Pa and I would like a loan to buy another quality mare."

"Where would you get her?"

"Pa has contacts. He's certain he can find exactly the mare he's looking for."

"If he has the right purchase price to offer."

Struggling to maintain her patience, Glory paused. Edmund understood the situation exactly. He knew why she had come. He was stretching out her discomfort—lengthening it word by word—because he was *enjoying* himself too much to bring it to a quick conclusion.

Forced to play his game, Glory smiled and said, "That's right. Pa and I hoped to start writing letters immediately so we could have Moon Racer sire—"

"Oh, I'm sorry, dear, but extending your father and you another loan at this time won't be possible."

Glory went cold as ice. "The Diamond C needs that loan."

"I'm sorry."

Glory forced herself to press, "Pa's counting on it."

Sympathy dripping with his every word, Edmund responded, "You have a loan coming due very shortly. You've asked for extensions in the past, and I've granted them against my better judgment."

"And we've met the payments."

"Forgive me, dear, but I'm in a position to know the Diamond C's financial situation. You *barely* met your last payment."

"Barely or not, you got your money."

"Yes, but as we've discussed, the situation in

this part of the country is changing. The trail herds—"

"We'll have the money for you when it's due, Edmund."

"Yes, I hope you will, just as I hope all the other ranchers in the area will be able to meet their payments. But, my dear, the situation is such that I'm unable to extend any further credit to the Diamond C until I can be sure."

"We need that mare now or our plans for the future will be set back severely. By the time Pa finds the right mare and she comes into season—"

"I'm sorry, dear. I do wish you the best, but business is business, you know."

Glory stood up abruptly. Unable to bear another moment of Edmund's bogus commiseration, she said coldly, "Then our business is concluded. Thank you so much for all your . . . *good wishes.*"

Glory jerked open the office door and started toward the street. She did not see the broad figure turning into the bank until it was too late to avoid a collision that almost knocked her off her feet. Aware that strong arms had saved her from a nasty fall, Glory looked up with an apology on her lips. The apology faded when a familiar green-eyed gaze met hers.

Oh, no, not again.

The concern in Quince Hunter's voice added heat to her anger when he asked, "Are you all right?"

"Of course I'm all right!"

Freeing herself from his support as the embarrassment of their former meetings returned to sting anew, Glory heard him say with a twist of his lips, "If you're in town to arrange for the 'compensation' you mentioned that first day, it won't be necessary."

His comment adding new fuel to her ire, Glory responded, "Actually, I'm glad we ran into each other today. I've been wanting to say something to you—something I couldn't say in front of Abby the last time we met." Lowering her tone so as not to be overheard, Glory continued tightly, "Don't delude yourself into thinking that your being a Hunter will affect me the same way it seems to affect everyone else in Diablo."

Stiffening noticeably, Quince said, "What's that supposed to mean?"

"It means I didn't appreciate your little act a few days ago."

Quince's light eyes grew cold. "What act was that?"

"Your pretense of being a saddle bum when we met."

"You made that assumption on your own."

"You deliberately misled me."

"You jumped to that conclusion."

"You didn't attempt to correct my assumption."

"I didn't feel the need."

"No. Instead you waited for the opportunity to embarrass me."

"That thought never occurred to me."

"You anticipated my embarrassment and enjoyed every minute of it!"

"You're wrong."

"No, I'm not."

"Believe me, *ma'am*, you are. I wouldn't waste my time."

Her fair complexion reddening to the exact shade of her hair, Glory snapped, "Unfortunately, I know better. But since that's your attitude, we have nothing else to discuss. I won't *waste your time* any longer."

Furious, Glory stepped around him with head held high. She walked out onto the street, muttering through clenched teeth the single word that described him so well.

"Bastard."

His jaw tight with irritation, Quince walked into the bank. Resisting the urge to slam the door behind him, he muttered under his breath the only word fiery Glory Townsend brought to mind.

"Witch!"

Edmund looked at the folder on his desk marked "Diamond C." He had reviewed it just that morning. The contents had been fresh in his mind when Glory Townsend walked through his doorway minutes earlier, and his satisfaction at her appearance had been true, indeed. Indulged by her crippled father, Glory had looked down on Edmund in a way no one else in town had ever dared, and it infuriated him. Swinging her trim hips in a long, confident stride and tossing her flaming mane, she was a beauty, all right. He had spent considerable time contemplating the pleasures her slender, white body could have afforded him, but she was a spitfire by nature, and he had decided she wasn't worth the effort it would take to tame her.

But Abby . . . that was another matter.

Sweet, innocent Abby. Abby of the budding beauty, of pure heart, of wonders hidden underneath baggy clothes. Abby, who looked more like her mother—the beautiful Beth—every day. He had spent hours pondering how he might tutor her in the pleasures of the flesh—then in contemplation of deviant joys he could explore with her as well. She would be an apt pupil. He would make sure of it when he—

Startled out of his reverie by the sound of heavy footsteps approaching, Edmund looked up a moment too late to prevent Quince Hunter from entering his office. Forcing a smile, angry at being caught at a disadvantage when his thoughts were elsewhere, he stood up immediately and offered, "Well, Quince, I heard you had returned. This must be my lucky day to be visited twice by old friends."

"Yes, this is your lucky day." But Quince was not smiling as he continued, "I arrived home a few days ago and I intend to stay, but I didn't come here to discuss my plans or to exchange pleasantries, Edmund." Pushing the door closed behind him, he continued, "I came here because I need to know some plain facts, and you're the man to talk to."

"Oh, is that right?" Edmund struggled to maintain a smiling facade. His dislike for Quince Hunter was increasing by the moment. To hide it, he asked agreeably, "How may I help you, Quince?"

"I need to know the extent of the Half-Moon's debt."

"Oh . . ." Edmund shook his head. "I'm sorry. That information is private—between your father and me. I can't divulge it without his permission." Pausing, his smile growing almost paternal, Edmund said, "Really, Quince, shouldn't you be talking to your father about this instead of me?"

Quince's expression tightened. "Knowing how my father has been behaving since his release from prison, do you really think that's possible?"

"I *am* sorry, Quince."

Glowering, Quince proceeded with lethal softness, "Then tell me something else. Why are you advancing my father loans against the Half-Moon when you know damned well he's just gambling the money away?"

"Gambling?" Edmund shook his head. "Jack said he's using the money to invest in the ranch, which sounded reasonable to me."

"Reasonable? When it's all over town that he's been spending most of his time with a drink in one hand and a pack of cards in the other?"

Pretending offense, Edmund replied, "I'm your father's friend, Quince, not his keeper."

"If you were really my father's friend, you wouldn't provide the means for him to put the ranch back in debt."

"Whatever you think, your father has plans. He's depending on me to help him follow through on them."

"My father has dreams that aren't based in reality, because they don't include a way to pay back his loans in the near future."

"Oh, well . . . that would be a problem for the bank, of course." Edmund shrugged. "I must think of the bank's financial stability. So many in the community depend on it."

"So I can take that to mean you won't be making any more loans to Pa unless he explains how he intends to pay them back?"

"I didn't say that, Quince. He is my friend, after all."

His jaw rock hard, Quince said with slow deliberation, "I want us to understand each other, Edmund. I'm telling you that my father is spending wildly and drinking heavily. He's gambling in an attempt to cover his expenses. If you lend him any more money, you'll be contributing to the ruin of the Half-Moon."

"Quince—your father's name is on the deed, not yours."

Quince straightened up, his gaze frigid. "Then I suppose we do understand each other, after all."

As Quince pulled the office door closed behind him, Edmund barely restrained his anger. No, he had never liked Quince Hunter . . . and one day soon, when all came to a final conclusion, he'd bring him to his knees.

He'd had enough.

Frustrated and angry, Quince walked out of the bank and turned resolutely toward the far end of town with a long, determined stride. The day had been a disaster from the moment he had stepped down onto Diablo's main street that morning—beginning with his brief exchange with Glory Townsend.

The red-haired hellion's image again flashed before his mind, and Quince's vexation increased. That brief encounter had clearly confirmed his previous opinion of his irritating neighbor. She was a witch . . . a virago . . . a shrew who stubbornly refused to surrender an irrational viewpoint that had no basis in fact.

Quince frowned unconsciously. Yet those moments when he had held Glory close to steady her, when she had looked up at him with her dark-eyed gaze briefly open, free of animosity and somehow defenseless, had struck a chord inside him that she seemed to touch with no effort at all. Despite the brevity of those moments, the incredible delicacy of her fair skin tinted golden by the sun, the sweet scent of her breath against his cheek, the warmth of her body pressed close to his, remained disturbingly vivid in his mind. During those fleeting seconds he had wondered how that delicate skin would feel against his lips, how her sweet breath would taste as he drew it into his mouth, how her body warmth would rise when he—

Cursing abruptly, Quince shook his head. He must be crazy!

Thrusting the fiery-haired termagant from his mind, Quince forced his thoughts back to the pressing problem at hand. His session with Edmund had been equally disastrous, leaving him with only one course of action. It galled him that despite his hypocrisy, Edmund was right. If Quince wanted information about the Half-Moon's finances, the person he should talk to was his father. No one knew better than he, however, that getting his father to talk to him would not be easy.

Quince's frown deepened. Pa had left the ranch right after breakfast. Questions about his intended destination had been answered with a cold-eyed stare—just as his own repeated attempts to engage his father in conversation since his return had been met with silence.

A solemn sadness ripped at Quince's gut. He wished it hadn't turned out that way between Pa and himself. He remembered a time when he had looked up to his father, when all he had ever wanted was to be like him in every way. He couldn't pinpoint the time when things started to change, but clearly imprinted into memory was Edmund Montgomery's increasing involvement in their lives as his father's deterioration began taking hold.

The familiar sadness deepened as Quince recalled the look in Ma's eyes when Pa came home drunk. Although they had argued, she had made excuses for him right up until the end, claiming Pa's "bad luck" had started affecting his judgment. He knew she never suspected that Pa's bad judgment would one day cause her death.

Quince stared at the Lone Star Saloon as he neared. However, he had learned from Ma's mistakes. He made no excuses for his father's behavior. Nor would he waste time working with the ranch hands and ignoring his father's problems while his father gambled away any chance for the Half-Moon's survival.

That thought in mind, Quince pushed his way through the Lone Star's swinging doors. His eyes narrowed as he glanced around the room. There were a few cowpokes at the bar, a card game in progress at a rear table, customers conversing with brightly dressed saloon girls, a couple strolling toward one of the upstairs rooms . . . yet Pa was nowhere in sight.

The upstairs rooms.

Quince's stomach twisted tight. Somehow he hadn't given a thought to the possibility that Pa might be spending his time and money on one of the women there—a woman who'd give him all the approval he wanted, for a price.

Leaning against the bar moments later, Quince sipped at the drink the bartender placed in front of him. He'd wait, and if Pa came walking down those stairs . . .

"How are you doing, handsome?"

A female voice at his elbow turned Quince toward the slight saloon girl standing beside him, and he frowned. He had neither the time nor the patience for what she had to offer.

About to speak those thoughts, Quince paused when the saloon girl said softly, "Don't you remember me?" She smiled, a shaky tentative smile that halted his intended rebuff. "I saw you in here a couple of nights ago. I came over, but you had other things on your mind, and you left before we could become acquainted." She took a short breath, then said, "My name's Blanche. Yours is Quince, ain't it?"

He remembered her, all right. Her name should've been "Persistence," because she hadn't moved from his side until he'd walked out of the saloon that night. Yet he also remembered that flash of desperation in her eyes—the same look he saw now when she forced her shaky smile wider and said, "Buy me a drink, why don't you?"

Quince shook his head, then said kindly, "Look, I don't have time for company today. You'd do better to find yourself somebody else who'll make your time worthwhile."

He wasn't prepared to hear that same desperation in Blanche's voice when she said unexpectedly, "Buy me a drink . . . please."

Silent, Quince looked at her more closely. Her blond hair didn't appear dyed; her darkly kohled eyes were a velvet brown; and underneath the heavy makeup of her trade and the green satin dress that displayed her generous bosom to great advantage, she didn't appear any older than Abby.

He signaled the bartender for her drink, then said in a softened tone, "Look, Blanche, I don't mean to hurt your feelings, but you're wasting your time."

"No, I'm not." Picking up her drink the moment it was placed in front of her, Blanche sipped it, then said, "The bartender's mad at me. I'm in trouble if I don't start getting some money into the till today." She shrugged. "You don't have to do nothin'—just stand there and let me talk to you a little bit."

"Blanche—"

"Please."

Unable to refuse the appeal in her eyes, Quince nodded. Movement on the upstairs landing drew his gaze as another couple exited one of the rooms laughing. Turning back toward Blanche store, he asked abruptly, "All right, so talk to me. Tell me who's in the upstairs rooms right now."

"The upstairs rooms?"

"The traffic seems to be pretty heavy there for this time of day."

Obviously uncertain, Blanche shrugged. "Madge is up there with one of her regulars. That's Willow coming down the stairs now. Violet ain't here anymore. O'Malley fired her, and Bonnie's in one of the other rooms."

"Who's she with?"

Blanche's gaze narrowed. "Why? Are you looking for somebody?"

"Yeah, I am." Quince paused. "Do you know Jack Hunter? He spends a lot of time in here, I understand."

"Your pa." At Quince's raised brow, Blanche explained, "Everybody in town knows the Hunters. Crystal worked here before she married Brent, your pa's a regular since he got out of prison, and you're Quince Hunter, the brother who was gone for five years—out fighting Injun renegades."

Quince unconsciously shook his head. "I forgot what a small town Diablo is."

"I know why your pa went to prison, too."

Quince stiffened.

"I'm sorry," she said. "That must've been hard,

but everybody says what a nice lady your ma was. You're lucky you had her for a while, though. I didn't know my ma, but I always wished I did."

Quince blinked at the idea that Ma's brief life had been a gift, despite the manner of her death. He'd never thought of it that way.

Movement on the second-floor landing again caught Quince's attention, and Blanche said, "Your pa's not up there. He hasn't come in yet today. He usually comes in later, when the card games get heavy in the back of the saloon."

Somehow relieved, Quince nodded. "Thanks. I appreciate that."

"I wish everything was that easy." Quince's silence prompted Blanche to continue, "I mean, I wish all problems could be settled that easy."

Quince almost smiled. "You're too young to have problems."

Blanche's eyes filled unexpectedly. Blinking away her momentary lapse with a laugh, she said, "I ain't so young—not anymore, anyways."

Surprised when one of the other girls brushed past him, then bumped into Blanche boldly, he heard the girl whisper, "Blanche . . . watch out. He's back."

Looking up a moment too late, Blanche gasped as a long-haired cowpoke grabbed her arm and pushed her backward against a table, then grated to the three silent fellows standing behind him, "So, you boys wasn't lying, after all."

"I didn't do nothing, Lobo." Panicked, Blanche pleaded, "I was just talking to this fella."

Grabbing the cowpoke's arm when he raised it

to strike her, Quince said, "Like the lady said, we were talking."

Unable to break free of Quince's hold, the cowpoke growled, "Let me go."

Quince held his gaze for a silent moment, then released him and said, "If you raise your hand to this lady again, you won't have time to think better of it."

Quince saw it then, the revealing flicker of the cowpoke's eyes. Snapping his hand to his holster the second before the man's hand reached his side, Quince drew his gun and whipped it across the cowpoke's jaw. Turning toward the three men behind the fellow as he fell heavily to the floor, Quince said softly, "I'd get your friend out of here if I were you." And when they moved to comply, he added, "Make sure you tell him if he tries something like that again, he'll be an even sorrier fella than he will be when he wakes up."

Acutely aware that the saloon had gone silent, Quince turned back to the bartender and said, "Another drink for Blanche here, and for me, too."

He noted Blanche's trembling as the unconscious cowpoke's friends dragged him out the door. The saloon came to life again. He waited for her to move back to the bar beside him before prompting softly, "You were saying?"

Glory walked out of the mercantile store, her jaw tight. She had been delayed in returning to the ranch because of the shopping list Pete had given her. Several of the items had been lodged in the back room of the store, waiting to be unpacked. Burt had been unable to leave the counter when the store was filled to capacity, and she had been forced to wait while talk about Quince Hunter's fight over a saloon girl at the Lone Star Saloon spread like wildfire.

Unable to restrain herself, Glory glanced toward the boldly painted establishment at the end of the street. It hadn't taken Quince long to fall in step with the Hunter line. Brent Hunter had married a woman who formerly worked in the Lone Star, Jack Hunter was rumored to spend more time now in that saloon than he did on the Half-Moon, and Matt had at one time been one of the Lone Star's best customers.

Pausing only to fasten her package onto her saddle, Glory mounted up and turned her horse toward home. A strange heat warming her skin, she remembered the strength of Quince Hunter's arms as he'd swung her up onto his saddle despite her protests that first day. He had done it with no effort at all. She recalled the sensation of those powerful arms closing around her that morning, preventing her fall. She wondered if his arms were wrapped around that saloon girl right now, and if he was looking down at her with the same penetrating, green-eyed stare that raised such intense emotions in her.

And then she wondered why she cared.

"Miss Glory! Wait a minute!" Running out of the store after her, Burt waved a small package, shouting, "You forgot the peppermint sticks Pete wanted."

Turning back toward Burt without a word, Glory accepted the package he held out to her. Impatient to escape her confusion, she dug her heels into her mount's sides and started him back up the street at a pace that sent pedestrians scrambling.

Chapter Five

The day had been clear and warm. Twilight was filled with the sounds of approaching night as Edmund turned his mount onto a familiar winding trail through a shadowed copse. He recalled the visitors to his office several days before—first Glory Townsend, then Quince Hunter.

A familiar anger tightened his jaw. Glory . . . so lovely with that flaming red hair and those smoldering dark eyes . . . so appealing with her tight, slim body and pale skin.

And so damned haughty!

Their brief conversation in his office that morning had run over and over again in his mind, each time igniting a hotter anger. But Glory's claim of financial stability hadn't fooled him. The loan on the Diamond C came due in four months, and the truth was that the ranch was all but his.

That thought brought him momentary satisfaction, and Edmund sneered. With the loss of their prize mare, the ranch's future was all but nil—but it was the present that he was determined to control, if only to teach Glory the lesson she deserved. It would not be difficult. Alone, with only a crippled father to turn to, she would soon realize that her future depended on him.

Taking care of Quince Hunter and the Hunter clan would take a little longer—but the satisfaction would be well worth the wait.

With those thoughts in mind, Edmund rode slowly as he sought the outline of a cabin in the isolated terrain. Locating it at last, aware that he was being watched as he approached, he whistled—one short, three long trills. He smiled when the cabin door opened and Kane stood framed in the light of the fireplace within, his rifle lowered to his side.

Edmund smiled as Kane raised thick, dark eyebrows at his approach. Edmund could see that the filthy bastard was practically salivating at the expectation of what he would propose.

Mentally counting the currency in his pocket, Edmund acknowledged to himself that Kane's services had always come at a high price, and that the price had escalated with each service performed. Despite his arrogance, however, Kane was good at what he did, and the money paid was well spent—at least, for the present.

Drawing his horse up in front of the cabin, Edmund dismounted. He reached into his pocket and withdrew a thick wad of bound bills to hold up for Kane's inspection. Seeing the anticipation in Kane's eyes, he walked inside.

"Come on inside, Jack."

Unwilling to admit even to himself how much he appreciated Crystal's words of welcome, Jack Hunter entered the cabin by the Half-Moon's north stream where Brent lived with his new wife. He smiled as he glanced at Crystal's rounded stomach. He'd taken unexpected comfort in the news that Crystal was pregnant with Brent's child. But then, the former dance-hall girl had been an unexpected comfort to him in other ways as well.

Entering the well-kept cabin, Jack said, "I was just passing by and thought I'd stop in."

"Brent's already gone to meet the hands in the west pasture. Something about driving the horses to a place where they can be sorted out more easily."

"Yeah, I figured they could handle that chore without me today."

He sat down, and she poured coffee into the cup she set before him.

"Brent's not happy with the way things have been going, Jack," Crystal said abruptly.

Pausing with the cup halfway to his lips, Jack frowned. "There isn't anything I can do to please my sons."

"I don't think that's true."

"It is." Taking a gulp of the scalding brew, Jack frowned, then continued slowly, "Thank you for not telling Brent or any of the others that I've been visiting you mornings."

Brushing back a strand of pale hair, Crystal said, "I want you to know that I've struggled with that, but Brent's so upset at some of the things you're done lately that he might want to put a stop to your visits, and I didn't think that would be fair."

"He doesn't understand."

"Maybe because you haven't explained your ambitions to him the way you have to me."

"Brent isn't like you. He's stubborn. He won't listen."

Crystal frowned, then continued more softly, "What about Quince? I met him briefly a few days ago when I went to the ranch house. He seems like a reasonable fella. You haven't given him a chance to try to understand."

"That would be a waste of time." The lines of fatigue in his face deepened as he continued. "When Brent and Quince look at me, I know what they're thinking. They're thinking about their ma."

"Jack . . ."

"I loved her, you know." His eyes grew moist. "Beth was the best thing that ever happened to me. She made possible all the good things in my life." At Crystal's silence, he shook his head. "Don't ask me what happened that last day. I was so damned drunk . . ."

"I'm sorry, Jack."

Jack took another swallow of coffee, then shrugged. "That's all water under the bridge. I served my ten years, and while I did, I got some ideas about how to make a success of the

Half-Moon like Beth and I always dreamed."

"I know, you told me."

Jack smiled briefly. "That's the trouble, I guess. You're the only one who ever listens to me when I talk—you and Edmund."

"Edmund . . ." Crystal shook her head. "I don't think he's the friend to you that he pretends to be."

"That's Brent talking, not you."

"If Edmund was really your friend—"

"I didn't come here for a lecture."

Crystal drew back, then continued slowly, "Did you ever consider that you aren't giving your sons a chance, Jack?" She smiled, the same smile that Jack remembered when he had walked into the Lone Star that first time after his release from prison, when Crystal was the only one who looked at him without condemnation. Somehow he had not expected that sympathetic dance-hall girl to marry his son.

"Jack?"

"I've got plans, Crystal. Big plans—a deal that's going to turn things around for the Half-Moon."

Crystal's smile faded. "Brent says you've already put the Half-Moon back into more debt than he can handle."

"That's only temporary. I'm a handy man with cards. I used to make my living at it. Things haven't been going too well yet, but I'll get a winning streak that'll take care of everything."

"Brent says you've been drinking again, too."

"Brent says a lot of things."

"Jack—"

"Don't you worry your head about it."

"You should tell Brent what you're planning."

"I will. I'll tell them all soon."

"But—"

"I've already made the deal, Crystal. I'm just waiting to hear back. It's too late to change anything, if that's what you're thinking." Jack paused. "I just wanted you to know—because of the baby and all."

He stood up abruptly. "I have to go. I've got an appointment in town."

"At the Lone Star?"

Anger flashing in his gaze for the first time, Jack replied, "I'll take care of things, just like I said."

Riding away, Jack did not look back to see Crystal's worried expression as she watched him go.

"I don't know how it happened, Pa."

The last thing Glory had expected to do that evening was to bring her father bad news. Shaken, she watched his face grow ashen as she described the morning's ghastly discovery.

The sun had been shining brightly on the pasture when Glory and the men rode through on their way to repair fences. The buzzing of bees and the chatter of magpies were the only sounds that broke the prevailing silence when they came upon the devastating scene.

Six brood mares lay dead around a water hole that the Diamond C had used without problems since its inception.

She remembered dismounting and examining

the animals, then turning toward Jan to say abruptly, "What could've happened here? The water hole must have been fouled, but how?"

"I don't know, Miss Glory." Jan had shaken his head, his ruddy complexion darkening as he said, "I can't figure it. Maybe underground seepage of some kind."

"Underground seepage."

That thought had remained with her, as had the knot of nausea in her stomach as the stiffening animals were dragged away and disposed of, and the water hole was fenced off.

The sun was setting when the weary band returned home, but Glory had known that the worst was yet to come. Her heart had sunk at the sight of her father wheeling himself out onto the porch, the welcome on his lips frozen by their somber expressions.

Glory continued softly, "I don't understand it, Pa. We've never had a problem like this before."

"Which mares were killed?" Byron asked.

"The three-year-olds we were expecting to breed soon."

Byron fought to control breathing that was becoming increasingly labored as he said, "That finishes off our breeding plans for next year. I'm afraid it'll finish off the Diamond C as well."

"No." Glory forced a smile. "We're not done for yet. The Diamond C has plenty of potential."

Byron's breathing grew more strained, and Glory felt the edge of panic. She continued more quietly than before, "We're all tired and hungry now. Everything will look better when we have some of Pete's food in our stomachs and we've had some time to think things over. Come on, let's go inside."

"I'm all right, Glory," Byron said. "You might take your own advice, though, darlin'. Supper's not ready yet. Why don't you go upstairs and freshen up? Jan can bring me inside."

"No, Pa, I—"

"Please, darlin'." Byron smiled. "We can talk about this later."

Not waiting for her reply, Byron addressed Jan, who stood silent behind Glory. "I'd appreciate it if you'd bring me inside while the other fellas wash up, Jan. There are some things I've been meaning to talk to you about."

Confused by her father's gentle dismissal, Glory followed at a distance as Jan pushed her father toward the study. She was about to turn toward her room when Byron said to the foreman, "Close the door behind you."

Glory walked slowly, deliberately, toward the closed study door. Pausing there, she listened to the conversation on the other side. She heard the agitation in her father's voice when he said, "Underground seepage be damned! Tell me what you think really happened, Jan."

"I don't know, sir." Jan's reply was hesitant. "All I know is that a tainted water hole like that is unlikely. This is more than bad luck, as far as I'm concerned."

"Did you have a chance to look around?"

"No, sir. There was too much work to be done—work that couldn't wait."

"I don't mind telling you that I'm starting to get worried. I want you and the men to be on your guard."

"Yes, sir."

"I don't want you telling any of this to Miss Glory. I could be wrong, and I don't want her unnecessarily concerned, but I want you to watch out for her, too."

"Yes, sir."

"I'm depending on you."

Aware that the conversation was drawing to a halt, Glory turned swiftly toward her room. She closed the door just as Jan was exiting the study.

Standing behind her bedroom door, Glory made a solemn resolution. Whatever was happening, she was going to make things right. She'd go into town tomorrow and talk to Edmund.

Her stomach twisted at the thought, but she raised her chin. She'd get Edmund to extend another loan to the Diamond C so they could replenish the breeding stock they needed, and she'd find a way to meet the payments on time if it was the last thing she ever did.

The sun was setting, tinting the gray of twilight with brilliant shades of pink and gold as Quince stared incredulously at Brent. Having spent the day working with Red and Curly in the east pasture, Quince had returned home hungry and weary a few minutes ago. The sight of Brent pacing in front of the ranch house had started the men mumbling, and caused apprehension to prickle down Quince's spine.

Quince had nudged his mount to a faster pace. Having seen Brent like that only a few times before, he had known his brother was just one step from losing control—a situation which Brent rarely allowed.

Seething, Brent waited for him to dismount, then asked, "Do you know where Pa is?"

"No. I thought he was working with you and Buck today."

Brent's smile was devoid of mirth as he said, "Same old Pa—out having a good time in town while everybody else is working."

Quince frowned at his brother's growing anger. "We don't know that for sure."

"No, maybe not, but I know for a fact how he's been spending some of his time." Pulling a wrinkled sheet from his pocket, Brent said coldly, "I got home early and started going over the ranch papers. I opened a letter addressed to the Diamond C that Jesse Wilkins dropped off on his way past the ranch this morning." Brent paused, his color heightening. "Do you want to know what it says?"

Quince waited, knowing there was no need to respond.

"It's a letter confirming the sale of stock to the Half-Moon, *twenty-five mares,* at a price for each that we couldn't afford to pay for even one."

Quince shook his head, incredulous. "That has to be a mistake. Even Pa wouldn't do something so crazy."

"It's not a mistake. The mares were bought north of here. The letter says they're almost ready to be picked up."

97

"Where did Pa get the money to pay for all this?"

"Where do you think?"

Quince cursed aloud.

"Right. It took ten long years to clean up the mess Pa made of things before he went to prison, and it's taken only a few short months for him to put the ranch back in the same spot again."

"How deep is the debt?"

Brent shook his head. "I don't know for sure. Pa wouldn't let me near the books after I saw his initial expenses. He has the books locked up now. If I hadn't happened to come back before he did tonight, I wouldn't even know what he was paying for those mares."

"What about the loan for the mares? What are the terms?"

"Terms? Do you think Pa ever considered *terms*? He thinks he's going to win enough money gambling to pay off the loan and make the Half-Moon the biggest horse ranch in this part of Texas."

"Maybe you're judging Pa too harshly. Maybe the terms of the loan—"

"I saw the loan papers." Brent's jaw hardened. "Pa must've gotten drunk after he signed them, because he left them on the desk."

"And?"

"He has to pay the loan back in six months."

"Six months! There's no way he can get a return on that investment in six months."

Brent stared at him without replying.

Quince felt the knot in his stomach tighten.

"And if he doesn't pay the loan back on time—"

"I don't have to tell you what happens then."

"Edmund wouldn't do that. He wouldn't foreclose on the Half-Moon."

"You know Edmund as well as I do, Quince. Are you sure he wouldn't?"

At a loss for words, Quince did not reply.

Brent shook his head. "If I could have gotten that contract with the army for those mustangs—"

"What contract?"

"Months ago, before Pa came home. With Victorio acting up again, the army needs horses that can stand the rigors of hard riding in this country. Mustangs might not be the best-looking mounts, but they do the job."

"Where do they need them?"

"Fort Griffin."

"Fort Griffin . . ." Quince's expression said it all.

"Yeah, and the fort's in worse shape than it ever was."

"Why didn't you get the contract?"

"I guess I should've realized there'd be a problem when the officer in charge agreed to meet me at Fort Sam Houston on the way to pick up Pa."

"What happened?"

"Lieutenant Barnes wanted money up front for his own pocket before he'd award the contract—more money than I could afford to pay."

"Did you complain to his superiors?"

"His *superiors*? That's a joke. They would've laughed in my face. That damned fort is a disgrace!"

"Is the contract still open?"

"I heard it was. There aren't many ranchers who'd pay the price Barnes was asking."

Brent searched Quince's expression for a few moments, then said, "If you're thinking about trying to get that contract without paying him, you'd be wasting your time. You'd be making a long trip to Fort Griffin for nothing."

"Do you have a better idea?"

"Yes, I do. I'm going to wait for Pa and I'm going to make him back out of that contract for the horses."

It was Quince's turn to look skeptical.

"Or I'll break that contract *for* him!"

Quince walked toward the house without responding.

"Where are you going?"

"I'm going to pack my gear. I'm heading out to Fort Griffin in the morning."

"You've been gone five years, but nothing has really changed, has it?" Brent snapped. "You still think you can handle things better than I ever could."

"No, that isn't what I was thinking, but you're right, Brent. It does look like nothing has changed at all."

Iona Montgomery sat balanced precariously on the edge of her bed, finding it difficult to maintain stability. It occurred to her as she faced Dr. Gibbs that life had become perpetually difficult of late. Proof of that fact was her embarrassment at having awakened that morning hardly able to lift her head—only to realize that she had fallen asleep in her afternoon clothing.

Iona fought to clear her mind. She remembered she had forced herself to dress despite her lethargy the previous day, and had gone to the dining room to be with Edmund when he returned for his afternoon meal. To her dismay, she had no recollection of the hours that followed. She had woken up a few minutes earlier in the condition she now found herself, with Dr. Gibbs at her door.

Dr. Gibbs's sharp tone penetrated her mental haze. He was angry, but she wasn't sure why.

"Iona, did you hear what I said?"

"I'm sorry. I didn't."

"I said your drinking has gotten out of hand."

"It's just a little sherry, Doctor."

Dr. Gibbs took a step closer. "You've been dosing yourself with laudanum, too, haven't you?"

"Laudanum?"

"Don't pretend!"

Iona's smile wavered. "It helps me to sleep when I'm anxious."

"You're anxious because you've been using laudanum to excess. I intended it to be used only for a limited time when I prescribed it for you. That's why I refused to provide it for you any longer. Laudanum can be dangerous, especially when combined with the liquor you've been consuming."

"I told you, I only drink a little sherry to calm my nerves."

"Sherry to calm your nerves. Laudanum to help

you sleep. Are you hearing what you're saying, Iona?"

"It's only temporary, until I'm feeling better."

"Iona—"

"What's the problem, doctor?"

Dr. Gibbs's head turned toward the doorway where Edmund had appeared unexpectedly. Embarrassed at her dishevelment, Iona raised a shaky hand to her hair as the doctor replied, "I'm attempting to advise my patient of the potential danger of her situation."

Edmund advanced toward them, and Iona smiled. Her husband was such a handsome man. And so thoughtful. She had considered herself the luckiest woman in the world when he began courting her, and she had silently resolved to be worthy of him.

But she had failed.

Iona's smile faltered. She could not forgive herself for that . . . for not being all that Edmund had hoped she would be.

Edmund took her hand and raised her to her feet. His gaze was tender as he said, "The doctor is obviously concerned, dear."

"It's nothing, Edmund—nothing important." Turning back to the frowning physician, Iona said softly, "I'm sorry to worry you, Doctor. I'm really fine, but you may rest assured I'll keep in mind everything you said."

Appearing unconvinced, Dr. Gibbs responded, "Iona, you must realize—"

"You heard what my wife said. She's fine." His level tone brooking no further discussion, Edmund continued, "Now if I may show you to the door?"

Waiting only until the two men had cleared her doorway, Iona sat back down on her bed. She could not seem to make Dr. Gibbs understand that she was simply tired. She slept poorly without her medicine, and without sleep, she was not at her best.

Iona sighed. But he was a good man. He meant well.

Iona reached over to the nightstand and pulled the door open. The crystal decanter inside sparkled in the limited light. A bit of sherry would settle her nerves, and then she'd dress to share a meal with her husband. She cherished those brief hours. Edmund and she seemed to share so little together of late.

Iona filled her glass with a shaky hand. Yes, a bit of sherry for her nerves and she'd be a new woman.

Unaware of the tear that trailed down her pale cheek, Iona forced from her mind the recurring thought laudanum could no longer suppress—that no matter how hard she tried, she would never be woman enough for the man she loved.

Iona's bedroom door was closed. Dr. Gibbs followed Edmund down the hallway to the street entrance. When Edmund turned toward him, he whispered harshly, "I'm warning you, Edmund—"

"You're warning *me*, Doctor?"

"You don't seem to understand the risk Iona is taking."

"What risk is that?"

"Simply put, laudanum and sherry can be a lethal combination. Iona cannot seem to grasp that concept."

"My wife knows what she's doing."

"I don't believe she does." Nervous perspiration trailed from his temples as the anxious physician continued, "I intended for Iona to use the laudanum only for temporary relief."

"I believe we've already had this conversation."

"Yet you continue to procure laudanum for her against my advice."

"Iona is miserable without it."

"She'd survive."

"She wants me to get it for her."

"You are not helping her."

"She's my wife. I am simply providing for her as our marriage vows prescribe."

"I don't think her daughter, Juliana, would agree with that statement if she were here."

"But Juliana isn't here, and Iona is my responsibility."

Drawing his rounded shoulders upright, Dr. Gibbs said with a twitch of his lips, "I must warn you that your conduct in this regard approaches criminality, Edmund. Should Iona suffer because of it, I'll be forced to tell the sheriff about our conversation today."

"Criminality?" Edmund appeared amused. "Apparently, I also need to make myself clearer than I did at our last conversation. Plainly put, I wouldn't speak to the sheriff if I were you. If you did, several possible incidents in your past might come to light."

Nodding as the doctor went suddenly still, he continued, "You see, my connections are extensive, Doctor. When I wired an inquiry back East a few years ago about the arrival in Diablo of a very knowledgeable physician, a man who seemed content to bury himself in our small town to treat the common rabble here when he obviously had a superior education and was qualified for so much more, my contact sent me a photograph of a doctor who was wanted for performing abortions that had caused the deaths of several women."

Edmund halted to assess the effect of his words. When Dr. Gibbs appeared frozen, he continued with a smile, "Of course, I realized at the time that your resemblance to the man in the photograph might have been mere coincidence."

Dr. Gibbs did not respond.

"So, since Diablo needed a physician and there were no present problems with your services, I saw no need to stir up any controversy. However, should that situation change . . ."

Edmund paused again, then flashed his benevolent smile. "I hope we understand each other more clearly now."

Dr. Gibbs nodded stiffly, then turned toward the door. He did not turn back when Edmund continued, "It's my hope that our conversation doesn't induce you to abandon our community, Doctor. Unfortunately, if it did, that photograph might find its way into the sheriff's hands to then be posted all over the West."

When Dr. Gibbs looked back at him sharply,

Edmund added, "Diablo does need you, you know."

His benevolent smile becoming fixed, Edmund watched as Dr. Gibbs left, closing the door behind him without speaking a word.

Glory breathed a relieved sigh when Diablo came into view at last. She glanced toward the sun making a slow ascent in the clear morning sky. She had pushed her mount harder than she should, so intense was her desire to reach town so she might return with news that would lift her father's spirits.

She had deliberately misled Jan when the men rode out that morning, telling him she'd be working with the hands in another pasture for the day. She had made sure to ride out with the others, but had left them as soon as was feasible, with the excuse that she was going to join Jan. Telling herself the deceit was necessary so she wouldn't be raising anyone's hopes needlessly if Edmund should prove immune to her pleas, she had then headed for Diablo as fast as her mount could carry her.

Glory mentally reviewed her situation as she had countless times during the sleepless night past. The loss of six brood mares could prove fatal to the ranch's financial health, but it was her father's physical condition that worried her. Supper last night had been a mostly silent affair. Conversation between the men had been strained. The expressions on their faces had been revealing, reflecting a concern almost as deep as her own when Pa put down his fork with a shaky hand halfway through the meal and with a flimsy excuse went to his room.

She had followed him, only to be dismissed with a smile of reassurance that he was merely tired— but Glory knew the truth. Pa was sinking rapidly. Doc Gibbs had prescribed a tonic to boost Pa's energy on his last visit to the ranch. He had also said to her in confidence that there was nothing more he could do.

Glory's throat choked tight. Pa was slipping away, but she'd be damned if she'd let him close his eyes for the last time believing that the Diamond C was slipping away, as well—or that he had failed.

Glory urged her horse cautiously down Diablo's main street, past a lively congregation in front of the sheriff's office. Amusement appeared to be the general reaction to a notice posted on the billboard there. Noting her inquisitive glance, Sheriff Dawson tipped his hat and called out, "Nice to see you again, Miss Glory. The fellas here have been reading the notice posted by a trooper from Fort Griffin this morning. They're finding it real interesting."

Fort Griffin. Glory shuddered. Everybody knew that fort's reputation.

Reading her expression accurately, the sheriff laughed. "That's what the fellas here have been saying. The commander is still looking to fill that contract for mustangs that everybody heard about months back. It seems they can't find nobody either able or willing to hook up with that lot."

Glory drew back on her mount's reins.

Raising his hairy brows when she dismounted and approached him, Sheriff Dawson questioned, "Don't tell me you're interested, Miss Glory? Hell—" He reddened, then said in a softer tone, "Excuse me for my plain talk, ma'am, but there ain't a uniform at that fort anybody can trust, much less when talking to a . . ."

Sheriff Dawson halted abruptly, his color deepening.

Much less when talking to a woman was how he had meant to conclude his statement.

Glory stared back at the burly sheriff. Knowing he meant well, she forced a smile. "I'm just curious, and I sure could use a laugh as much as anybody else."

His relief apparent, Sheriff Dawson turned to the men clustered in front of the posted announcement and said, "Make way for the lady, fellas. It ain't gentlemanly to keep this joke all to ourselves."

Her smile growing stiff, Glory eased her way closer to the notice. She read it through once, then read it again.

Nodding a thank-you at the burly sheriff, she returned to her horse and mounted—then rode back up the street in the direction from which she had come.

Chapter Six

Sadly, Fort Griffin was all it was rumored to be, and more.

His gaze narrowing as he guided his mount cautiously through the grounds, Quince assessed the fort more closely. The early morning sun shone on rows of wooden barracks appearing to number almost ninety or more, all in an advanced state of disrepair. The surrounding structures were no better. The roads and walkways were littered with all manner of refuse, as were parade grounds that were badly neglected. Civilian buildings were primitive and poorly tended at best, and a surprising lack of discipline was notable among the milling military personnel. His stomach lurched at the smell of sanitary conditions that fouled the air, completing an atmosphere of overall deterioration that to his mind had advanced to the point of no return.

Quince was aware that although Fort Griffin had never reached the military standards intended for the post, it had at one time functioned well in forays against the Kiowa and Comanche and as a base in the Red River campaigns. He also knew that once hostile incursions waned, the fort had temporarily rivaled Fort Worth as a cow town. Not surprisingly, with the decline of military activity had come long periods of boredom for the soldiers, which had spawned corruption in the ranks and the phenomenal growth of The Flat.

The Flat, a town adjacent to the fort, where all manner of vice was rumored available to fill empty hours, had a reputation all its own.

However, after several hard days on the trail with Brent's harsh words ringing in his ears, Quince had just one goal in mind. Heading toward one of the stone structures that was official in appearance, he drew up at the hitching post, dismounted, and walked up the steps.

The military clerk in the outer office looked up from his desk as Quince announced, "I'm here to see the fort commander."

The fellow assessed him with a critical, sweeping glance, then responded, "Why do you want to see him?"

Annoyed, Quince replied, "That's my business."

The clerk snapped back, "If you don't tell me what you want—"

"Never mind, Corporal. I'll see him."

The familiar voice turned Quince toward the

commandant's door. A broad smile spread across his lips when he saw the officer standing there.

"Well, I'll be damned." Stepping forward, Quince accepted the hand Major Jonah Tremain extended to him in greeting. He shook it warmly and asked, "What are you doing in this hellhole, Jonah?" Following him into his office, Quince waited until the door was closed behind them before continuing. "The last time I saw you, you were flat on your back in bed with an Apache bullet in your leg."

Grinning, Jonah replied, "And the last time I saw you, you said you were going to Texas to keep an appointment that had been waiting for five years. I didn't know then that I'd be following right behind you."

Quince eyed his friend more closely. Jonah's skin was still pale, but his eyes were clear and his limp, as he had preceded him into the office, had been hardly discernible.

"So, why are you here?" Quince asked.

"Orders. Victorio's been acting up, and the officers at this fort had been ineffective in taking the necessary steps to combat the threat he poses." Jonah paused. "Bluntly put, the fort's reputation reached the ears of higher-ups and I was sent here to 'handle' the situation."

"Handle the situation." Quince shook his head. "That's a pretty tall order, from what I can see."

"The fort was in worse shape when I first got here. There was no discipline or organization at all, much less incentive among personnel to get the job done unless it filled individual pockets along the way."

"You're expected to turn everything around?"

"Not exactly." His even features sober, Jonah continued, "The higher command has accepted the fact that with the present shortage of funds, the situation here is beyond total redemption. My job is to get the necessities accomplished."

"What about your injury?"

"A scratch. It's almost healed." Jonah continued, "The education I received in dealing with Geronimo made me the most experienced Indian fighter available who also has an organizational background. The men at the top think I'm the man to figure out what we'll need to be effective against Victorio. They also expect me to secure whatever's necessary, any way I can, so I can follow through."

Silently doubting Jonah's light dismissal of his injury, Quince asked, "What do you mean by 'whatever's necessary'?"

"Supplies, military equipment, and the armaments necessary to wage a successful campaign. I've already taken steps in that regard, but what's needed most of all here are decent mounts for the men. It would be impossible to chase Victorio down with the nags most of these men are riding. Victorio would run them into the ground in a matter of days. A contract to supply horses to the fort has been offered locally, but the fort's reputation has evidently made ranchers in the area think twice about doing business here. I've sent men out to post notices offering the contract in different communities, but so far, no one has responded."

"You're looking for saddle horses with stamina, horses that are accustomed to the territory. You're talking mustangs."

"Damned right. One thing I learned while chasing Geronimo is that when it comes to hard riding on local terrain, mustangs leave the pampered horseflesh I was accustomed to riding in the dust."

"You've got that right."

"As soon as I can get those horses . . ."

Jonah halted abruptly. The light of sudden realization entered his eyes as he continued more slowly, "I never did ask what brought you to Fort Griffin, did I, Quince?"

Dispensing with formalities, Quince responded simply, "How many mustangs do you want me to deliver?"

Blanche walked out the Lone Star's back door toward the convenience in the rear yard. It had been a long and difficult day. A group of cattle-company wranglers had stopped off for some recreation in Diablo while making their way back home. The pace had been hectic from the moment she had entered the saloon, and it looked like it was going to be a long night.

Blanche unconsciously sighed. She was only seventeen and she felt like ninety. She was tired. Her skin was crawling from the touch of callused hands, and from the realization that the evening had barely begun.

Her thoughts returned to Quince Hunter, as they had countless time since she had last seen him. She didn't remember ever being treated as gently as Quince had treated her. She didn't recall ever feeling as safe as she did when she had looked up into his eyes. He had actually listened to her when she talked, as if he was interested in *her* instead of what she had to offer. During the few, short hours they had spent together, she had told him more about herself than she had ever confided to anyone, and his responses had been so kind. For a while after he left, she had actually started to believe she might be worth something, after all.

Unfortunately, that feeling hadn't lasted long.

Telling herself she was wasting her time, she had found herself glancing hopefully at the saloon entrance each time the doors squeaked open. When days passed and Quince didn't return, she actually began fantasizing about what it would be like if he loved her; how it would feel to lie in his arms knowing he wasn't just passing time like the others; how she would feel knowing she meant more to him than any other woman in the world. She began wishing—

Gasping as an arm slipped unexpectedly around her neck from behind, Blanche heard Lobo's voice rasp in her ear, "I knew you'd come out here sooner or later. I figured it was just a matter of time."

Panic gripped Blanche as she struggled to breathe. O'Malley had kept Lobo out of the Lone Star since his last episode with Quince. He had done it because Lobo was trouble, but she had known it wasn't over for her yet.

Darkness began closing against her eyelids as Lobo's grip tightened and he whispered, "You're going to pay for what you did to me, but I ain't going to kill you—oh, no. You're worth more to me alive than dead." Loosening his hold when Blanche started going limp in his arms, he snapped, "Are you listenin' to me?"

When she was again fully conscious, he continued, "You get paid tonight, and I'll be waiting in the alley to collect after you finish up. I'll let you keep the change you've got tucked down deep in your bosom, though." He laughed when she reacted physically to his statement. "Yeah, I know about the little bit extra some fellas have been slipping you. You'd better keep them real happy, because that's all you'll have to live on."

Tightening his hold so that Blanche was again struggling for breath, Lobo hissed, "Don't try reporting me to the sheriff or you'll regret it. Don't think you can get away from me, either, because I'll come after you. And as far as that Quince Hunter is concerned, he wouldn't have beat me to the draw if I hadn't been woozy from drinking—so keep that in mind. If there's a next time, it'll be different."

His voice growing menacingly sweet, Lobo whispered with his wet lips against her ear, "Tell me you understand what I'm saying, Blanche, honey."

Unable to speak, Blanche managed a feeble nod.

"Tell me you're going to do what I say, darlin'."

Terrified, Blanche nodded again.

Releasing her so abruptly that she fell to her knees, Lobo stood over her as she struggled to catch her breath and said, "Remember, I'll be waiting in the alley when you're done tonight. If you don't show up, I'll come and get you—and that won't be no fun for you at all."

Blanche was still gasping for breath when Lobo disappeared around the corner of the building. Finally managing to stand, she shuddered at the realization that he had meant every word.

Wearier than she could ever remember feeling, Glory entered Fort Griffin as the afternoon waned. Accompanied by Jan, Robbie, and Shorty, she had ridden long and hard for several days to get there. Far more difficult than the journey, however, had been the hours she'd spent beforehand convincing her father she needed to make the journey.

Concern about her father's health loomed ever larger in Glory's mind. Leaving him had been hard, but she had known the army contract was the only feasible way to raise the money needed to replace their breeding stock. She had stressed that point over and over again with him. She knew he balked only out of concern for her welfare, but she also knew she could trust no one but herself with the task of securing the contract.

Her father had agreed, on the condition that Jan, Shorty, and Robbie accompany her. She had consented for his peace of mind, but it had been more difficult than she had imagined to travel with insistent bodyguards at her side.

Relieved to have finally reached her destination, she approached the stone building to which she had been directed, one of the few among the many ramshackle wooden structures that comprised the fort. She was surprised when ushered into the commandant's office to see the handsome, spit-and-polish officer who stood politely upon her entrance and motioned her to a chair. She was devastated minutes later to learn that the contract was no longer available.

Obviously sincere, Major Tremain said, "I'm sorry, ma'am. I know how difficult your journey must have been. I regret that you made it unnecessarily, but the contract was awarded this morning."

"This morning . . ." Glory took a deep breath. "You're sure? I mean, you're certain you can count on the stock being delivered on time?" Somehow unwilling to surrender without a struggle, she pressed, "My men are skilled and dependable wranglers. We can deliver the mustangs to you saddle broken and ready to ride by whatever reasonable date you ask."

"I have no doubt that the conditions of the contract will be met."

"You can't be sure if you're not familiar with the outfit you gave the contract to. There are too many uncertainties involved." Desperate, Glory leaned toward the young officer and said, "You *can* be sure with the Diamond C."

"I know the person I contracted with very well. He's totally dependable. His word is his bond."

"Major—"

"Ma'am . . . I'm sorry." Obviously unwilling to discuss the matter further, the major stood up. He smiled sympathetically when she stood as well, then added, "I know you're tired from your journey. I wish I could offer you accommodations at the fort, but"—he shrugged—"conditions here aren't very favorable, as you're probably aware. You'll do well to try the new hotel in The Flat. Despite The Flat's reputation, the hotel is reasonably safe, and it has a restaurant where you and your men will be able to get a decent meal. I'm sure things will look better to you afterwards."

Drawing her pride around her, Glory forced a smile. "Thank you for your courtesy, Major." She added, "I'll leave my address with your clerk. I hope you'll wire the Diamond C if the contract falls through for any reason. We'll be happy to handle it for you if it does."

"I'll keep that in mind, ma'am."

The sincerity in the handsome major's gaze momentarily thickened the lump in Glory's throat. Forcing it aside, she left the office with her head high and a smile on her face that lasted only until they reached the horses, when she turned to Jan and said, "What are we going to do now?"

Quince leaned against the bar of the Silver Dollar Saloon, whiskey glass in hand as he looked around himself. The smoke-filled room was filled almost to capacity with itinerant cowpokes, ranchers, fancy-suited professionals, military personnel who appeared to mix with no restrictions of rank, gamblers, saloon girls, and other miscellaneous characters who defied description. A heavy-handed piano player banged out a steady stream of unrecognizable tunes from the corner of the room, adding to an overwhelming din of conversations conducted at a shout, roars of laughter, and the shuffle of dancing feet. An earlier tour of The Flat had revealed that business appeared to be brisk in all the other saloons as well.

Quince was momentarily amused. With The Flat close by, Jonah had his work cut out for him.

An unconscious smile flickered across Quince's lips. He had been damned glad to see his friend again. They had spent a good part of the afternoon talking, taking more time than he knew Jonah could spare, but neither of them had been of a mood to cut the visit short. Once the contract particulars were dispensed with, they had conversed as old friends, bringing each other up to date with smiles, laughter, and a few frowns. He had been relieved by the knowledge that with Jonah controlling the contract, he need no longer worry about corruption. As for the Victorio problem, he knew it could not be in better hands.

He had left the fort in early afternoon and had taken a room at the hotel Jonah had recommended so he could get a good night's sleep before starting back home. Fortified with a good meal and strong coffee, however, he had been distracted by the hoopla outside the restaurant window and had found his way to the bar where he presently stood.

Rejecting the advance of another buxom saloon girl, Quince downed his drink and signaled for a refill. It occurred to him belatedly that he hadn't even considered the saloon girls' invitations. It annoyed him to realize that once the pressure of Half-Moon affairs had been relieved from his mind, his thoughts had begun drifting in a direction where they too often strayed of late.

Fiery hair that glittered in the sun's rays, dark eyes that blazed with heat—*and a tongue sharper than the blade of his knife.*

Yet he was unable to suppress the image that inevitably followed, of smooth, white skin tinted a mellow gold by the sun; of a long-limbed, feminine body that had fit so well into his arms; and of a fleeting vulnerability in those black, blazing eyes that had somehow touched his soul.

A familiar knot tightened in his gut when he remembered the flush that had transfused Glory Townsend's white skin when he had held her close to steady her. He wondered if that heat would smolder if he—

Irritated by his growing fixation on a woman who so clearly despised him, Quince emptied his glass and tapped the bar for another. Determined to wipe Glory's image from his mind, he scanned the crowd for the woman in the blue satin dress whom he had just turned away. He spotted her in a corner and was about to beckon her toward him when his attention was caught by three men who had just pushed their way through the swinging doors.

Quince squinted through the heavy smoke. Two of them were unfamiliar, but the size of the third fellow made him unmistakable.

Glory had called him by the unlikely nickname, Shorty.

* * *

Glory assessed the small hotel room critically. The scarred dresser and chair and the washstand that leaned dangerously to the left were adequate, but the bed squeaked with her every move when she had sat on it briefly, and the linens were suspiciously wrinkled and stained. Dark smoke wafted upward from the two small oil lamps that lit the room, further darkening the already smudged ceiling above and leaving the air uncomfortably heavy to breathe.

Glory gave a caustic laugh. If she didn't know better, she'd think the sympathetic major had been joking when he said the best and newest hotel in the area was in The Flat.

The major had been right about the restaurant downstairs, however, and Glory had been glad. Jan, Robbie, and Shorty had been almost as despondent as she to learn that they had been only a few hours too late to get the army contract. They had been sorely discouraged, and she knew they deserved better than to spend another night serving as her protectors.

For that reason she had insisted that they take some time for themselves in town. She had listened impatiently to Jan's cautions after finally convincing them she just wanted to be alone. She had been appeased by their promises to dismiss the Diamond C's problems for a few hours while they cut loose.

The growing uproar on the street distracted her, and Glory walked to the window to look down on the activity below. She'd never seen a mix of people quite like those thronging the street—and she'd never seen such determined and abandoned merrymaking. She glanced into a doorway and saw a wrangler wrapped in a passionate embrace with a woman who clung to him as if he were her lifeline. When they separated at last, they walked down the street with the woman tucked into the curve of the wrangler's arm and then disappeared from sight.

Swept with a deep-seated emotion she couldn't clearly identify, Glory remembered the strength of Quince Hunter's arms when he lifted her up onto his horse despite her protests that first day. She remembered the warmth of the arms surrounding her, holding her secure although she was muddied and disheveled after suffering the humiliating and devastating loss of Cinnamon. She had reacted with anger to the comfort his arms afforded. She had wanted to escape him because she had somehow believed his strength emphasized her weakness.

She recalled the second time she was in Quince's embrace, when he'd caught her in his arms to prevent her fall. She remembered looking up into his eyes, somehow sensing he was able to see past her facade of strength to the panic beginning to expand inside her.

Anger had again been her response. It had been followed by an ache deep inside when she later learned Quince had gone straight from their encounter to a Lone Star saloon girl who was so important to him that he had fought to protect her.

Confused, Glory turned away from the window. She had spoken the truth when she told Jan she wanted some time alone. She was hurting. She needed to come to terms with the myriad emotions and uncertainties assaulting her.

Glory looked up at the sound of a knock on the door. Jan and the others couldn't be returning already. Their intentions were good, but their sympathetic glances were more than she could presently bear.

Determined to send them straight back to the nearest saloon, Glory unlocked the door and pulled it open. The words froze on her lips at the sight of Quince Hunter standing in the opening.

Reacting sharply to the embodiment of the image she had ejected from her thoughts only moments earlier, Glory snapped, "What are you doing here?"

His muscular frame filled the doorway, and his expression was sober as he looked at her without any immediate response.

Struck by a thought that made her take a spontaneous step backward, Glory muttered incredulously, "Oh, no . . . you can't be the one."

"I met Shorty and your men in the Silver Dollar down the street. They told me you came here to get the army contract."

"You're the person who got the contract, right?" She gave a bitter laugh. "You found out I was going after it somehow and made sure you'd beat me to it."

"That's not true."

"Isn't it?"

"Why would I do that?"

"You're saying it's merely a coincidence that you're here?"

Retreating an automatic few steps when Quince advanced toward her, Glory frowned as he pushed the door closed behind him. "I didn't tell you you could come in here," she said. "Get out."

"We need to talk."

"We have nothing to talk about. You have the army contract and I don't. End of story."

"Damn it, Glory—"

"I told you not to swear at me."

Grasping her arms, Quince held her fast as he said, "You're being unreasonable. I knew you were disappointed that you didn't get the contract, and I came here to talk to you."

"Why?"

Glory forced herself to ignore the concern that tightened his strong features—the way he searched her face when he replied, "Believe me, I had no idea you wanted the contract."

Somehow unwilling to relent Glory said, "Would it have made a difference if you did?' "

"No, but—"

"Then we have nothing to talk about."

"What do you want me to say, that I'm sorry I got the contract when you didn't? Because I'm not. The Half-Moon is in debt. It needs that contract to survive."

"Like I said, we have nothing to talk about." Glory turned away from Quince's penetrating stare.

Still holding her arms fast, Quince said, "Look at me, Glory." And when she refused, "Look at me, damn it!"

Turning back toward him, Glory hissed, "I told

you not to swear at me! Now let me go."

"No."

"I said—"

"I know what you said."

She spat, "What do you want me to say, that the Diamond C needs that contract as much as the Half-Moon does, that the ranch's future depends on it, that my father's health depends on it?" Glory continued, "What did you expect me to do, *beg* you to give me the contract so you could laugh in my face?"

"I'd never laugh at you."

"I'd never give you the chance."

"I know you wouldn't."

"Then why don't you go?"

Glory was unconscious of the tear that had trailed down her cheek until Quince wiped it away and whispered, "Don't cry, please."

"I'm not crying."

"Damn it, Glory . . ."

Slipping his arms around her, Quince drew her close. The world went still when his hard body touched hers. She felt his callused palms caress her back, heard the soft words of comfort he murmured against her hair. His warmth filled her, choking off the protest that sprang to her lips. She heard the catch in his voice when he drew back abruptly, just far enough to look into her eyes and whisper, "I came here to talk to you . . . just talk."

She was somehow mesmerized by his light-eyed gaze as it dropped gradually to her lips, as he slowly lowered his mouth to hers. Her gasp echoed in her ears when he brushed her lips with his. She felt her mouth clinging, then heard his soft groan when he covered it fully with his own.

A sweet lethargy overwhelmed her senses as Quince's kiss deepened; she accepted the caress of his mouth. She separated her lips, and a spontaneous moan reverberated deep inside her as his tongue swept hers and the taste of him filled her. She slid her arms around his neck, and he pulled her flush against him, crushing her closer still. His heartbeat pounded against her breast, echoing her own. She felt him harden, and she pressed herself tightly against his heat.

Pushing her away from himself unexpectedly, Quince held her at arm's length. His chest heaving with powerful emotions, he said, "I didn't come here to . . ." His jaw tight, he began again, "I only wanted . . ."

Incapable of protest when he suddenly pulled her back into his arms to devour her mouth with his, Glory returned his kiss. She was breathless, overwhelmed by wonder, giving kiss for kiss, caress for caress. A sweet singing began inside her, and she abandoned herself to it. She—

A loud knock on the door shattered the moment.

"Miss Glory, are you awake? Are you in there, ma'am?"

Glory jerked back from Quince's embrace at the sound of Jan's voice. Sanity returned with a cold slap, and she flushed a hot red as she called out, "Yes, I'm here, Jan."

"Are you all right, ma'am? The boys and me just

126

wanted to check on you before turning in for the night."

"Yes, I'm fine."

"We'll see you in the morning." Then, "Don't worry, ma'am. Everything will turn out all right."

"I know."

"Good night, ma'am."

"Sleep well, ma'am."

" 'Night, ma'am."

"Good night, boys."

Breathing raggedly, waiting only until the sound of her ranch hands' heavy footsteps faded and she heard their door snap closed, Glory looked up at Quince and said coldly, "Please go."

"Glory, this is all wrong. You don't have to be embarrassed—"

"No?" She shook her head, momentarily unable to go on. "I don't know what happened a few minutes ago, but it was a mistake. I won't make excuses for myself. The fault is all mine, but I'll tell you this. It won't happen again."

"It won't happen again," she repeated, the knot inside her twisting to the point of pain.

"Glory—"

"I asked you to go."

"But—"

"Go!"

His jaw suddenly tight, Quince said, "If that's the way you want it."

Motionless as the door swung closed behind him, Glory slowly closed her eyes.

Chapter Seven

The ranch yard was silent and deserted in the fading light of the setting sun. Pausing as he prepared to mount, Brent turned back toward Quince to reply, "So you got the army contract. What do you expect me to do about it?"

Quince returned Brent's stare coldly. He was in no mood for his brother's ill humor. He had left The Flat at daybreak several days earlier and had arrived back at the Half-Moon at mid-morning, missing the opportunity to talk to his brother before the ranch hands and he left for the day's work. He had ridden home at a pace calculated to put his latest disastrous encounter with Glory out of his mind—but the effort had failed.

In retrospect, he realized it was the single tear straying down Glory's cheek that had undone him. He had taken her into his arms—and for a few minutes while Glory responded instinctively to his touch, he actually began thinking things could be different between them. He remembered the elation that swept his senses when she slid her arms around his neck and pressed herself closer, when she returned his kiss full measure, revealing a sweet passion that tore at his heart. The beauty of those moments, however, was short-lived. With a knock at the door, humiliation, anger, pain—emotions all too familiar in exchanges between Glory and him—returned.

Aware that Brent still awaited his response, Quince replied just as sharply, "What did I expect from you? Not much, I suppose, except cooperation."

"Cooperation is in short supply on the Half-Moon. I thought you knew that."

"Look, Brent, I'm tired of arguing. Major Tremain needs those horses to mount a campaign against Victorio. Lost time could mean lost lives."

"I can't help you."

"What do you mean, you *can't*?"

"Pa's leaving tomorrow morning to pick up the mares he bought. He's going to need the ranch hands to do it. I'm going with them, because if there's any way of getting out of the deal, I'm going to see to it that Pa takes it."

"How long do you think it'll be before you get back?"

"Who knows?" Brent shrugged in disgust. "Edmund set it all up. Instead of picking up the horses at one location like we thought, we're going to have to ride all over Texas to get them."

"You're taking all the men?"

"Pa's insisting on it. He says the mares are too valuable to chance losing even one of them. He's leaving Red and Navidad behind at the ranch to keep an eye on the women."

"The *women*?"

"Crystal, Abby, and Frances."

"Isn't Abby going with you?"

"No."

"Why not?" Quince asked.

"She's a woman."

"She's also one of the best wranglers the Half-Moon has, and she's proud of it."

"Pa doesn't want her working like one of the hands."

"It's a little late for that, isn't it?"

"Maybe, but I agree with Pa on this."

"Abby deserves—"

"She's not going."

Quince's expression grew frigid. "You'll never change."

Holding his gaze without flinching, Brent said, "I don't care what you do about the army contract. You took it on. You're responsible for it, but the ranch hands have too much work ahead of them to be a part of it—and Abby's staying home with the women where she belongs."

Dismissing him without another word, Brent mounted up and turned his horse toward his cabin beside the stream.

"I'll go after those mustangs with you, Quince."

Her narrow jaw rock hard and her eyes bright

with determination, Abby stood opposite Quince in the ranch yard. His first day back from Fort Griffin was ending in an agitation that had become the norm for him at the Half-Moon. He had accepted that discomfort for himself, but Quince knew he could not dismiss Abby's distress.

"Brent's been after me for a long time to 'act like a lady,'" Abby said, "but it's gotten worse since Papa came home. Truth is, I've worked with the ranch hands around this place for as long as I can remember, and I'm not about to change who I am just because Papa and Brent seem to think I should."

"I know that, Abby."

"I'm not going to let anybody force me into being somebody I don't want to be."

"I know that, too."

"So I'm going with you."

Quince looked down at his sister and felt a familiar warmth. Not only did Abby look more like their mother every day, but she had the spunk and determination that had been so great a part of Beth Hunter's character underneath her womanly softness. If Brent had any sense, he'd realize that and give Abby a chance to find her own way.

"Quince?"

"I'll be glad to have you ride with me, Abby, but there's no way we'll be able to do it alone."

"Can you wait until Brent gets back with the hands?"

"Brent made it clear that the contract is my responsibility. He's not going to let me use the ranch hands, no matter when he gets back. Besides, I can't wait. Major Tremain needs those horses. We both know the mustang herds have been dwindling over the years. We might have to travel farther north than we think to find enough of them. If I don't get those horses to the major by the time he's ready to move against Victorio, he'll have to go with the mounts he has available. Not only will we lose the contract then, but it'll be a disaster for the campaign."

"Maybe I can talk Papa into letting us use some of the hands."

"Don't waste your time."

"What are you going to do?"

"Don't worry about it. I'll go into town tomorrow morning. I should be able to find five or six wranglers who'll be only too glad to sign on. By the time Pa and Brent get back, we'll have the mustangs rounded up and be on our way home."

Abby said unexpectedly, "I'm sorry about all this, Quince."

Slipping his arm around his sister's narrow shoulders, Quince leaned down and said, "I thought I told you not to worry. Come on—Frances should have supper ready by now, and I'm hungry."

Drawing Abby along with him, Quince turned toward the ranch house. He had wanted to alleviate Abby's concern with reassurances, but he was only too aware as they entered the house that taking his own advice not to worry was far beyond him.

*   *   *

"Don't worry, darlin'. It'll be all right."

Byron Townsend spoke with a soft confidence that did not deceive Glory as she sat opposite her father in his small study. It had been nearing sunset when she and the hands returned from Fort Griffin a few hours earlier bearing the bad news that they'd failed to get the army contract. She was tired and discouraged, as were the men who had accompanied her. They had all eaten supper in silence while Glory noted that her father was thinner and more drawn than he had been when they left. She had hoped securing the army contract would slow the obvious decline of his health, but that wasn't going to happen.

"I'm sorry, Pa." Glory forced herself to follow with, "But I haven't given up. I'm going to Diablo tomorrow to talk to Edmund again about a loan."

"No, I don't want you to do that!"

The sudden sharpness of her father's tone surprised her. She scrutinized him intently as she inquired, "Why, Pa?"

"Edmund told us he won't give us another loan unless we meet our next payment, and he won't change his mind."

"I know, but—"

His voice softening, Byron continued, "No buts, darlin'. We've made it this far. We'll manage. Go on and get some rest now. You deserve it. We can talk again tomorrow."

Deciding it was best to leave the matter to be discussed at a better time, Glory stood up, then leaned over to kiss her father's cheek. "Good night, Pa."

"Good night, darlin'."

Glory was about to enter her room when the sound of a soft knocking turned her back toward her father's study. She saw Jan push open the study door, then walk inside and draw the door closed behind him.

Jan wouldn't have gone to see her father unless Pa had sent for him.

Glory had taken two steps toward the study when she halted, then sighed in resignation. Pa was more upset about their situation than he had let on, but he didn't want her to worry. He needed another man to talk to. She couldn't begrudge him that.

Glory entered her room and closed the door behind her. She had said as little as possible to her father about Quince getting the contract instead of them. She supposed her father had sent for Jan in order to find out exactly what had happened. If so, she was glad. She didn't want to discuss Quince. She couldn't.

Her thoughts slipped back to the morning the ranch hands and she had left The Flat. Quince was already gone by the time they went down to breakfast in the hotel. She had been relieved that she didn't have to face him, that Jan and the hands wouldn't have any inkling what had transpired between Quince and her. She had also been forced to accept the realization that Quince wanted to forget the previous night as much as she did. She had told herself she was glad Quince had made his feelings clear.

She was still glad, and in the time since, she had

resolved to dismiss the whole episode from her mind.

Glory turned toward her bed. Yes, she'd forget everything that had happened when Quince came to her room. She was resolved.

It was nearly midday when Diablo came into Quince's view on the horizon. Frowning, he remembered the solemn mounted group that had ridden away from the ranch house after breakfast that morning. Pa had been angry, no doubt after another heated discussion with Brent, who did not hesitate to voice his disapproval of Pa's "irresponsible" purchase. The ranch hands had been uncomfortable with the situation, their loyalties torn between the man their father had once been, and the son who was losing his fight to save the Half-Moon.

Quince remembered the injured look on Abby's face when the men had ridden away. He silently renewed his resolution to see the misery of feeling she didn't belong erased from his sister's eyes—one way or another.

He was keenly aware, however, that he presently had a more urgent problem to solve.

His gaze narrowing as he rode down Diablo's main street, Quince surveyed the crowded boardwalk where shoppers moved from store to store. He saw wagons drawn up to hitching posts where merchants loaded supplies for smiling women, a milk wagon making its final stops at the far end of the street, the inevitable groups of loitering drifters and merrymakers who were much the worse for wear after a night on the town, and a few itinerant wranglers leaning against storefronts, men with too much time on their hands than was healthy.

Quince glanced at the men standing near a bulletin posted outside the sheriff's office. Dismounting, he tied his mount's reins to the hitching post and stepped up onto the boardwalk to find that the notice was one obviously posted by one of Jonah's men prior to Quince's journey to Fort Griffin.

He listened to their laughing comments:

"I heard about this notice. It's a joke, ain't it? There ain't nobody in this town crazy enough to have anything to do with the military at Fort Griffin."

"They ain't trustworthy, that's for sure."

"Jake Forester learned that the hard way when he tried to do an honest job for one of the officers there. He never got paid, and there wasn't nothing he could do about it."

"When he tried to complain, the commander said he'd have him thrown in the brig if he made any trouble."

"That's a helluva thing . . ."

"That commander's got gall to post a notice here. I'm surprised somebody didn't rip it down already."

"Hell, no! We don't want to do that. This is the best laugh this town's had in a dog's age."

Quince turned away and began walking slowly down the main street. He passed the same drifters and itinerant cowpokes he had glimpsed on the way in. They looked back at him with bloodshot eyes and sour expressions that spoke volumes, and Quince continued on by. It appeared Fort Griffin's reputation was going to make it more difficult than he'd thought to hire dependable wranglers.

He had almost reached the doors of the Lone Star, where he'd planned to make some inquiries, when he stopped, unwilling to continue the farce any longer.

Turning, he started back in the direction from which he had come.

"He turned around. He's going back up the street!"

Standing inside the Lone Star's swinging doors, Madge looked at Blanche as she rushed to join her. Incredulous, her thin brows arched almost comically on her brightly painted face, the seasoned saloon girl shook her head. "He was heading here, I know he was."

Standing beside Madge, Blanche watched as Quince's long-legged stride quickly covered the distance back to the opposite end of town. Madge's heavily kohled gaze was sympathetic when she offered, "Maybe he's coming back. Maybe he just forgot something."

Quince mounted, turned his horse, and nudged him into motion. Hardly aware she was speaking aloud, Blanche said, "He's leaving town."

"No, he can't be. He just got here."

Quince disappeared from sight, and Madge frowned. "I'm sorry, honey. I don't know what happened. I saw him the minute he rode down the street. There's no way to miss that big fella, you know. I called you as soon as I saw him. He wasn't in town no more than a couple of minutes, I swear."

"That's all right, Madge." Blanche blinked back the sudden brightness in her eyes. All the girls knew how she felt about Quince. They couldn't miss the way she glanced hopefully at the door every time it opened. They felt sorry for her. They didn't know about Lobo, because she hadn't told them. She hadn't told anyone; she was too afraid—and ashamed.

Blanche shrugged. "I guess Quince has better things to do than waste time in the Lone Star."

"He'll be back."

"Sure."

Her smile forced and her heart breaking, Blanche walked back to the bar.

The Diamond C ranch house hadn't changed much since Old Man Potter's day, Quince thought as he approached the log structure with an assessing eye. His trip to town earlier that morning had been a long, unnecessary ride that had wasted valuable hours.

His gaze narrowing, Quince scrutinized the house a moment longer. It was large, probably six rooms or more, built for a growing family when Old Man Potter was younger. It was obviously well maintained now, with steps leading up to a newly added porch. He looked at the outbuildings, noting they were in good repair. He scrutinized the mares in the corral beside the barn. It took no more than a glimpse for him to see that those mares did not match the quality of the animal that had sunk into the quicksand bog that first day.

Continuing his approach, Quince saw a short, heavily whiskered fellow come out onto the porch, then disappear back into the house. Within minutes he was back, pushing a sober-faced gentleman in a wheelchair.

Aware of their keen observance of him, Quince dismounted and walked up to the porch. The first to speak, he extended his hand toward the wheelchair-bound man and said, "You must be Mr. Townsend. My name's Quince Hunter, sir."

The old man accepted his hand and shook it firmly despite his obvious frailty. His gaze acute, he responded, "If you came to make a social call, you picked a poor time, Mr. Hunter. I'm the only one home. The hands are all out working, and my daughter is with them." He paused, then said, "But this isn't a social visit, is it?"

"No, it isn't." Quince studied Byron Townsend briefly. He saw a mental sharpness that had not been affected by the man's obviously wasted physical condition. He noted also an impatience in his gaze that prompted Quince to respond bluntly, "I came to make you a business proposition, sir."

Townsend studied him for long, silent moments before turning toward the whiskered fellow behind him to say, "This is Pete, our cook." Waiting until Quince had acknowledged him, Townsend said, "Mr. Hunter and I have some business to discuss, Pete. If you could take me to the study, then get us some coffee, I'd be very appreciative."

Quince followed the wheelchair inside.

Byron turned his chair toward Quince Hunter when the door closed behind Pete. He waved him to a chair and scrutinized him a moment longer. Glory had mentioned Hunter briefly—too briefly to suit him. He had questioned Jan about the circumstances surrounding their visit to Fort Griffin and The Flat, but Jan had had little to add.

From what Byron could see, Quince Hunter appeared to be a serious, somewhat intense young man. He was tall, with a powerful physique that reflected hard work. Byron supposed some women might be drawn to his rough masculine appeal; they might consider him handsome in his way, although the light eyes assessing him keenly in return were certainly his best feature. Yet there was something about him, an air of authority and bold resolve, that set the fellow apart from the average wrangler—a quality that had nothing to do with his physical appearance or his courteous, direct manner. He seemed to be a fellow who could be trusted to speak his mind frankly and be candid in his responses.

Yet Glory had evaded Byron's questions about this man.

He began cautiously, "You said you had a business proposition to offer, Mr. Hunter."

"Mr. Hunter is my father's name." Hunter did not smile, "My name is Quince."

"All right, Quince, but my question stands. What's this all about?"

Byron noted the flicker in Quince's gaze before he began. "Your daughter went to Fort Griffin hoping to get the army contract to supply horses. You know, of course, that Major Tremain awarded the contract to me a few hours before she got there. I met her afterwards. She told me the Diamond C needed the contract in order to meet its bills."

Silently surprised that Glory had revealed the Diamond C's uncertain financial position to a man who was a virtual stranger to her, Byron said, "That's all true, but why has that brought you here?"

Quince responded without hesitation, "There's no point in trying to hide the Hunter family history, Mr. Townsend. Everybody knows why my father went to prison for ten years. I'm sure everybody's heard about the trouble in the family since he got out, too—about my father's drinking and gambling, and his spending sprees."

"Diablo is a small community."

"To put it plainly, I have the contract to supply the army horses, but the Half-Moon wranglers will be busy with something else, and I won't be able to use them to meet it." Ignoring Byron's surprise, he leaned forward, continuing, "So this is my proposition. I have the contract, and you have the wranglers. If we join together, we can both come out ahead."

"What are you offering?"

"An equal split of the profits between the Half-Moon and the Diamond C."

"You'll be supplying one wrangler to our

seven—and you want to give the Diamond C an equal split?"

"*Two* wranglers to your seven. My sister is going, too. But there's no room for bargaining on that point—it's still an equal split, or I'll hire wranglers in Diablo and hope for the best."

Byron held the younger man's gaze, his expression cold.

It had been a long, difficult day. Glory rode in weary silence with the men as they drove range stock back toward the ranch-house corral. The easy work she had expected—cutting horses needing attention out of the herd in the east pasture—had turned into a nightmare. The herd had been nervous and wary, difficult to manage. Fresh wolf tracks discovered nearby had later explained the herd's skittishness, but the situation had extended the day's work. The circumstances had been complicated further by her own distraction as painful memories of the evening in The Flat continued to haunt her.

Rounding the curve toward the Diamond C ranch house at last, she refused to let herself think past the hot meal that would be waiting, and the seclusion of her silent room, where she hoped to turn off the world around her.

The ranch house came into sight, and Glory's thoughts stopped cold. She saw her father waiting on the porch in his wheelchair, flanked by Pete and—

Oh, no, it couldn't be him!

But it was.

*   *   *

"I won't do it!"

"Then the boys will have to go without you."

Glory stared at her father, incredulous. His pale face was composed into unyielding lines. She had seen him this way before. She knew that neither hell nor high water could move him when he was in this mood, and she was momentarily speechless.

Grateful that Quince had had the decency to leave immediately after her father announced his decision to accept Quince's proposition, Glory had not spared him more than a stiff goodbye. She had then followed her father into his study, where her protests began.

Determined, Glory asked, "Did you ask yourself why Quince is doing this, Pa? Why he's ready to give up half the profit from the contract when he could have it all?"

"I didn't have to ask. He told me."

"What did he say?"

"He needs the Diamond C wranglers in order to meet the contract."

"Why can't he use his own wranglers?"

"Something obviously happened between him and his family at the Half-Moon. He had intended to use his own men, but it didn't work out that way."

"His own family doesn't trust him."

"I don't think that's the case."

"You can't be sure."

"What do we have to lose? We need the money, and Quince needs us. It's been my experience,

Glory, that nothing binds more tightly than mutual need."

Her father's comment striking a chord inside her, Glory raised her chin. "You don't really know him. He may not be what he appears to be."

Byron's gaze pinned her. "Are you trying to tell me something?"

"No." Shaking her head, Glory took a backward step. "It's just . . . I mean . . . the whole situation seems wrong somehow."

"Right or wrong, I'm going ahead with it." His pale face flushing with sudden unexpected anger, Byron spat, "I'm tired of being under Edmund Montgomery's thumb. I'm tired of having him pull the strings so he can watch us dance. I don't want to leave this world knowing that he'll still have control over you when I'm gone, and if there's any chance of ending it now, I'm going to take it!"

"Pa!"

"I'm sorry, Glory." Breathing rapidly, Byron continued, "That's the way it is. I won't press you to go with the men, of course. Jan can handle things, but you'll be taking my place here sooner or later—"

"Don't talk like that, Pa."

"All right, I won't. But aside from that, every available hand will be needed to make sure things work out with the success I'm hoping for. I'd go myself if I could."

The glimpse of distress in her father's eyes was more than she could bear. "All right. I'll go," Glory said abruptly.

Byron searched her expression before asking,

"You're sure? If you have an objection of some kind and would rather stay behind with Pete and me—"

"No, you're right. I should go."

The tension in Byron's thin frame gradually relaxed. "If this works out well," he said, "we'll have the money we need to replace the mares, and we might even have a chance to get ahead of our bills. If the army is favorably impressed, it could lead to a whole new source of income for the Diamond C."

Glory nodded, unwilling to extinguish the hope in her father's eyes.

His breathing gradually returning to normal, he continued, "I've already told Jan to instruct the men to get their supplies together tomorrow. Quince wants to get started the following day."

"I'll be ready."

"We stand a chance of getting ahead of things financially, Glory. That's important."

"I know."

His expression softening, Byron said, "I'm sorry to put this burden on your shoulders, Glory. I know it isn't fair."

"Oh, Pa."

He hesitated, then said unexpectedly, "You do know I love you very much, don't you, dear?"

Blinking back the heat of sudden tears, Glory whispered, "Of course I do."

She took a breath. Aware that she was in tenuous control of her emotions, she forced herself to smile and said, "I'm hungry. I'm going out to see what Pete made for supper. Are you coming?"

"In a few minutes."

Glory's smile faded into uncertainty as she pulled the study door closed behind her.

Edmund drew his watch from his pocket and frowned down at the face. Doubting its accuracy, he shook it, then glanced out the window of his office at the sun gradually reaching its apex in the cloudless sky. His mood was foul. Feeling a hardening need, he had paid a visit to his favorite whore the night before—a woman living a distance from town who tolerated all manner of perversion for a price, but her mood had been black and the scene had turned ugly. He had refused to accept the screaming tirade that had ensued and had used his fists to quiet her. He had then counted out the additional price she had demanded for her silence.

He had awakened that morning with the memory still stinging. Then he had arrived at the bank and learned from gossip circulating rapidly through town that Quince Hunter had secured the army contract to supply horses to Fort Griffin. He had been further stunned to learn that Quince was using Diamond C wranglers for the job.

Edmund ground his teeth in suppressed anger. No one had to tell him what that would mean— money to help pay Jack Hunter's rapidly rising debts, and a way for the Diamond C to meet its pressing financial problems.

Damn the man! Everything had been going according to plan until Quince Hunter came home. The Diamond C had virtually been in the palm of his hand, and the Half-Moon had been rapidly coming under his control. The army contract could set his plans back indefinitely—and he was in no mood for a delay in the satisfaction he so clearly envisioned when both ranches were his.

Edmund reached down into his desk drawer for the Diamond C and Half-Moon folders, then cursed under his breath when he remembered he had left them at home. He stood up and snatched his hat off the stand on his way out his office door.

Entering his house minutes later, he walked directly to his study. He stopped abruptly when he saw that the folder was not on the desk where he had left it.

A hot rage flushed his face as he called out, "Hilda, come in here!" Struggling to conceal his anger when the woman appeared at his study door, he said, "I believe I left a folder on my desk last night. Did you move it?"

"No, I didn't."

His jaw twitching, Edmund spat, "Then where is it?"

Hilda took a backward step. "I don't know, Mr. Montgomery."

About to lose control, he snapped, "I know where I left it. It's not there. Can you tell me where it is, then?"

"Edmund . . . ?"

Edmund froze at the sound of Iona's voice in the hallway. He knew instinctively that his wife's drunken interference at that point would push him over the edge. Aware that Hilda was witnessing the rapid deterioration of the facade he had carefully cultivated, he turned toward her and said in as normal a voice as he could manage, "I'm sorry, Hilda. The folders are important. I'm concerned that they've been misplaced. I hope you understand."

"Of course, Mr. Montgomery." Hilda took another backward step. "If you'd like me to search the house—"

"That won't be necessary." He forced a smile. "You may go."

Iona remained in the hallway when Hilda disappeared from sight. With an attempt at patience, Edmund asked, "What do you want, Iona?"

"I . . . I heard your voice, dear." Her feeble smile nauseated him as she continued, "You sounded upset. I thought I might be able to help—"

"Go back to bed."

Momentarily speechless, Iona said, "But you were looking for something."

"I said, go back to bed."

"Edmund . . ." Iona took another unsteady step toward him. "Are you looking for the folders you left on the dining room table last night?"

Edmund went rigidly still.

"I didn't want them to get lost, so I took them. I had intended to put them in your study, but I felt shaky and went directly to my room."

"Where are they?" Barely restraining his contempt, Edmund pressed, "Are they still in your room?"

"Yes, I'll get them."

Brushing past her without responding, Edmund

walked directly to Iona's room and pushed open the door. Repelled by the sickening odors of alcohol and sweet perfume, he saw the folders balanced on the edge of the nightstand. He snatched them up and turned, almost colliding with Iona who had come up behind him.

Her face drawn into lines of concern, she asked, "Are you angry with me, Edmund?"

"Get out of my way."

"Edmund—"

"I said, get out of my way!"

Thrusting her roughly aside, he strode down the hallway. He had almost reached the front door when he heard Iona call out, then the sound of a thud.

Disgusted, he turned and saw her lying on the hallway floor, struggling unsteadily to stand, Edmund took firm hold of his emotions and walked back toward her.

Iona was stammering her apologies, further deepening his loathing as he attempted to draw her to her feet. He saw the look of pain on her face when he stood her upright at last and her leg collapsed underneath her. Knowing he had no recourse, he picked her up. Revolted by the press of her bony body against his, he carried her down the hallway toward her room as he called out, "Hilda, send someone for Dr. Gibbs. Mrs. Montgomery has fallen."

The Half-Moon ranch house was silent as the sun began brightening the clear morning sky. Red had already eaten and left for his chores in the barn, leaving the table exclusively to Abby and Quince. Dressed for travel, his saddlebags packed and supplies already loaded on the spare mounts necessary for the mustang hunt, Quince glanced at his sister. She was consuming a hardy breakfast with gusto, and he could not help smiling. She was excited. She was looking forward to their journey into mustang country with great anticipation. He only wished his own feelings were as uncomplicated as hers were at that moment.

He remembered his thoughts while he'd approached the Diamond C with his contract proposition in mind two days earlier. Finally discarding the thought of hiring itinerant wranglers whose skills and dependability were uncertain, he had told himself that making an offer to the Diamond C was the most logical answer to his problem. He had resisted the thought that he was using the situation as an excuse to see Glory again, however brief the contact might be. Yet he was unable to deny the drumming that had begun inside him when Glory rode into sight of the ranch house where he and Townsend awaited her return. It had taken only one glimpse of her set expression, however, to make him realize that any effort to change the situation between them would be a waste of time.

He had left the Diamond C immediately after Townsend summarized their agreement for his men, but he had no regrets about striking the deal. He had seen the anxiety in Townsend's eyes at his first mention of the contract, then the glimmer of hope that had gradually grown there. He liked the

old man. It rested well with him that the deal
would benefit them both.

Quince took his last gulp of coffee as Abby set
down her fork. They stood up without a word.
Abby grinned when they reached the horses and
prepared to mount. He saw her grin dim when
Joey Weatherby, the blacksmith's son, rode unexpectedly into view.

Her expression was sober when Joey tipped his
hat to them both and said, "I've got a message for
you, Miss Abby. Mr. Montgomery asked me to
ride out. He wanted me to tell you that Miss Iona
fell and hurt herself yesterday." Quince heard
Abby gasp as Joey continued. "The doc said she
hurt her leg pretty bad. It's all swollen and she
can't walk. Hilda says she has her own family to
take care of and can't look after Miss Iona the way
she'll be needing. Mr. Montgomery said to tell you
Miss Iona asked if you could come and stay with
her until her leg is better."

Quince watched the play of emotions across
Abby's white face during the extended silence that
followed. He saw the almost imperceptible quiver
of her lips, then the deep breath she took before
she turned toward him, her eyes bright. He knew
what she was going to say before she whispered,
"Iona needs me, Quince. With all she did for me
after Mama was gone, she never even once asked
for anything in return." She swallowed, then said,
"I can't refuse her."

Nodding, aware of the sacrifice Abby was making, Quince untied the supply horse from her saddle and secured it to his own. She was mounted

when she turned again toward him and said, "I wish . . ." Then, "I'm sorry, Quince."

"Don't worry about it, Abby. Tell Iona I hope she feels better." He winked. "You'll have your work cut out for you when we bring those mustangs home and start breaking them to the saddle."

Quince watched with regret as Abby and Joey disappeared around the bend in the road. Then mounting, he spurred his horse into motion.

The Diamond C riders were waiting when he approached the ranch house, standing beside the porch where Townsend was seated in his wheelchair. A quick glance revealed that their alternate mounts were in the corral, readied for their journey. He explained the reason for Abby's absence as he dismounted, noting the brief hardening of Townsend's gaze at the mention of Edmund's name.

Declining to comment, Townsend responded, "You met Jan, Shorty, and Robbie at Fort Griffin." Motioning to the other men, he said, "These fellas are Miles, Riggs, and Slim."

Six of them.

Quince was about to ask about the seventh man when Glory walked out onto the porch with saddlebags in hand. She was dressed in riding gear.

Quince's mind froze.

"My daughter is going with you, of course."

Somehow he had never considered she would be a part of their party.

"She's going in my place."

"No."

"Why not?"

"Mustanging is hard, dangerous work."

"My daughter can handle herself, and she's no stranger to hard work." Townsend frowned. "Frankly, I'm surprised at your attitude, especially since your sister was supposed to be a part of this party."

"Abby's an accomplished wrangler. She works as hard as any man."

Speaking up for the first time, Glory interjected, "So do I."

When he did not reply, she stated flatly, "I'm going, whether you like it or not."

Silently cursing when a look at the old man revealed he would not relent, Quince signaled the party to mount. He paused only to tip his hat to Byron in a silent farewell before moving into the lead.

He didn't like this—not one damned bit!

Edmund made his way through the secluded terrain, vexed that he did not have his usual cover of twilight in approaching as he neared the log cabin he had visited many times before. His surly mood of the last few days had not abated with the added annoyance of Iona's injury and the confusion following, which had delayed his contact with Kane.

The only positive note had been Abby's arrival at his house to care for Iona that morning. After sending Joey to get her, he had allowed his fantasies to build with the hope of using the opportunity to awaken Abby's response to him—but the possibility now appeared practically nil. Abby had secluded herself in Iona's room after arriving, hardly showing her face. He was uncertain if she was deliberately avoiding him, but he had already decided that if she was, he would make sure the price she eventually paid for her affront would be harsh.

His mind turning to matters at hand, Edmund whistled the necessary signal as he approached the cabin: one short, then three long trills. He waited until the door opened to expose Kane's unmistakable figure, his ever-present rifle hanging at his side.

In no mood for pleasantries, Edmund dismounted and walked into the cabin without a word. Kane smiled at his obvious agitation, the amusement in his voice adding to Edmund's irritation when he said, "You ain't your usual self. What's the matter? Got something stuck in your craw?" Kane laughed. "Well, you came to the right place. Old Doc Kane will remove it if the price is right."

"Price is no problem, but you know that very well. Timing may be difficult, however."

"What are you talking about?"

"Quince Hunter and the wranglers from the Diamond C started out on a mustanging expedition this morning."

"So?"

"I want it to fail."

"So?"

His annoyance increasing, Edmund spat, "It's not a one-man operation."

"That's never stopped me before."

"I can't tell you exactly where they're headed, either. You'll have to track them somehow."

"There ain't nobody I can't trail if I've got a good enough reason."

Reaching into his pocket, Edmund pulled out a roll of bills that curved Kane's wet lips into a hungry smile. Inwardly repulsed, Edmund said, "This should give you the incentive you need. I'll double this amount when you come back if you do the job right."

Snatching the roll out of Edmund's hand, Kane flicked his thumb across the edge, then looked back up at him. His response was simple.

"Get your money ready."

Chapter Eight

There were fifty of them or more.

Maintaining a safe distance from the herd, Quince watched the milling mustangs through his field glasses. He studied the irregular formation carefully. Two-year-old males recently ousted from the herd were gathered in companionable comfort on the far side, a respectful distance from the main stallion, whose attention did not stray from his mares. Upon closer scrutiny, Quince noted that there were two separate herds—two separate harems each with its own stallion standing guard. Although unusual, he knew it was not unheard of that stallions might choose to water their mares at the same place and time while keeping the groups separate as they awaited their turns to drink.

Quince smiled, aware that the situation would

work out well by enlarging the initial herd even before the excitement of the run picked up lesser herds along the way.

He turned at the sound of movement behind him. Glory had nudged her mount up closer to get a clearer view, while making sure to keep her distance from him. It had been that way for the two days it had taken to sight the herds. Glory had maintained a cool reserve, speaking only when necessary. Her attitude toward him was in sharp contrast with the easy familiarity between her and the Diamond C wranglers, who appeared to easily accept her as a peer.

Unfortunately, he didn't. Awareness of the dangers the next few days would bring and Glory's obvious determination to work alongside the men nagged incessantly at his peace of mind.

The herd started moving, and Quince gestured with his arm, signaling the wranglers for caution. The stallions weren't aware of their presence. He knew they wouldn't travel much farther than fifteen miles from their water source before circling back if they felt confident about their safety. He also knew it was time to return to camp for a last night of undisturbed rest before beginning the four- or five-day run necessary to bring the mustangs under control.

Handing Slim his glasses with a few whispered instructions about maintaining a careful watch, he signaled the other men to follow him. He noted that Glory nudged her mount to Slim's side for a few words that raised an unexpected smile to the silent wrangler's face.

Quince's gut squeezed tight at the familiarity of their exchange. Determined to ignore his reaction, he urged his horse into motion.

"I ain't never seen you have so much trouble finding a trail before."

Kane's head jerked up toward the rider beside him. Lefty's yellowed teeth flashed in an amused smile at his obvious annoyance. Aware that the other three men in the party were awaiting his response, Kane spat, "Do you think you can do any better?"

"It ain't my job."

"That's right. Your job is to shut up and do what I tell you."

His companion's responsive snort started a chuckling behind him, and Kane's temper flared. He had used Bart, Sloan, Whistler, and Lefty on other jobs he couldn't handle alone. They did what they were told with no questions asked, but he couldn't turn his back on any of them, and as far as he was concerned, they weren't worth a damn.

Allowing his pointed gaze to linger on Lefty a few moments longer, Kane returned to his scrutiny of the trail. If it hadn't been for the size of the roll Montgomery had flashed at him and for the promise to double that amount when the job was done, he would have told the bastard to forget it. His reassurances to Montgomery aside, he didn't like starting out a step behind in any job. As it was, he was two steps behind—the two days it had taken him to locate the men now riding with him, and then to find Quince Hunter's trail.

Kane's heavy brows knit tighter. Despite the size of Hunter's party, the trail wasn't easy to follow with so much time having elapsed. But the trail was getting clearer. He knew that as soon as they reached a less traveled area, the signs would be distinct and they could make up time.

"You think we'll find them?" Persisting in his heckling, Lefty continued, "If we don't, do me and the boys get paid anyway?"

His disposition darkening, Kane replied with a hint of menace, "Don't worry about your money. I'll find the trail and we'll get the job done, like we always do. But you boys won't have to worry." He added more softly, "If something goes wrong, I'll just take care of you all in my own way."

Satisfied by the uncertain silence that followed, Kane concentrated on the trail ahead.

The Diamond C wranglers had already eaten and were camped for the night. The men were conversing in small groups, their anticipation under control as they checked their equipment for the day to come. Having already designated Slim's replacement on lookout and having checked his own equipment as well, Quince watched as Glory prepared her bedroll on the opposite side of the fire.

Without realizing his intent, he stood up, walked to her side, and said, "We need to talk."

Casual conversation among the wranglers stopped as Glory stood up and replied, "All right. Go ahead."

"Privately."

Her gaze cold, she nodded.

Aware that Glory was right behind him, Quince advanced to a spot where they could be neither seen nor heard from the camp. Then he turned toward her and said, "There are some things we need to set straight between us. You may be comfortable with this arrangement, but I'm not. As far as I'm concerned, you shouldn't be here."

Glory's clear skin heated visibly as she replied, "Is that right?"

"Yes, that's right. The next few days are important. We'll either gain control of the herd or lose them completely. Let me tell you now, I don't intend to lose them."

"Neither do I."

Ignoring her response, Quince continued, "We'll be driving those horses at a gallop for as much as seventy-five miles a day. We'll be letting them stop only every eight miles or so, for no more than fifteen minutes. We'll be alternating positions so we can get fresh mounts and keep ahead of them. When the herd starts to tire, our minds have to be clear enough so we can anticipate their reactions when we try getting them to turn on command."

"What are you saying?"

"We can't have any distractions."

"So?"

"You're a distraction."

Quince saw anger surge in her dark eyes as Glory said, "No, I'm a wrangler."

Suddenly infuriated, Quince grated, "You're a distraction, whether you want to admit it or not!"

"Only to you!"

"Maybe."

"Then that's your problem."

"It may be my problem, but I'm the boss here. I hold the contract. I'm the one who's responsible for the safety of everyone here *and* for meeting the terms agreed to with the army."

"And I'm as good a rider as you are!"

"That's what you tried to tell me when you were stuck in that quicksand bog."

"Bastard!" she spat. Quince noted the trembling that beset her slender frame as she continued in a harsh whisper, "You're determined not to let me forget that morning, aren't you?"

"That's right. For good reason. The pace is going to be hard and fast when we're driving those mustangs. I don't want to have to worry about you going down in the middle of them."

"You don't have to worry about me!"

"Somehow I'm not convinced."

Her eyes flashing, Glory returned, "What do you want from me? Do you want to hear me say I'm afraid?—because I'm *not*. Do you want to hear me admit that I won't be able to keep up with the men?—because I *can* keep up with them." Pausing, her chest heaving, she rasped, "Or do you want me to beg you to let me be a part of the run?—*because I won't!*"

"I'm not asking—"

"You'd better not!"

"I'm telling you—do you understand, *telling* you how it's going to be tomorrow."

"You're not telling me anything."

Taking a step closer, steeling himself against the remembered scent of her, Quince repeated, "I'm telling you how it's going to be—or I'll make one of the men sit out the run with you."

"There's not a man around that campfire who'd obey that order."

"Those men are experienced wranglers."

"Yes, they are."

"They know there can be only one boss on a run."

Raising her chin, Glory spat, "What makes you think you're the person they'd choose to back?"

Quince paused, inwardly marveling at the sheer passion of Glory's responses. There was no doubting her spirit—but it wasn't her spirit that concerned him.

Quince replied, "They'd choose me because I'm the best man for the job." When Glory did not immediately respond, he continued tightly, "I know what I'm doing because I've done it before. I know how to handle these mustangs. I know what to expect from them. This territory is familiar to me, and I can anticipate every move the herd is going to make. I know when to push and when to let up, and I know when to back off if my men are endangered. Can you honestly say you can do the same?"

The blink of Glory's eyes was as revealing as the silence that allowed him to continue. "Are you willing to take a chance with your men's lives to satisfy your pride?"

"Pride!"

"To prove your point?"

"That isn't what I'm doing."

"Isn't it?"

Quince studied Glory's expression in the extended silence that followed. He saw the almost imperceptible twitch of her lips before she responded, "All right, I'll concede that you should be in charge when we start the mustangs running."

" 'In charge' means we do things my way."

Glory nodded.

"That means you follow *my* orders."

She nodded again.

He stared down at her. "Then listen carefully, because this is the way it's going to be. I want you in my sight at all times."

Silence.

"You ride close to my side wherever I go."

No response.

"You don't stray for any reason."

Glory grew rigid.

"You take your breaks when I take my breaks. You change horses when I change horses. You—"

"All right!"

Refusing to relent despite her obvious agitation, Quince pressed, "If you ride out of my sight for one minute—"

"I already told you, I agree!"

Taking another step toward her, Quince grasped her arms and rasped, "I mean what I'm saying, Glory. If you—"

"Take your hands off me."

"Glory—"

"You heard what I said."

His chest heaving, Quince rasped, "The question is, did you hear what *I* said?"

"I heard you. Now take your hands off me."

Quince dropped his hands back to his sides. "Are you finished?"

It was Quince's turn to nod.

A sudden sadness overwhelmed him as he watched Glory turn away from him without another word and walk back to camp.

Standing silent in the darkness, Quince stared after her as she disappeared from sight. He had won the battle—a total victory—yet the moment left him colder than he could ever remember feeling.

Abby looked out Iona's bedroom window at the shifting night shadows. It had been a difficult day. She had arrived at the house two mornings previously to find Iona smiling bravely despite her leg's grotesque swelling. It had taken her a few minutes to realize that the sickeningly sweet fragrance in the room was not due entirely to Iona's choice of perfume. Instead, it came from the sherry which was her constant companion, and the medicine that she'd insisted Dr. Gibbs prescribe for her, medicine with an overpowering scent of cloves.

Abby looked at the bed where Iona slept, then sighed. It wasn't easy seeing Iona this way. She remembered tearful days during her childhood when Iona had been her lifeline in a sea of sadness. It was painfully clear to her now that Iona was the one who was drowning.

A knock sounded at the door, and Abby felt a familiar surge of distaste. Fearful of waking Iona and starting anew the cycle of sherry and the medicine which Iona insisted was essential for a good night's sleep, she opened the door. She forced herself to smile as Edmund inquired softly, "Is she sleeping?"

"Yes." His arrival at the door after Iona had fallen asleep had become a ritual which Abby was beginning to find intensely uncomfortable. Conscious of the nightwear she had borrowed from Iona, she clutched the neckline closed and said, "She seems to be a little better, but she still has some pain."

"You are such a dear." Edmund reached out to stroke her cheek. "You do know how much Iona and I appreciate your help, don't you?"

Inwardly cringing at his touch, Abby took a backward step. "I'm glad I can help. Iona's always been so good to me."

"You said she's sleeping." His handsome face forlorn, Edmund urged boldly, "Why don't you come out of that room and sit with me for a while. Iona's been unwell so often lately. I've become quite lonesome. We can take some time to console each other."

"No." Her flesh crawling, Abby shook her head. With a belated attempt at a smile, she added, "Thank you, but it's late and I'm tired. The bed Hilda made up for me in here is very comfortable. Besides, I want to be nearby in case Iona needs me."

The ice in Edmund's eyes sent a chill down her spine as he replied, "Very well, if that's the way you want it—good night."

"Yes, good night."

Releasing a relieved breath when the door was

again securely closed, Abby turned back toward Iona.

Dear Iona.

Poor Iona.

Walking silently to the window, Abby stared out at the full moon glowing in the dark sky. She wondered how Quince was faring and wished with all her heart that she was with him.

The campfire glowed in the darkness. Sounds of heavy slumber joined the sounds of night as Quince turned restlessly in his bedroll.

Unable to sleep, he had seen Robbie throw back his blanket and go to relieve Slim in watching over the mustangs. He had been awake when Slim returned and began snoring within minutes.

Through it all, Glory had remained motionless, breathing evenly in sleep.

Quince stared at Glory's fiery hair as it glistened in the flickering light of the campfire. What he had intended as a few simple statements to settle an uneasy situation had turned into yet another angry session that had done little to assuage his concerns about her safety—or the ache inside him each time he looked her way.

Glory sighed in her sleep. She turned, briefly exposing a smooth cheek and softly parted lips.

And the sleepless night stretched on.

Dawn had just broken through the night sky, but the wranglers mounted behind him had been up for more than an hour.

Quince scanned their sober faces, then turned

back to scrutinize the mustangs grazing a distance away. The herds had returned to the watering site as expected and were milling quietly. He had led their party in an approach downwind of the horses, aware that it would allow him to situate his riders at points where they would have maximum control once the run began. Glory sat her horse beside him in stony silence, a position she had assumed as soon as they were mounted. Not desiring a resumption of the previous evening's conflict, he had chosen not to comment.

Quince turned back to the men behind him. His expression sober, he whispered into the hush, "Remember, maintain your positions if possible. We'll be allowing the horses fifteen minute breaks every six to eight miles—just long enough for them to get their wind. Then we'll get them back up and running again. Watch for the signal to start turning them. We'll make the turns gradually over a distance of miles so they won't realize we're running them in circles. When we get back in the vicinity of our camp, you can start dropping back one at a time to change horses and replace the guard we left there. If you have a problem, signal as best you can. If a part of the herd tries to break loose, run it harder. Each time we stop for the night, we'll edge a little closer to the herd so they'll become gradually accustomed to seeing us there. Don't push control. It'll come."

Quince scrutinized the men a moment longer. He saw acceptance of his orders, a tension that acknowledged the importance of the next few days, and an excitement that raced hotly through his own veins as well.

His tone reflecting that anticipation, he said, "All right, get into position. I'll signal when to start."

Quince watched as the men rode quietly in various directions. Turning at the sound of restless movement beside him, he saw the resentment in Glory's eyes the second before she averted her gaze. He was about to speak, but decided against it. There was nothing he could say that would alleviate her frustration, just as there was nothing she could say to lessen his legitimate concerns.

Quince waited, tension building as the men one by one reached their appointed positions. Gradually raising his arm, Quince felt his heart leap before he brought it down with a rebel yell that shot the scene into action.

"What's the matter, dearie?"

Blanche felt Anne Pals studying her as she stood up from the boardinghouse breakfast table. Blanche had lingered longer than the rest because she had been hungrier than the others; she had missed her boardinghouse supper the night before and hadn't had the money to buy a meal elsewhere.

"Dearie?"

Blanche smiled at Anne. The gray-haired, full-breasted widow was nice. She was fair to all the saloon girls who lived there, even if that didn't often set well with her church group. Blanche knew if it was up to some of the church people, they'd have Anne throw the girls out onto the street. Blanche frowned at that thought, realizing it might become a reality if things didn't change with Lobo.

Aware that Anne was waiting for her response, Blanche moved away from the table. She attempted to disguise her pained limp as she replied, "No, nothing's wrong. I'm just tired. I got in later than usual last night."

"I know. I heard you."

Blanche's expression froze.

"You had some trouble getting the alleyway door open, didn't you? I guess I'll have to have somebody check that lock again. It sticks every once in a while."

Blanche managed a nervous smile. It wasn't the jammed lock that had caused the commotion. It had been the person waiting in the dark for her. Lobo had been drunk. He had tried to force his way up to her room with her, even though he knew Anne didn't allow it. She had fought him off, but she knew her efforts would have failed if he hadn't been so unsteady on his feet. She had twisted her ankle while trying to get away from him, but had slammed the door behind her in time to shut him out. Her relief at that moment, however, had been short-lived. She didn't fool herself. There would be a next time.

Blanche turned toward the door, then hesitated when Anne said, "You're limping. Did you hurt yourself?"

"Twisted my ankle is all. I'll be all right."

Out on the street, Blanche walked laboriously toward the general store. It was early. The street was devoid of the usual morning shoppers, and she was glad. She didn't want to call attention to herself; she certainly wasn't looking her best. She had dressed quickly. Her fair hair was hanging loose, and she knew that without the makeup of her trade, her skin was pale and the circles under her eyes were almost blue from lack of sleep. But she also knew she couldn't go to work later that day with her dress torn from Lobo's groping hands.

Blanche unconsciously reached toward the coin secreted in her bosom. A smiling cowboy had slid it into her hand just before leaving the Lone Star the previous night. It would be more than enough for the thread she needed in order to make her repairs.

Engrossed in her thoughts, Blanche stepped down off the boardwalk between two stores, then gasped as she was snatched off her feet from behind and dragged backward into a shadowed alleyway. She fought the hand that clamped over her mouth to stifle her screams and struggled wildly as she was thrust painfully back against the alleyway wall. Then she went suddenly still at the sight of Lobo glaring furiously down into her face.

Tremors of fear raced down her spine as he spat, "You thought you got away from me. Well, you didn't." His sweaty body pinned her, holding her motionless as he continued, "You think you're too good for me now that O'Malley's keeping me out of the Lone Star. You think you can keep pushing me away, that the money's enough, even when I got something else in mind for us. Well, you can't."

Finding her voice at last, Blanche said shakily, "No, that ain't it, Lobo. You were drunk last night and you scared me. Besides, I figured I didn't have no more money to give you."

"I wasn't after your money last night, and you know it."

Blanche rasped, "Anne don't let us take nobody up to our rooms."

"I ain't just nobody."

"No guests—that's a rule or Anne will throw me out."

"I ain't no guest neither."

"Lobo—"

"We don't need to use your room anyways." His hand roughly kneaded her breasts. "We can do what we need to do right here."

Blanche scanned the narrow corridor between the buildings. It was filthy, rank, and littered with debris. She shuddered.

"What's the matter? This place ain't good enough for you either? Well, it's good enough for me."

Scraping her back mercilessly against the wall as he dragged her deeper into the alleyway, Lobo grated, "I'm going to teach you a lesson you'll never forget, and I'm going to do it now."

He was tearing at her dress when Blanche started fighting him in earnest. Swinging her arms wildly, punching and biting, she struggled to escape the imprisoning press of his body. Frantic, she did not see the first blow coming.

Stunned when Lobo's fist struck her jaw, Blanche felt the bitter taste of blood fill her mouth. She was somehow unable to move when a second blow hit her, then a third. She doubled over as his powerful pummeling slipped lower.

Unable to catch her breath as the blows continued, she sank slowly to the ground. Merciful oblivion was consuming her when Lobo's voice drifted into the spiraling darkness with the words, "This ain't the end of it."

The clouds of dust raised by pounding hooves grew larger with each passing hour.

His head bent low over his mount's neck as he rode, Quince pushed the mustangs on relentlessly. They had been riding hard for the greater part of the day, with only planned stops to rest the horses before resuming the run. To her credit, Glory had kept up well and had stayed close to him at all times.

Glancing back at her as he had done countless times during the long day, he saw that she held a straight line, allowing not a single horse to separate itself from the herd, and he was somehow proud.

The men had maintained their points well, making the gradual turns on his signal. The exchange of mounts had also gone smoothly, with the men alternating as they slipped out, then rejoined the run with a fresh horse and a minimum of time lost.

Glancing overhead, Quince saw with relief that the sun was beginning to slip toward the horizon. They would soon turn the run again and head back for the watering place, where the exhausted herd would be most comfortable and wouldn't balk when his men kept a visible vigil during the night.

The sun was casting elongated shadows against the ground when the herd finally slowed to a halt beside the water hole. Retreating a distance from the milling mustangs, aware that Glory followed close behind, he waited for the hands to join him. He assigned the watch, then turned back toward the camp.

Seated at the campfire after a simple meal, Quince observed the men in silence. They were tired, already preparing their bedrolls. He heard Glory comment to Jan that she needed to check her primary mount's hoof. Quince watched as she turned toward the spot where the horses had been hobbled for the night. Waiting until she had disappeared from sight, he followed her. She looked up from her horse at the sound of his step and waited for him to speak.

At a sudden loss for words, he said simply, "You did a good job today."

"Did you expect anything different?" Not allowing him a chance to respond, Glory added, "Oh, I forgot. You did."

"Glory—"

"I have to check my horse's hoof."

"If he's having a problem—"

"He's all right."

"If he falters during the run—"

Her expression tightening, Glory rasped, "You still want me out of the run, don't you?"

"No, I don't."

"You'd like to see me sitting the whole thing out."

"That's not true."

"That's good, because I'll be riding right beside you."

Quince did not reply.

"And before this is all over, I'll make you eat your words!"

"I didn't come to argue with you, Glory."

"Then maybe you'd better leave."

Glory's abrupt statement hung on the air between them. The silence was long and strained as Quince searched her face, seeing there the familiar animosity that seemed to mark all conversation between them. He hadn't intended it to be that way when he had sought her out. He had intended . . .

Yes, what had he intended?

Knowing that that question now stood no chance of being answered, Quince turned slowly and walked away.

"What's the matter, boss? Are you all right?"

Pete's question sounded in the darkness of the porch behind Byron Townsend, rousing him from his thoughts. The ranch was unnaturally quiet with the absence of Glory and the ranch hands. They had been gone only three days, and Byron was already becoming anxious for their return.

Too anxious.

"Boss?"

Byron turned toward his balding cook and forced a smile. "I'm fine, Pete. I was just wondering how things were going with Glory and the men."

"You don't need to worry." His leathery face sober, Pete responded in the manner of a friend. "That Quince Hunter don't look to be the kind who'll let anything get past him."

Byron nodded.

"He'll take good care of Miss Glory, too."

"He didn't want her to go with them."

"He don't know Miss Glory. He thought she would cause him problems when they went after them mustangs. With her being so female and pretty, there's no way anybody would know how tough she is when she needs to be."

"I have a feeling he'll learn."

"I think you're right."

"I'm uneasy, Pete."

"About Miss Glory?"

"About the whole thing. There have been too many accidents lately for me to be able to chalk them all up to coincidence."

"Does Miss Glory know how you feel?"

"No."

"But—"

"I told Jan to be on the lookout for trouble."

"You didn't say nothing to Hunter?"

"I wasn't sure it was necessary. This is his contract. It has nothing to do with the Diamond C. We wouldn't have gotten involved if it wasn't for the situation at the Half-Moon."

"So what are you worrying about?"

"I don't really know. It's just a feeling."

"Don't worry, boss. Like I said, it don't look to

me like nothing will get past that Hunter fella."

"I've been counting on that, Pete."

"Besides, they'll be back before you know it."

Byron nodded.

"Do you want me to take you inside now?"

"No, I'll stay out a little longer."

"Boss?"

"Yes?"

"Don't worry. It'll be all right."

Waiting until Pete went into the house, Byron rubbed the persistent ache in his chest. He needed to see the Diamond C on stable ground—soon. His suspicion that fate wasn't alone in working against him would not relent. He had asked Jan to scout the area where Cinnamon had bolted out of Glory's control, but Jan had been unable to find anything suspicious. Neither had he discovered anything to further Byron's suspicions after the poisoning of the mares at the water hole. Yet Byron couldn't shake the thought that there was more to those "accidents" than met the eye.

Quince Hunter's offer to share the army contract had initially seemed the answer to Byron's prayers. He had wanted Glory to be a part of it. He had believed the experience was essential to prepare her for the future. During the long, quiet hours since their departure, however, anxiety had tempered his enthusiasm for the endeavor.

His only consolation was the recollection of the look in Quince Hunter's eyes when their party mounted. He had seen strength, intelligence, and determination to assure the success of their venture. As for Glory's safety—he had seen something else in Quince's eyes, something that had almost dispelled his remaining insecurities despite the obvious animosity between them.

What more *did* he expect from her?

Seething as Quince disappeared into the darkness, Glory raised her horse's hoof and checked it carefully. The stone she had removed from his shoe earlier that day did not seem to have caused any damage, and she was glad. Her assurances to Quince aside, she was aware of the danger if a horse should stumble during a run.

Glory's throat felt tight as the familiar question returned to harass her. What more *did* Quince expect from her? He already had everything he wanted. She had been reduced to the status of a second-rate wrangler who couldn't be trusted to do her job. She had accepted that position rather than put additional stress on a difficult situation, even though Quince's reminder of the circumstances of their first meeting had pained her deeply.

As if she could ever forget that day.

Yet when he had looked down at her a few minutes before, his light eyes so intent, her heart had begun an unnatural pounding that she knew had nothing to do with anger. Even now, she could almost make herself believe that she had seen something in his gaze, a kind of . . .

No.

Halting her straying thoughts, Glory dropped her horse's hoof and straightened up. She wouldn't fall into that trap again. She had made a fool of herself once before when she had felt alone and unsure, and had imagined that Quince could somehow soothe the ache inside her. If she hadn't been entirely successful in erasing the memory of those moments when he had held her close, when his mouth had claimed hers—she was determined to prove to herself that she could.

Resolved, Glory turned back to the campfire.

And before she was done with him, she would make him eat his words—every last one of them.

Chapter Nine

"What happened to you, honey?"

Madge's hoarse voice filtered through the mottled haze that clouded Blanche's vision. Disoriented, Blanche struggled to clear her mind. She attempted to speak, but the effort was beyond her. Her head ached. Her vision was distorted. She seemed somehow unable to form words with her lips, and every breath caused her pain.

"That's all right, don't try to talk." Madge's brightly painted face moved in closer. "One of the Double Bar H riders heard you moaning in the alleyway near the general store and got the doc."

Blanche blinked in an attempt to look around herself.

"You're upstairs in the Lone Star. The doc came here after he got done taking care of you as best he could. He said you'd be needing care for a while and he wanted to know where the best place for you would be. We figured this was it, 'cause there'd always be somebody around during the day and through most of the night." Madge shrugged. "O'Malley said it would be all right, and one room less for our customers ain't going to make no difference. Me and the girls will just have to work a little faster to handle business, that's all."

Blanche winced with pain.

"Who did this to you, Blanche?" Anger flashed in Madge's eyes. "You can't see yourself, but the truth is, you look like hell. Your face is all banged up. The doc says you have a couple of broken ribs. He says it's a miracle your nose ain't broken and you still have all your teeth."

Blanche was unaware of the tear that had slipped out of her eye until Madge said, "Don't go crying, now. The doc says you're going to be all right. Your ribs will heal, and when the swelling goes down, your face should look as good as new."

There was a knock on the door, and Madge went to answer it. When she turned back, she had a plate in her hand.

"Bonnie brought you some broth," she said, " 'cause you've been unconscious for a while and you need to eat something. The doc says you won't be able to have nothing solid for a few days."

Blanche closed her eyes. She felt sick, too sick for broth or anything else. The doc said she'd be herself in a while, but what was the use? Lobo would only find her again.

"Open your eyes, honey." Suddenly whispering, Madge said, "Tell me who did this to you. Me and the girls will fix him."

Blanche opened her eyes. It took all her strength to shake her head.

"You're afraid, is that it? Well, I ain't afraid."

With a supreme effort, Blanche shook her head again.

"All right, you don't have to tell me." Putting down the spoon when Blanche refused it, Madge said, "I'll let you sleep a while. The doc says that'll be the best thing for you for the time being but you got to eat something when you wake up, you hear?"

Blanche took a painful breath.

Madge said unexpectedly, "This wouldn't have happened if that Quince Hunter had been around. I saw the way that big fella looked at you. He wouldn't have let it happen."

Blanche's sadness cut deeper. Madge didn't know the truth. Quince had been nice to her; he liked her, but he didn't really care—not the way she cared about him.

"He's out mustanging, you know. He got the army contract with Fort Griffin. The whole town's talking about it, saying he was crazy to take it. But if you ask me, that fella knows what he's doing." Madge paused, then said, "He'll come looking for you when he comes back, I know he will. Then you won't have to worry about nobody hurting you no more."

Blanche closed her eyes again.

"You're tired. Go to sleep. I'll be back." Blanche

felt Madge touch her arm. "Don't you worry. Nobody's going to hurt you here."

The door clicked closed behind Madge, and Quince's image flashed through Blanche's mind. She wasn't fooling herself about him anymore, but just thinking about him made her feel better. Nobody had ever been nicer to her than Quince Hunter, and Madge was right in one way. If he'd been around, he wouldn't have let Lobo hurt her.

But he wasn't around.

Blanche took another painful breath.

He wasn't.

Quince dismounted, hobbled his horse, and turned wearily toward the camp. Three consecutive days of running the mustangs had wearied the animals. There wasn't much fight left in them. The problem was, he and his men were pretty well spent, too.

His gaze drifted toward Glory as she hobbled her horse nearby. She didn't fool him with the brave front she was putting on. She fell asleep each night as soon as her head hit the bedroll. Any woman less stubborn than she would admit she was at the point of exhaustion—but Glory wasn't just any woman.

Quince followed Glory's slim figure as she unsaddled her horse.

Not just any woman.

There was more truth in those words than he had been prepared to acknowledge. His original concerns aside, it didn't really surprise him that she had worked as hard as the men during the four grueling days of running mustangs. He had been unprepared, however, for her insistence on taking her turn on watch. He had balked at that, stirring another brief conflict. When he finally relented, he had consoled himself that she would be safe, since he had been assigning the watch in pairs. In pairing her with Jan, he had been sure he'd be able to rest easily. But he hadn't. He had lain awake and restless from the moment she left until she rode back into camp the next morning. The weary droop of her shoulders as morning reached afternoon had gnawed at him, leaving him uncertain if he was more angry with her or with himself for letting her wear him down.

Scrutinizing Glory more closely, Quince saw the toll the difficult days were taking on her. Her slim body was even thinner, her complexion was pale underneath the sun-tinted color of her skin, and her dark eyes were shadowed with exhaustion. To his eye, she looked fragile, and he ached at the sight of her.

Quince's gaze lingered. It wouldn't be much longer. He had scanned the herd carefully as it settled down to water and graze. It was time to turn them back toward Diablo. He'd tell the men tomorrow, and with any luck, he'd be splitting the herd between the Half-Moon and the Diamond C in two days.

Glory lingered behind as the other wranglers drifted back to camp. Waiting until they were out of earshot, she turned toward him. His stomach knotted. He knew what was coming even before she said, "I'll take the second watch tonight."

"No."

"I said—"

"I don't care what you said. Robbie and Miles are taking it."

"It's my turn on watch."

"No."

Glory's eyes were suddenly blazing. "You're determined, aren't you?"

"That's right, I am."

"You can't stand being wrong about me making good as a wrangler."

"That has nothing to do with my decision."

"It damned well does!"

"It has to do with my judgment of your physical condition."

"By that you mean I'm not in condition to handle the watch tonight because I'm a woman."

"That's part of it."

"So you admit it!"

He was beginning to admit that and a lot more to himself—but he was silently grateful she didn't ask him to explain the rest of his reason.

Instead, she repeated, "I'm taking the second shift."

"Robbie and Miles are taking it."

"Robbie's tired. I'll take it with Miles."

"Miles is just as tired as Robbie, and you're more tired than either of them."

"No, I'm not!"

"Yes, you are, damn it!"

"I won't let you treat me this way. I won't let you infer I can't keep up just because I'm a woman, or because when we met that first day, when Cinnamon . . ."

Glory's voice choked off. She struggled visibly to control her emotions. Rigid from the effort, she managed, "I'm taking the second shift with Miles, and that's the end of it."

The tremor in her voice was suddenly more than he could bear. Despising his weakness, he said, "All right, do what you want."

Not waiting for the flash of triumph in her eyes, Quince strode back to the camp without another word.

"Are we going to get this over with or not?"

Kane turned slowly toward Lefty, who sat mounted at his right. The bright light of a full moon illuminated Lefty's heavy features as he glared at Kane boldly. The amused mockery Lefty had displayed earlier in their journey had turned to open discontent as they had wandered, losing Hunter's trail time and again.

Lefty pressed, "The boys and me are getting tired of riding around. First you couldn't find Hunter's trail. Now we finally caught up with them and you're holding back. Hell, them horses are ripe for the picking!"

"You're a damned fool!"

Lefty's face flushed hot. "I don't like being called names."

"Why not, when they fit?"

Lefty's hand moved toward his hip, and Kane growled, "Go ahead, go for your gun and we'll settle this here and now."

Waiting only until the blink of Lefty's eyes signaled silent retreat, Kane scoffed, " 'Ripe for the picking.' Sure, we should try stampeding the herd right now—in the dark."

"There's a full moon. It's almost as bright as day."

"That's a stretch that can't cause nothing but trouble." Taking a moment to sweep the silent men behind him with his burning stare, Kane continued, "We don't know nothing about this territory, and them wranglers have had days to scout it out. We need to make sure we can scatter them horses for good when we stampede them."

"So, how are you going to do that?"

"By using my brain, that's how."

"Yeah, that says a lot."

Kane went dangerously still before replying, "It says I'm going to wait until morning, so we can look over the terrain and know where we're riding. It means I'm going to figure out what Hunter's planning to do so we can find the best way to stop him—permanently."

"How long is that supposed to take?"

"As long as I decide it'll take."

"I ain't intending to grow old here, you know."

His eyes as cold as death, Kane replied, "Keep it up and you won't need to worry about growing old."

Turning toward the men shifting nervously behind him, Kane grated, "Anybody else got any complaints?"

When there was no response, Kane spurred his mount into the shadows, confident they would follow.

*   *   *

She was a stubborn, exhausted little witch. She had taken the second watch just to prove a point to him that she had already proved countless times during the past few days. And she was near the point of collapse—he knew she was.

Quince glanced around the campfire. The men were all sleeping soundly. Shorty, Robbie, and Slim hadn't even raised their heads when Glory and Miles got up to take over the watch. Jan and Riggs had returned and were already snoring.

Quince reviewed again the conversation he had had with Glory a few hours earlier. Why did things get so complicated when he tried to talk to her? How did everything he said seem to turn into an accusation? Why couldn't he make her understand that his need to keep her in sight during the long, strained days of mustanging hadn't been because he still doubted her, but because her safety was important to him for reasons he had never anticipated?

And what was he doing here, lying in his bedroll trying to sleep when she stood no chance of sleeping at all?

Mounted minutes later, Quince rode slowly across the moonlit terrain. He saw Miles astride his horse, watching the herd. He rode past him with a nod of acknowledgment, annoyed at the realization that Glory had chosen to take the far, more isolated watch point.

No, she wouldn't make it easy on herself. Not her.

He approached the watch site slowly, careful not to disturb the herd. He saw the restless twitching of the mares as they turned to watch him. Aware that a single false move could be a costly mistake, he dismounted and secured his horse to a low-lying shrub, then walked the rest of the way. The knot inside him tightened when he saw Glory sitting her horse, so exhausted that she was hardly able to hold herself upright.

He walked closer, and she twisted around toward him. Obviously angry that he had gotten so near without her realizing it, she snapped, "What are you doing here?"

Suddenly as angry as she, he grated, "I came out to relieve you."

"It's not time yet."

"Yes, it is."

"I told you, I won't let you treat me any differently than the rest of the men."

"I know what you told me. Now go back to camp and get some sleep."

"No."

"You say you want to be treated like the rest of the wranglers," he spat, "but you don't want to take orders like they do."

"I'd take your orders if they were fair."

"They're fair."

"Not to the others, they aren't."

Quince stared at Glory. She was hardheaded and impossible to reason with!

As silent as he, Glory glared back at him. Suddenly furious, he reached up and swept her down off her horse. Holding her fast, he grated, "You're not like the others, Glory. You're a woman. Can't you get that through your head?"

He felt her shudder before she snapped, "That doesn't make any difference. I'm as good as any man."

The hard core of his anger slowly melting, he responded, "You are, but—"

"I can do anything any of the other wranglers can do."

Anger rapidly turning into something that tore viciously at his control, he replied, "I know you can."

"I'm not tired."

He drew her closer. "I know."

"I don't need to be relieved."

"All right."

She shuddered again. "I can take the rest of my watch."

Yes, anything . . . if she'd just let him hold her.

She looked up at him as she said with the last spark of bravado, "I'm not tired at all."

I'm not tired at all . . . yet she looked so weary and vulnerable that he could stand it no longer.

The last of his restraint slipped away. Quince whispered, "All right, you're not tired. You don't need to be relieved. You're as good as any man. Just stop talking, Glory. Damn it, just stop talking and let me love you."

Slipping his arms around her, Quince kissed her, the way he had always wanted to kiss her. She made no resistance when he separated her lips and stroked her tongue with his, drinking in the taste of her. She did not protest when he pressed his kiss deeper, consuming her with a voracious hunger. She was as breathless as he when he drew away from her briefly to whisper how much he wanted her, what torment it was to have her so close, yet so far from his grasp. He kissed her again, promising never to let it happen again, never to let her slip away while she was so near.

He felt her surrender to his kiss, to his touch. Her skin scorched his lips as his kisses slipped to the white column of her neck, to the sweet hollow at its base. The sound of her impassioned gasp when he first tasted the velvet warmth of her breasts was burned forever into his heart.

Suddenly clear was the reality that this was what he had wanted. This was what he had needed—to hold Glory, to make her his.

She was lying underneath him, her sweet flesh pressed to his, her heart pounding against his chest, when he entered her.

Glory gasped as Quince filled her. Hesitating, he looked down at her with whispered words of concern. The same concern was reflected in his eyes. She stroked his cheek, reassuring him. She offered him her lips, wanting him. He groaned as he thrust himself deeper, and his groan resounded inside her.

She felt his heat and shared it as he began moving within her. Matching her rhythm to his, she reveled in the searing moments of intimate union. She clutched him closer as the heat between them flared to a scorching blaze. The flames soared higher, their intensity more brilliant. She felt the moment approaching as Quince's strong body quaked and she was swept up with him into a shuddering burst of sustained ecstasy. Their release left her lying limp and breathless, replete in his arms.

Quince lay atop her, his moist flesh pressed intimately to hers. She felt him stir, then heard him whisper huskily against her lips, "Glory, look at me."

Her breathing still uneven, she looked up into his impassioned gaze as he said, "I want you to know I never doubted you—not really. I *resisted* you, with all my strength, but you wore me down without even trying. I wanted you near me—not because I thought you couldn't make it without me, but because I knew you would. I wanted you to want me. I wanted you to need me the way I needed you.

"Quince—"

"Don't talk, not yet." Quince's strong features softened in a way that touched her heart as he continued, "Words always seem to come between us. Just . . . just tell me you want me."

Somehow unable to do otherwise, Glory whispered, "I want you."

"Tell me you need me—here and now, while I'm holding you in my arms."

Never more aware of that truth, she said, "Here and now . . . I need you."

She saw his gaze flicker before he replied in a

voice hoarse with emotion, "I hope so, Glory, because those words are more true for me than I ever imagined they could be."

Her response coming naturally, Glory whispered in return, "Then make love to me, Quince. Here and now, before anything can come between us. Make love to me."

He responded silently with a look of love and tender compliance.

Dawn had not yet touched the night sky when Glory opened her eyes with a start. Momentarily disoriented, she realized she lay on the ground with Quince beside her, a blanket covering their nakedness.

Meeting Quince's gaze in the light of cold reality, Glory forced herself to whisper, "Quince, we have to be getting back soon, and I need to say . . . this . . . everything that happened last night . . . none of it changes things, you know." To his slow frown, she responded, "I'm still a wrangler here, and that's the way I want to be treated."

Quince hesitated briefly before nodding, "All right."

"On the runs, on the watches, on the way back to the ranch—"

"I said, all right."

"I don't want the men to know."

"I understand."

"It would make them uncomfortable."

He nodded again.

"When we get back . . . we can decide then

what . . . I mean where . . ." She stopped and searched his face, then said, "We can decide then where we go from here."

"Anything you say."

Glory frowned. She wasn't used to this. He was too agreeable. And his lips were lifting into a smile.

"Quince . . ."

The uncertainty in her tone sobered him, and he responded, "We'll take it slow if that's the way you want it."

She wasn't sure.

He searched her expression. "If that *is* the way you want it."

She wasn't sure of anything anymore, except that when he looked at her the way he was looking at her now, when he took her into his arms as he was doing now, she felt as if she belonged there.

And when he kissed her—as he was doing now—she had no doubts at all.

Kane turned toward the men mounted beside him as dawn streaked the sky. He had scouted the terrain and the herd. He had formed a plan and had detailed it to his men. Lefty, his expression sullen, was still mumbling about being forced out of his bedroll before dawn. Bart, Sloan, and Whistler had remained neutral. Kane sneered. Those three were smarter than he had thought. They knew he had a long memory. They knew that Lefty was in for trouble when this job was done, and that payback would be heavy when it came.

Turning again toward the herd, Kane scrutinized it more intently. The herd was bigger than he had expected, and the mustangs looked ready to be started back toward the ranch. He needed to act hard and fast. Drastic measures would be necessary.

Using his field glasses, he confirmed his earlier assessment that the herd consisted of several smaller herds that had been picked up during the runs. The individual stallions were easy to spot where they stood apart, watching for encroachment on their mares.

That couldn't be better.

Turning toward the men behind him, Kane said, "Are you ready?"

"Sure we are."

"We're waiting on you."

"Just tell us when."

"Yeah . . . just tell us when."

That last reply from Lefty registered in Kane's mind as he replied, "Hunter's wranglers haven't ridden out from the camp to take their positions around the herd yet. There's time to get the stallions fixed in your rifle sights before you shoot. Remember, don't fire until I give the signal or you'll give them a chance to bolt. If that happens, you'll never hit them. It's important to take all the stallions down with the first shot. No misses. That way, with the stallions gone and with the wranglers not in position to control the herd when we stampede it, them mares will start running wild. They'll scatter all over creation, and Hunter's wranglers won't stand a chance of rounding them back up again." Kane paused, then added, "And if Hunter's men get in your way, use your guns."

At a sign of movement in the distance, Kane grated, "Hunter's getting his men together. They'll be riding out soon. Get your rifles aimed at them stallions and make it fast."

Kane smiled coldly as his men reached for their rifles. He watched as they raised them toward the unsuspecting stallions.

"Remember . . . wait for my signal!" he ordered.

"It looks like the herd is ready."

Quince's statement hung on the early morning silence of the camp. Glory watched him as he scrutinized the wranglers gathered around him. There was no trace of the previous night's passion in his sober expression. Because of Quince's close scrutiny of the watches, it had not seemed unusual when he and Glory arrived back at the camp together, with Miles drawing up behind them. The men hadn't asked any questions, and she had been relieved.

Standing among the wranglers now, Glory was as surprised as they when Quince said, "We'll be starting back home today. We'll take our regular positions around the herd and get them running like always, but we'll begin changing direction as soon as the pace becomes stabilized."

He cautioned, "Keep them tight and follow my lead. We'll test out the herd first—check for resistance. I don't expect any trouble at this stage of the game, but if something should come up, remember—follow my lead. If all goes well, we'll be splitting the herd up between the Half-Moon and the Diamond C in two days."

Nodding in assent, the men began walking toward their mounts. They stopped in their tracks when Quince addressed Glory directly. "I want you in my sight at all times, Glory. No straying for any reason. Today especially, we can't afford distractions."

Feeling the flare of familiar anger, Glory replied, "I'm a distraction, of course."

The flash of intimate heat in Quince's glance was unexpected. It raised a flush to her cheeks that forced her to continue curtly, "All right. Whatever you—"

The bark of rifle fire in the distance turned all heads sharply toward the herd. Incredulous, Glory saw the stallions drop motionless to the ground— all four of them!

And the terrified herd was up and running.

Reacting instantly, Quince raced to head off the frantic herd as it tore blindly forward. He glanced at Glory, who rode beside him toward the frenzied mustangs. When they reached the mares, he looked back at the sound of new gunshots to see an unknown rider attempting to split the herd. He saw another unknown rider firing wildly into the air.

Drawing his sidearm, Quince turned in time to see a gun leveled in his direction. He fired, and did not look back when the rider disappeared underneath the stampede.

Panicking when he realized Glory wasn't riding beside him, Quince glanced around to see her pushing her mount through the wild-eyed mustangs in an attempt to head them off. Fear choked his throat when her horse stumbled, then righted itself miraculously to continue its forward surge. He shouted, calling her back, but his voice was lost in the thundering din.

Unable to free himself from the swelling crush, Quince saw Glory close in on the panicked lead horses. He knew that one slip . . . one false move . . .

Riding abruptly into sight ahead of the herd, Jan fired rapidly into the air, and the lead mare began turning. He saw Glory reach Jan's side, firing as well, and he took a relieved breath.

With a glance behind him, Quince saw that the men were beginning to reach their stations around the herd. Shouting and firing into the air, they were attempting to tighten the main body of the herd when one of the unknown riders flashed back into view, his gun pointed at Glory.

Firing without hesitation, Quince saw the man slip out of sight under the mustangs' hooves. Turning to scan the herd, he saw another unknown rider with his gun drawn, then another—until a shot from Shorty's gun left only one of them still in the saddle.

Whistler fell from his horse and disappeared under the stampede, and Kane shouted an epithet that was lost in the din of the melee. His men were dropping like flies.

He glanced around himself. He was alone, damn it!

Leaning low over his mount's neck to avoid any bullets aimed his way, he maneuvered his mount out of the wild fray. Breathing rapidly minutes later, he watched, concealed on the sidelines as the herd pounded past with Hunter's men gradually bringing it under control.

Kane seethed. It was all Montgomery's fault! It had already been too late to do the job right when Montgomery came to the cabin to hire him. Montgomery hadn't given him enough time or information. It was his fault that they'd been outnumbered almost two to one by Hunter's wranglers. If he'd had time to prepare . . . if he had known more about the whole situation, it would have turned out different.

Still seething, Kane saw a rider appear in the dust left behind by the herd. He watched as Lefty galloped in his direction, then pulled his mount to a sliding halt beside him.

"Hiding, ain't you?" Lefty spat, "I always knew you was a coward! You got the rest of the fellas killed while you stood on the sidelines, all safe and sound, but that ain't going to happen to me. I'm going to make sure I get what's coming to me, and when I do—"

Kane drew his gun and pulled the trigger. He did not react to Lefty's startled expression when the bullet struck him, or to the heavy thud when his body hit the ground. Nor did he say a word as he turned his horse and rode away.

Quince stood over the bodies of the two unknown riders, then looked up at the wranglers opposite him. The exhausted herd was settled for the night and the long day was coming to a close. Intensely aware of the disaster they had so narrowly escaped, Quince had left guards with the mustangs and ridden back with the other wranglers to check on the fallen men who had attacked them.

Glory had remained at his side, silent through the ordeal when they found the first two bodies earlier. Identification of the battered bodies was impossible, and they had buried the men and continued on. Strangely, only one of the next two bodies they found was similarly battered. The other was virtually unmarked except for the bloody circle on his chest.

Quince felt Glory's shudder as she looked down at them. Frowning, he asked, "Does anybody recognize these fellas?"

"I never saw either of them before."

"Me neither."

"I don't know who they are."

"Rustlers, I guess."

"Rustlers? Maybe . . ." Quince glanced at Glory. Her face was pale. She had had enough. He said abruptly, "Whoever they are, let's bury them and be done with it."

Uncaring of the men's reaction, Quince slid his arm around Glory and urged, "Come on, sit over there. You don't need to be a part of this."

Her fair skin pale, Glory looked up at him. Her gaze unreadable, she leaned into the curve of his arm without protest as he led her away.

Chapter Ten

The Half-Moon ranch house came into view, and Quince knew he had never seen a more welcome sight. He glanced at Glory, who rode silently beside him, then turned to survey the herd, which was still intact after two long days of travel. Those days had required that they pay constant attention to the uneasy mustangs, which had balked at every opportunity.

His respect for the Diamond C wranglers had never been greater; Quince looked at each of them in turn. Extended days of travel had not altered their devotion to their work. They were good men, loyal to the Diamond C and to Glory.

Glory.

Quince scanned her sober face. She had been deeply disturbed by the discovery of the rustlers' bodies. They had had no time to talk alone since then. He wasn't sure what she was thinking. It worried him.

His gaze lingered. On the surface, it was as if the night Glory had spent in his arms had not happened at all. His mind told him they had to act that way for the present, but his heart did not agree. He ached for her. He despised holding himself apart from her. Awareness of her fatigue troubled him further as she rode beside him with shoulders held almost painfully erect.

He admired her courage.

He respected her tenacity.

He suffered for the exhaustion he read in her gaze.

He yearned to comfort her, to take her into his arms and tell her she need never worry again, because he'd always be at her side, wherever that promise took them.

He wanted to tell her he loved her.

Those words rang truer inside him each day. They lay on his tongue, aching to be spoken. He wanted—

The approach of a familiar horseman halted Quince's thoughts. Drawing to the side of the herd, he waited as Brent neared. His brother's expression clearly communicated his displeasure even before he said, "Where do you think you're taking those mustangs?"

"To the west pasture. We're going to leave half the herd there, then drive the other half to the Diamond C."

"Take them all to the Diamond C. We don't want them here."

Quince met Brent's gaze coldly. Always the "older brother." Always *his* way or no way. Quince responded, "Not this time. Half of those mustangs belong to the Half-Moon, and here's where they're going to stay until they're ready to be delivered to Fort Griffin."

"No Half-Moon wrangler is going to waste his time breaking those horses to the saddle, if that's what you're thinking."

"Waste his time?"

Brent's tight smile was caustic. "You'll never collect a penny from the military at Fort Griffin, and you know it."

"I do, huh?"

"If you had a lick of sense in your head, you would've realized that before you signed the contract."

"I wouldn't have signed that contract if I didn't know Major Tremain was as good as his word."

"I was at Fort Griffin the same day Quince was there, Brent," Glory interrupted unexpectedly. "I met Major Tremain. He's a real gentleman. He seemed honest and dependable to me."

"I'm sorry, Glory, but you're wrong," Brent replied, obviously restraining his impatience. "There's not an officer in Fort Griffin anybody can depend on. If you want the Diamond C to take a risk with that contract, that's up to you, but no Half-Moon wranglers are going to work their hands raw without a chance of getting paid."

Addressing Quince again, Brent said, "Tell those wranglers to turn that herd around now. Those mustangs aren't going to stay on Half-Moon land."

Quince did not respond. He hadn't wanted it to come down to this—the same kind of direct confrontation with Brent that had driven him away from the Half-Moon five years earlier—a confrontation between brothers where there could be no true winner, whatever the outcome.

But it wasn't five years earlier.

Quince felt Glory's restless movement beside him as Brent urged his mount closer. "Turn those mustangs around, and do it now," he repeated.

The sound of an approaching horseman forestalled Quince's reply. He turned toward Jack Hunter's unexpected approach, noting that his father's lined face was tight as he reined back, glanced between them, and demanded, "What's going on here?"

"I told Quince to move these mustangs off Half-Moon land," Brent said. "That contract he has with the army isn't worth the paper it's written on."

"I signed a contract with Fort Griffin, and I'm going to honor it," Quince replied levelly, his voice devoid of emotion. "I'm going to deliver these mustangs to the fort, on time, saddle broken, and ready to ride."

"I told you—"

Interrupting Brent, Jack said, "And I told *you*— you don't speak for me or the Half-Moon. I'm the boss here. My name's on the deed, I do my own talking, and I make my own decisions. I don't expect to have to tell you that again."

Turning toward Quince with no lessening of his frown, Jack said, "You know how I feel about mustangs. They don't have any place in the Half-Moon's future."

Jack paused, his gaze narrowing as he stared at Quince. He proceeded unexpectedly, "But you signed that contract in good faith and you're bound to it. Making it hard for you to fulfill it doesn't make much sense."

"Pa—"

Jack's attention went back to Brent. "As a part of this family, Quince has as many rights on the Half-Moon as anybody else here."

Incredulity rang in Brent's voice as he returned, "They're mustangs, Pa! 'Range varmints' to your way of thinking."

"Quince isn't expecting to raise them on the Half-Moon—just saddle break them."

"He won't get a cent out of Fort Griffin when he's done."

Not bothering to reply, Jack looked at Quince and said, "Put them in the west pasture, like you wanted. Half-Moon wranglers will help you break them, too. Just make sure you keep them away from my brood mares. That's where the future of the Half-Moon lies—with them."

Quince stared at Jack with the belated realization that his father was cold sober. He did not waste time wondering how long that sobriety would last as he tipped his hat to the old man and spurred his mount into motion.

Quince turned toward Glory when she rode up behind him. Her relief was apparent. Also relieved, he was unable to dismiss his lingering regret when Brent rode away without another word.

Edmund walked along Diablo's busy main street, his foul mood progressively worsening in anticipation of the day. The deterioration of his careful plans for the future continued. Jack Hunter had returned from purchasing the twenty-five mares that he couldn't afford, and the loan papers had been carefully filed, but the situation hadn't turned out to be the triumph he had imagined. The mares were high-quality breeding stock, if he were to believe Jack's glowing report when he had come to town a few days ago. Involved with settling the mares in, Jack had not even stopped off for a drink on that occasion. In the time since, he had dispensed with his routine of drinking and gambling to the point that he was beginning to look like a reformed man. Edmund consoled himself that the situation would change drastically when the first payment on the note came due, but he was beginning to worry that something else would go wrong before then.

The situation at home was not much better. Abby had been staying with Iona, only a bedroom away, for more than a week. She avoided him whenever possible, and shrank from his touch when she could not. She had remained civil and polite in their conversations, but would not allow him to get close—while Iona, the pathetic sheep that she was, continued to solicit his attention in every way she could. Hope had flared briefly when Abby had come to him last night to discuss Iona.

She had left when he avoided her questions, but that moment had clarified his realization that Iona was the key to winning Abby's confidence. He had resolved to find a way to exploit Abby's concern, telling himself he would succeed with her ultimately, but his agitation had not been subdued.

Rounding out his expanding vexation was the amount of time since he had heard from Kane. He didn't like it. The bastard had had plenty of time to get the job done. If it wasn't for the payment waiting for him when he returned, he would almost believe Kane had taken the money and—

As if summoned from his thoughts, Kane stepped into his path on the boardwalk in front of him. Forcing a professional smile despite his anger at the fool's stupidity, Edmund extended his hand and said, "Well, Mr. Kane. Have you reconsidered opening an account in the Diablo State Bank? I can promise you your money will be safe if you do."

"Right." Kane did not bother to return his smile as he said, "That's what I wanted to talk to you about—in your office."

"Surely. Follow me."

Making certain to nod pleasantly at each questioning glance along the way, Edmund continued briskly down the walk with Kane beside him. Entering the bank, he called out to his head teller in a voice calculated to be overheard by the customers standing in line, "Mr. Kane has some questions about opening an account, Wilfred. If you need me, I'll be in my office."

He turned viciously toward Kane the moment

the door closed behind them and hissed, "What are you doing here? You know better than to contact me in public. If I'm associated with you, especially now—"

Interrupting him, Kane grated, "Hunter will be bringing the mustangs back to the Half-Moon any day now."

"What?"

"You heard me."

"What do you mean? You were supposed to make sure his plans failed."

"It didn't work out."

"What happened?"

"What do you think happened? The boys and me followed Hunter and them wranglers out there like we was supposed to, but there was too many of them for us to get control of the herd."

"I told you—"

"You didn't tell me nothin'! They had eight men, and we didn't. They had four days' head start on us, and by the time we got there, there was no way we could do what we wanted to do."

"Excuses!"

"Yeah, well they may be excuses, but that's all you're going to get from me right now."

"They didn't see you, did they?" Edmund demanded. "Because if they did and you're here now—"

"They didn't see me."

"What about your men?"

"They're all dead."

"Dead!"

Kane stared coldly into Edmund's eyes. "They knew the risks."

Momentarily silent, Edmund gave a tight laugh. "And you don't have to split the money I advanced to you. That worked out well, didn't it?"

With a threatening step toward him, Kane said, "I risked my life dodging bullets for that money."

"For all the good that does me."

Kane's swarthy coloring darkened. "Too bad, ain't it? I guess you'll have to come up with another scheme to make sure them ranches end up in your pocket."

"And I suppose when I do, you'll guarantee satisfaction just as you did this time."

"Like I said, this was your fault."

Disgusted with Kane's excuses, Edmund snapped, "Listen to me, Kane. I'll pay you, and pay you well, but I won't stand for failure and I won't listen when you refuse to admit your failures."

"You ain't had no cause for complaint up till now."

"One time is more than enough."

Taking another step, Kane was eye to eye with Edmund when he said, "It's enough for me, too. There ain't no way either Hunter or them Townsend wranglers will get the best of me again. That I *do* guarantee."

His control returning at the realization that Kane deplored his failure as much as he, Edmund responded, "All right, but don't go far. You'll be hearing from me again soon."

Taking a moment to affix a suitable facade to

his patrician features, Edmund pulled open his office door and offered Kane his hand in full view of the outer office as he said, "I'm sorry we couldn't do business today, Mr. Kane. Stop back again. The Diablo State Bank is always at your service."

"I'm fine, dear, really I am."

Abby looked at Iona, who sat in the elaborately upholstered chair that dominated the corner of the Montgomery living room. She didn't look fine. Thinner than she had ever been, Iona looked incredibly small and pale—totally lost in the oversized chair. The circles under her eyes had darkened to an almost frightening degree, yet she seemed unaware of her deteriorating physical appearance. She didn't sound like she was fine, either. Her voice was weak and shaky, her words beginning to slur despite the sweet smile on her lips that never seemed to falter.

Abby ached inside. She had tended to Iona for more than a week while the older woman recuperated from her fall. Worried about her in ways that had nothing to do with her accident, Abby had made sure to remain in the room while Dr. Gibbs visited. She had heard him caution Iona about the amount of sherry she was consuming and her use of laudanum, but nothing changed. Iona insisted on her sherry and the "medicine" that allowed her uninterrupted sleep.

Abby had secretly questioned Dr. Gibbs about Iona's condition, only to have him reply that he couldn't do any more for her than he was presently doing.

Desperate, she had tried to talk to Edmund the previous night, but he had evaded her concerns, and his attempt to "console" her had sent her back to Iona's room in a hurry.

Yet Iona was now insisting she was almost well.

"Really, dear, you needn't stay any longer."

"It's no hardship for me to stay until you're more steady on your feet," Abby replied. "There isn't anything for me to do at home that somebody else can't handle until Quince comes back. I'm sure Brent and Pa hardly realize I'm gone."

"Oh, I'm sure you're missed whenever you aren't around. You are such a dear girl, but you heard what Dr. Gibbs said yesterday. My leg is much better. I'll be able to manage quite well even if I might be limping for a while. In any case, Hilda will be here in the event of an emergency during the day, and Edmund . . ." Iona's smile faltered for the first time. "Edmund is usually close by."

Abby withheld her reply. Yes, Edmund was usually close by—while Iona was asleep, when he had no trouble avoiding her.

Noting her hesitation, Iona pressed, "If you stay any longer, I'll feel even more guilty than I do now for forcing you to tend to a tedious old woman when you should be out enjoying your youth."

"I'm happy to help you, Iona."

Her gaze moistening, Iona replied, "I know you are, but it's time for you to get back to your own life." Her smile again wavered. "I will expect you to visit me, though. I'll look forward to it."

"Iona—"

"Please, dear. I don't want you wasting any more time here. But I will ask you to help me back to my room before you go, so I can take a nap."

A nap. Abby knew what that meant—more sherry and more "medicine."

"Abby?"

Having no recourse, Abby took her arm. When they entered her bedroom minutes later, Iona said unexpectedly, "If you could help me to my desk, I think I'd like to write a letter to Juliana before I sleep."

Abby's lips tightened. Juliana, who had not come home to visit her mother in years.

Iona's eyes again misted. "You know, dear, you're not alone in the type of loss you suffered. Juliana had a difficult start in life when she lost her father so young, yet she proved her courage by striking out on her own and doing extremely well for herself. I'm very proud of her. I so look forward to the excitement of her letters."

Dear Iona.

Iona was seated at her desk when Abby hesitated again.

"Go, dear. I'll be fine. Don't worry about me." At Abby's continued hesitation, Iona added in an earnest whisper, "You do know I love you as if you were my own child, don't you?"

Unable to answer for the thickness in her throat, Abby kissed Iona's withered cheek and walked out the door.

* * *

Kane's earlier visit weighed heavily on Edmund's mind. It continued to irk him as he turned to the papers on his desk, and his mind wandered. The fool had not only failed in his mission, but he had deliberately approached Edmund again on the street. He didn't like having Kane blame him for his own inadequacies, but most of all, he disliked Kane's attitude. He had always known the repulsive fellow would push him a step too far one day. It appeared that the day was approaching more quickly than he had imagined.

The sound of a conversation being conducted in deafening tones in the bank doorway interrupted Edmund's thoughts. Looking up in annoyance, he saw a cowpoke laden with trail dust talking to Burt Spindle, who had apparently been about to enter the bank with a deposit. The fellow was obviously inebriated and intent on telling Burt his tale.

About to dismiss the incident with disgust, Edmund went suddenly still at the mention of the name *Hunter*, then listened as the cowpoke continued, "Yeah, I seen him on the trail back to the Half-Moon a little after daybreak—Quince Hunter with that Townsend woman and her wranglers from the Diamond C. They was driving a herd of mustangs in front of them."

Always alert for gossip, Burt prodded, "It was a sizable herd, was it?"

"Yeah, it was big enough. From the looks of it, them wranglers didn't have too easy a time of it, neither."

"What makes you say that?"

"They was looking mighty weary."

"Well, maybe Hunter wasn't so crazy, after all, to take that contract from Fort Griffin."

"You think so?" the cowpoke sneered. "I'm thinking all Hunter did was find himself a lot of work that he ain't never going to get paid for."

"I don't know about that." Burt shook his head doubtfully. "If those horses are delivered on time, there's no way the army can renege on a signed contract."

"He ain't home free, though, is he? He'd better get them horses delivered on time—saddle broke and ready to ride—because them officers at Fort Griffin are just looking for an excuse not to pay him."

"Maybe—"

"No maybe about it!" the swaying cowpoke said hotly. "Them army officers never had trouble backing out of things before. All I can say is, I'm damned glad Hunter didn't come to me when he was looking to hire wranglers for that mustang hunt. I would've told him he was wasting his time."

The conversation continued, but Edmund's attention lapsed. He had heard all he needed to hear.

The mustangs needed to be delivered on time—saddle broken and ready to ride.

Smiling, Edmund stood up and started for the door. He had picked up the posted notice offering the Fort Griffin contract after it was ripped from the sheriff's wall a few days ago. He had folded it and stuffed it into his pocket for some reason which he did not now recall. If he remembered correctly, he had later shoved it into his desk drawer at home. That sheet now contained information which might be useful to him in the next few days.

You'll have to come up with another scheme to make sure them ranches end up in your pocket.

Kane, repulsive fellow that he was, had been right. Edmund would have to come up with a new plan. But first he needed another look at that notice.

Glory's heart leaped when the Diamond C ranch house came into sight at last. The Half-Moon portion of the mustang herd had been cut and left behind. The Diamond C mustangs had already been driven into a fenced pasture where they would remain until the men were rested enough to begin breaking them. With that business aside, she was anxious to see her father again. She knew he would be worried about her, but most of all, she was worried about him.

The image of the rustlers' battered bodies flashed unexpectedly before her mind, and Glory shuddered. The awful moments while she stood looking down at them had left her strangely shaken. Almost undone, she had leaned fully into Quince's support when he slipped his arm around her and led her away.

Her response to him had returned to haunt her. She had sensed a change in her wranglers after that, a concession to her sex that had not existed before. One night in Quince's arms and she had behaved like a weak, helpless female—an image she had worked for years to overcome. She had despised herself for that display of weakness and had promised herself she would erase whatever doubts those moments had raised. She owed her wranglers that confidence; but most of all, she owed her father that consolation in the face of a future that was still uncertain.

She allowed her gaze to linger on Quince, who spurred his horse briefly ahead to herd straying mustangs back into line. An indefinable ache stirred again inside her as she watched him chase the mustangs down, his strong features intense and his powerful body leaning instinctively into the chase. She remembered the strength of his arms as they had wrapped around her and pressed her intimately tight against his naked flesh. Her own response had been instinctive when his expression had softened to warm honey and his mouth had sought hers. Her throat tight, she recalled surrendering to emotions so new and profound that they were undeniable, then awakening in Quince's arms to see similar emotion in his light eyes.

Then had come the hard crush of reality.

She had seen the question in Quince's eyes as they drove the mustangs home—as she had deliberately held herself aloof from him while conflicting emotions raged within her. Quince had said he wanted her, that he needed her, and she had returned those words to him in the passion of the moment; yet the future was tenuous, too tenuous for either of them to afford—in Quince's word— *distractions*.

That was the reality to which she was bound.

She needed to tell him that, to make him understand.

Two figures appeared on the ranch-house porch as they neared, interrupting her thoughts, and Glory took a deep breath. Spurring her horse to a faster pace, she dismounted minutes later, acknowledged Pete, then said to her father with emotion barely held in check, "We're back, and everything's fine, Pa."

She bent down and kissed her father's cheek, then turned at a sound to see both Quince and Jan standing on the porch behind her. Her father's hand trembled as it reached for hers. His voice was shaky, too, when he said, "Welcome home to you all." She noted the dimming of his smile when he scrutinized Quince and Jan more closely and said, "So, it didn't go as smoothly as I hoped it would."

The first to speak, Quince sketched the events of the hunt briefly and accurately. Jan was adding the details when Glory was suddenly overcome by weariness. Aware that she would spend the evening hours confirming those same details with her father, she patted his shoulder, knowing he hardly realized she was leaving as she walked into the house. She had advanced only a few feet into the parlor when she heard a step behind her.

"Glory . . ."

Turning, she was unprepared when Quince pulled her into his arms and covered her mouth with his. His driving hunger rebounded inside her as he crushed her closer, pressed his kiss deeper.

The warmth of him . . . the power he exuded . . .

the hot, blinding emotions he brought to life each time he touched her . . .

It was Quince who pulled back abruptly. Breathing raggedly, he whispered against her lips, "I don't know what you've been thinking these past two days, but I know what I've been thinking. And I'm telling you, this isn't over between us."

"I need to talk to you, Quince." Glancing toward the porch when her father called her name, Glory rasped, "But not now. My father wants me."

"I want you, too."

Glory's heart skipped a beat. "He's calling me."

"Why are you afraid to let him know about us?"

"I'm not afraid."

"Then tell him. Your father wants to see you happy, Glory. I can make you happy."

"This is all happening too fast. He'll be worried."

"It's not too fast for me."

"Quince, please."

Quince was stroking her back, drawing her tight against his heat, against the hard proof of his passion. She swallowed as he whispered, "It's not happening too fast for your father. It's too fast for you—that's what you're saying, isn't it?" His light-eyed gaze was direct. "But you want me anyway, don't you?"

When she did not respond, Quince cupped her cheek with his palm. He kissed her again, refusing to yield his possession of her lips until they parted of their own accord to allow him access. She was as breathless as he when he drew back again at the sound of her father's voice.

"Your father's calling you."

Yes, he was.

Feeling somehow abandoned when Quince released her, Glory took firm hold of her conflicting emotions. She forced a smile when she walked back out onto the porch. Intensely aware of Quince's presence behind her, she responded with pure strength of will when she was drawn into the conversation there. She remained silent when the discussion halted, then acknowledged Quince's brief glance in her direction when he said goodbye.

Glancing up at the sky as he rode out of sight, she was somehow startled to see it wasn't even noon—that the lifetime that had passed since she had mounted her horse at dawn had consisted of only a few short hours.

Iona sat at her desk, struggling to finish her letter to Juliana. She paused to steady her hand. The tremors were almost constant now. They embarrassed her, as did her instability, which she knew had no relation to her injury. She had tried desperately to hide the tremors from Abby, but she knew she had not succeeded.

Abby was truly worried about her. Iona wished she could have relieved the dear girl's concerns, but she knew the effort was beyond her. She needed the sweet sherry that had become her constant companion in recent months. It blurred the sense of inadequacy she felt each time she saw distaste in Edmund's eyes. It made her feel almost worthwhile again.

Iona sighed unconsciously. Edmund was so kind, yet she had seemed less and less able to please him lately, no matter how hard she tried. That thought haunted her whenever she lay down to sleep. It allowed her no rest. It was only the laudanum that Dr. Gibbs decried which granted her respite. She couldn't give it up—not yet.

Iona took a steadying breath and a firm hold on her pen as she signed the letter. It had taken a long time to admit to herself that she had not done as well as she should have by her daughter. The knowledge had gnawed at her over the years, making her even more anxious for the affirmation of Juliana's love and respect that her letters represented.

That agitation had grown stronger of late. There were so many things she should have said to Juliana that she had left unspoken. Uncertain of the reason, she only knew she felt a driving need to express them to Juliana now, so her daughter would know what had always been in her heart.

Folding the letter carefully, Iona inserted it in the envelope, addressed it, then stood up. She would give it to Hilda to post at the first opportunity.

The slam of the front door and the sound of Edmund's step in the hallway turned Iona toward the clock on her dresser. It was early. It wasn't time for him to come home yet. She wasn't ready.

Standing uncertainly, aware that she still held the letter in her hand, Iona took a few steps toward the bed, then stopped. Edmund wouldn't be happy to see she had written to Juliana without his knowledge. He wouldn't understand that she had needed to say some things to her—things that could be said only by mother to daughter.

Edmund's footsteps neared her door. He would be angry. She didn't want him to be angry with her.

Reaching her dresser as his knock sounded, Iona pulled open the drawer and shoved the letter underneath the lacy unmentionables there. She turned, a smile on her face as she bade him enter.

There she was, the drunken witch!

Furious, Edmund glared at Iona, who was supporting herself unsteadily with her hand on the dresser. He had come home believing the horrendous day was about to take a turn for the better, only to learn from Hilda the moment he arrived that Iona had sent Abby home.

Unwilling to have Hilda witness his reaction to Abby's departure, he had sent her out of the house on a pretext, then had stood in the doorway for long seconds in an attempt to calm his rage. Abby was gone. He had needed only a few more days to reach her—he was sure of it—but Iona's interference had effectively canceled that opportunity.

Edmund shook with ire. No, he wouldn't stand for it! Iona would summon Abby back to stay with her, and he would see that she did it now.

His anger in tenuous control, Edmund looked at Iona as she waited for him to speak. Her darkly circled eyes were wide with apprehension at his unconcealed wrath as he grated, "Hilda told me you sent Abby away this morning." Repulsed when Iona nodded assent with her sickening smile, he spat, "Why?"

"I . . . I couldn't take advantage of her by asking her to stay any longer. She's a young woman. She . . . she has a life of her own."

"Unlike you—a useless hag with no life at all."

Iona gasped.

"Listen to me, old woman!" Edmund took a threatening step toward her. "You will send for Abby. You will tell her you made a mistake, that you need her here a while longer."

"But—"

"Be quiet and listen, you drunken fool!" Edmund demanded, his chest heaving. "You will tell her you were hasty in sending her away. You will tell her you need her here a little longer. You will ask her to come back to stay with you—and you will do that today, do you hear?"

"B . . . but it isn't true. I'm well! Other than my limping, I'm almost the woman I used to be."

Taking Iona by the shoulders, despising the feel of her bony frame beneath his palms, Edmund turned her roughly toward the mirror. "Take a look at yourself, Iona. Take a *good* look, then tell me again you're almost the woman you used to be!"

Holding Iona fast in front of the mirror, Edmund felt a surge of satisfaction as she shuddered. He watched grimly as she attempted to turn away. He said, "Have you seen enough?"

Releasing her when she nodded feebly, Edmund

saw her grip the dresser again for support as he repeated, "Send for Abby. I don't care how you manage it, but do it!" His gaze held her fast as he added, "I promise you will regret it deeply if she isn't here when I return."

Edmund strode out of the room and slammed the door behind him. Stopping only to take the Fort Griffin notice out of his desk drawer, he walked back down the hallway and out onto the street.

Trembling violently, Iona clutched the dresser, barely holding herself erect as she stared at the doorway Edmund had strode through moments earlier. She jumped at the sound of the front door slamming shut behind him.

She shook her head in abject denial. No, this had not really happened! Edmund had not talked to her as if he despised her. He had not called her names and threatened her. He had not forced her to look in the mirror to face the appalling wretch she had become. This was all a dream—a nightmare from which she would awaken!

She staggered to her bed and sat abruptly when her legs refused to support her. None of this was true. None of it. She needed to sleep, to allow this nightmare to run its course so it would be over and done. When she awakened, she would be able to face her life again.

Iona glanced at the night table and the sherry that glistened there. She reached for the bottle with a trembling hand and poured the tumbler half full. A sob escaped her throat as the horror of Edmund's tirade returned. No, sherry wasn't strong enough to ease her revulsion at the moments past. Laudanum was her friend. It would dull her mind and induce sleep. It would erase the memory of the frightful image of herself that she had seen in the mirror.

Filling the glass to capacity, Iona drank long and deep, then settled back against her pillow. Drowsiness came quickly—the advent of a merciful slumber that she knew would follow. A smile returned to her lips. When she awakened, the nightmare would be over.

When she awakened.

Iona closed her eyes to the tranquillity that dulled her senses, to the velvet cloak of sweet serenity that gradually settled around her to grant a final, everlasting peace.

"I want to know the truth, Jan."

Intensely sober, Byron Townsend faced the ruddy-skinned wrangler standing opposite him in his study. Glory had gone to tend to her horse, giving him the opportunity to speak to his foreman alone. Noting Jan's hesitation, he pressed, "The truth—no holding back. That story about the rustlers—"

"You know everything there is to tell."

"But there's something everybody's thinking and not saying."

"Maybe."

"There's no 'maybe' about it. I saw Quince Hunter's face when he talked about those rustlers.

It bothered him how they just happened to find you all."

"Coincidence, maybe."

"That's one too many maybes for me."

"None of them fellas was familiar to us—as best we could tell, anyways. Since they was strangers, we all figured they heard about Quince getting the contract and decided to cash in at the last minute on our hard work."

"That would mean they deliberately tracked you down. It doesn't make much sense, considering how everybody seemed to think Quince was crazy for believing Fort Griffin will come through with payment."

"Maybe they figured it was worth taking the chance."

"More maybes."

"I don't know, boss. You should talk to Quince about it, man to man, and see what he thinks."

"You think so?"

"Yeah."

"You like him, don't you?"

"He's smart. He's a fine hand with horses, and he seems like a real fair man to me."

"What about Glory? She doesn't have too much to say about him."

"There's no saying what Miss Glory's thinking. They were at each other's throats one minute and real quiet the next. There's just one thing I know— she made sure Quince remembered that she's the boss here."

Byron smiled at that. "My girl's got a lot of spirit." His smile faded. "I've got a feeling she's going to need it." He continued, "But you're right. I need to talk to Quince alone about a few things. In the meantime, I'm depending on you. There's just so much I can put on Glory's shoulders right now."

"I know, boss."

"Remember, this is all between you and me."

"You can depend on it."

He knew he could.

Yet as Jan drew the door closed behind him, Byron made himself a promise. If what he was thinking was true . . .

Edmund was breathless when he reached his front door. Joey Weatherby had come running into the bank minutes earlier to tell him something was wrong with Mrs. Montgomery. His first reaction was that if the drunken witch had begun crying her sad tale to the world, he needed to stop her.

Pausing briefly to gather his thoughts, he was about to enter when Hilda pulled the door open. Her full face was blotchy, her eyes red-rimmed as she said, "I'm sorry, Mr. Montgomery. I didn't check in on Mrs. Montgomery when I returned from my errand. I should have. Maybe then she'd still be . . ."

Annoyed when Hilda was unable to continue, Edmund pressed, "Where is she? In her room?"

"Yes." Hilda sobbed. "I called the doctor right away when I found her, but he said her heart stopped. I'm sorry. I didn't know she was so sick. I thought it was just the sherry. I thought she—"

Walking past his tearful housekeeper, Edmund

turned into the hallway toward Iona's room.

He slowed his pace, fighting to compose himself as Hilda continued blubbering behind him. Iona was dead. All her many assets, with the exception of Juliana's small trust fund, were now officially a part of his own personal fortune—and he was finally rid of the millstone that had hung around his neck for years.

Yes, he needed to compose himself. It would not do to approach his wife's deathbed with a smile.

Iona's bedroom door opened unexpectedly. Dr. Gibbs stood there, his expression emotionless. Walking past the doctor, Edmund approached the bed and looked down at his wife.

Damned if she wasn't still smiling that sickening smile!

"She died in her sleep, Edmund."

"I see."

"Sherry and laudanum—a dangerous combination."

"I know."

The doctor's voice sank to a hiss as he pushed the door closed. "I warned you about this! I told you what would happen if you continued to supply Iona with laudanum."

Turning to the doctor's flushed countenance, Edmund said, "I have no regrets, and neither should you. Iona chose to drink and chose to take laudanum. No one poured it down her throat."

"You're a cold-hearted bastard, aren't you? You couldn't care less that your wife is dead."

"Actually, I'm relieved." Waiting for his admission to register fully in the doctor's incredulous expression, Edmund continued, "I feel free to tell you that because I know my secret will be safe with you—since you have so many secrets of your own."

"I was not responsible for the deaths of those women back East. They were in trouble. They were desperate. They begged me to help them. I warned them of the risks, but they didn't care."

"A sad story."

"It wasn't the same with Iona."

"I suppose it wasn't—but I doubt that anyone would believe you if Iona's death was ever questioned."

Dr. Gibbs went still.

"I don't suppose it will be, though. Everyone knew Iona's condition was . . . delicate."

Dr. Gibbs did not reply.

"I suppose I should have someone notify Charlie Herbert so he can ready a coffin. We'll have the funeral as soon as possible."

Dr. Gibbs cleared his throat, then said, "Iona spoke often of a daughter."

"Juliana," Edmund sneered. "Yes, I'll notify her of her mother's death—eventually."

Allowing his gaze to linger an extended moment on Edmund's pleased expression, Dr. Gibbs picked up his black bag and started for the door.

"Thank you, Dr. Gibbs." As the doctor drew the door closed behind him, Edmund was unable to stop himself from adding, "Your help was invaluable here. Please console yourself with that thought."

Waiting until he heard the front door shut behind the silent doctor, Edmund turned back to the bed and looked again at his wife's motionless body.

She always was a pitiful-looking wretch.

Affixing a suitable expression on his face, Edmund walked out into the hall.

Abby went still as Joey Weatherby rode into sight. She had arrived back at the Half-Moon a few hours earlier and had been told by Frances that Quince had returned, had driven the Half-Moon's share of the mustang herd into the west pasture, and had then gone on to drive the remainder of the horses to the Diamond C. Frances had also reported with her characteristic bluntness that Brent and Quince had had another run-in, which Jack had settled.

With both Brent and her father nowhere to be found, she had ridden out to look at the herd, and excitement at the herd's potential had briefly driven her worries about her brothers and Iona from her mind. She had returned to the ranch house only minutes earlier, her excitement dimming as her concerns returned.

Joey's appearance had stopped her thoughts cold. The last time he had come to the ranch had been when he was sent to tell her that Iona had fallen and needed her help.

Watching as Joey drew up near the porch and dismounted, then approached with hat in hand, Abby felt a shiver move down her spine. She held her breath as he cleared his throat, his youthful face twitching nervously as he said, "I have some bad news for you, Miss Abby. It's about Miss Iona."

Trembling, Abby listened as his voice droned on.

A brilliant full moon lighting his way, Dr. Gibbs climbed into the saddle and headed out of town. His departure at that late hour was a relatively common occurrence since he was often called to sick patients in the middle of the night. No one would give it a second thought when he didn't return for a few days, as was sometimes his practice when the illness was severe.

No one would be able to guess from the clothing and personal articles he'd left behind that his saddlebags had been carefully packed with essentials, or that he had turned his horse loose as soon as he reached the nearest railhead and had boarded the first train for parts unknown. Still considered a "tenderfoot" by most of the people in town, he had been warned countless times about the danger of going off alone when called to a patient at night. When his horse was found wandering, the townsfolk would assume he had had the accident they had warned him about, or that he had met with foul play. It would not be the first time that a body was never found in the wilderness.

Dr. Gibbs glanced nervously behind him as Diablo slipped into the distance. He had apparently succeeded in leaving town unseen. He was glad. In his present state of mind, he was in no mood for explanations. It had been painful to watch helplessly as Edmund manipulated his desperate, unsuspecting wife into the grave. It had been chilling, however, when he realized that the true reason Edmund had maneuvered him into remaining in Diablo had been to use his past against him in the event Iona's eventual death was considered suspicious.

In another town, with another name change, he hoped to strike from his mind the poor woman who had refused to acknowledge, right to the end, the depth of her husband's perversity.

In another town, he hoped to leave Edmund Montgomery and Diablo, Texas, forever behind him.

Chapter Eleven

Concealed behind a curtain at the upstairs window of her room at the Lone Star, Blanche was afforded a clear view of the scene as Iona Montgomery's funeral procession moved toward the First Street Church yard. The line of mourners was long and somber.

She had heard about that lady's unexpected death. The rumors had saddened her. Some said Edmund Montgomery's wife had drunk herself to death, and Blanche had been confused. Why would someone who had everything she wanted do that to herself? Blanche had never met the woman, but she had seen Edmund Montgomery in Diablo, and his pious attitude when meeting her on the street had somehow not matched the look in his eyes. It had made her wonder.

The procession continued behind the plain

wooden coffin. Her heart leaping, Blanche spotted Quince the moment he came into view. Her bruised lips moved into a smile. With him standing a few inches taller than most, and with those powerful shoulders and his way of walking that made a woman stop and take notice, it would be impossible to miss him. She remembered the first time he'd looked at her with those light eyes. They'd made her wonder how it would feel to be held in his arms.

She still wondered.

Suddenly still, Blanche saw a small woman step into view at Quince's side. She was crying. Quince slid his arm around her, and a familiar ache began inside Blanche. The woman buried her face against his chest, and he leaned down to whisper something into her ear. The woman looked up at him, allowing her a clearer view of her face, and Blanche took a relieved breath. She had seen that young woman around town. She was Abby, Quince's sister. She remembered hearing that Abby had been close to Iona Montgomery.

Brent Hunter and Crystal, her rounded stomach clearly reflecting her condition, came into view. Jack Hunter followed, walking alone. A red-haired woman appeared in Blanche's line of vision, and she saw Quince look up. Only one woman had hair that blazing color. It must be Glory Townsend from the Diamond C, who had gone mustanging with Quince.

She saw the way Quince watched Glory Townsend—so intently—his gaze never leaving her slim figure as she made her way to Edmund Montgomery's side and spoke to him briefly, then left the column of mourners.

Glory Townsend disappeared from sight, and Blanche relaxed, then frowned at her own reaction. Was she jealous? If she was, she was wasting her time. She needed to face the hard truth that if all the Glory Townsends in the world were suddenly wiped off the face of the earth, Quince still would not look at her the way she wanted him to.

Blanche turned to assess her reflection in the mirror. The dark purple bruises around her eyes were just beginning to fade, but the swelling in her cheeks and lips had lessened during her long days of convalescence. She didn't look like a monster anymore. Bent over the way she was from the pain in her ribs, she just looked pitiful,

No, he especially wouldn't look at her now.

The procession moved out of sight into the churchyard, and Blanche's thoughts drifted. She couldn't work in her condition. If it wasn't for O'Malley's unexpected charity, she wouldn't even have a place to stay. Anne Pals had packed up her things, sent them to the Lone Star, and moved someone else into her room when the rent came due and she'd had no way of paying it. She had been a little surprised at that. She had thought Anne liked her—even though she'd always known that with Anne, business was business.

Worst of all, she couldn't hide from Lobo forever. It scared her to think what would happen when she went back to work and he showed up again.

Quince moved back into view in the church

yard, and Blanche's heart leaped again. It pleased her just to look at him, to know that somebody like him had even remembered her name. She wished—

Blanche forced herself to stop wishing. She turned resolutely away from the window with the sharp reminder that wishes never did come true.

Abby sobbed as Iona's coffin was lowered into the ground.

Quince tightened his arm around her and whispered against her hair. He knew she hardly heard what he was saying. He had come home shortly after Joey Weatherby told Abby of Iona's passing and had found Frances frantically attempting to console her. Although a little surprised at his haste, he was glad Edmund had decided to have the funeral the next morning. He knew it would be easier on Abby that way.

Quince glanced at Edmund as Reverend Crawford said some final words. He unconsciously assessed the mourners as the silent column turned to follow the minister back toward Edmund's residence.

Edmund's fellow deacons walked directly behind Reverend Crawford. It was no secret where their sympathies lay as they eyed Edmund mournfully. He knew that the whispers about Iona's "problem" would begin again the minute the last shovelful of dirt fell on her grave.

Brent walked in front of Quince, holding Crystal's arm as he guided her carefully on the uneven ground. Crystal had acknowledged him pleasantly, but Brent had hardly looked his way.

Pa stood to the side of the column, pretending he didn't care that he was still shunned by the respectable citizens of Diablo. Quince could not help wondering if his father was remembering the funeral he had been unable to attend ten years earlier while he sat in jail with blood on his hands. Pa had chosen to ride his own horse to town, and Quince was glad. He wasn't up to a long buggy ride home with him.

Countless other mourners followed, representing the town's respectable citizens—as well as those beholden to the Diablo State Bank who had not dared to be absent.

Edmund himself was composed—perhaps a little too composed for his sorrowful display in front of the mourners earlier to ring true.

As for Glory, she had made an appearance but had shown little emotion when speaking to Edmund. Her sympathy had seemed sincere only when she had hugged Abby briefly before returning to the Diamond C. She had spared only a nod in his direction. Staring after her for long moments, he had felt frustration, anger, but most of all a hunger that nagged with every thought of her. No, it would not end here.

It occurred to him as he turned his sister back toward the street that Abby was the only true mourner in the long line of people heading toward Edmund's house for the repast Hilda was preparing.

"Abby . . ."

Quince looked up to see Edmund standing beside them. Wearing a dark, meticulously tailored suit, he was dressed in sharp contrast with the Western garb worn by most, as well as the outdated dress Abby had worn out of respect for her departed friend.

"Abby, dear . . ." Abby reacted with a frown as Edmund continued, his hand stroking her shoulder, "I know how strongly you felt about Iona. I hope you'll sit beside me when we go back to the house so we may share the solace the mourners offer."

Quince felt Abby cringe as Edmund attempted to slip his arm around her. He saw the flash of anger in Edmund's eyes before he continued smoothly, "Your presence would be a great comfort to me."

"As a matter of fact, Abby just asked me to take her straight home." His jaw tight, Quince stared at Edmund, his cold gaze imparting more than his words as he continued, "She doesn't have the heart for conversation right now."

"Of course . . . whatever is best." Turning back to Abby, Edmund said, "I'll miss you, Abby." Leaning forward unexpectedly, he kissed her cheek. The fact that his kiss had grazed Abby's lips before reaching that chaste spot did not escape Quince's notice.

Rigid with anger, Quince was staring at Edmund's departing figure when Brent appeared at his elbow and said, "Let's get out of here."

He knew it had not missed Brent's notice when Abby wiped away Edmund's kiss with the back of her arm, then started walking toward the buggy without a word.

Crystal and Abby were seated in the buggy when Brent turned toward Quince and said, "If that bastard touches her again—"

Completing Brent's sentence, uniting them as brothers where nothing else had seemed able, Quince grated, "—he'll be damned well sorry!"

Jack Hunter watched from the churchyard as Quince snapped the buggy's reins against the team's back and the vehicle jumped forward.

He had watched from a distance as Quince supported Abby through that morning's ordeal, comforting her in her distress. He had watched from a distance as Brent tended to his wife while glancing with concern at Abby. He had watched from a distance as Brent and Quince seated Crystal and Abby in the buggy and then conversed briefly, sharing sober thoughts as brothers should—their past differences apparently behind them for the moment.

He had no place there.

For a few short days after bringing his recently purchased mares back to the Half-Moon with Brent, he had started to believe his future was brightening. The hours recently past, however, had revived vivid memories that had changed his thinking.

Jack looked around himself. The mourners had filed past, leaving him alone in the churchyard. They had returned to Edmund's house to be with him for a few hours to share his grief.

He had no place there, either.

He had no place anywhere.

Jack turned toward the street and started walking briskly toward the Lone Star. There, for the price of a bottle, anybody belonged.

Quince closed Abby's bedroom door behind him, then started back down the hallway toward the yard. The ride home from the funeral had been silent and difficult. Crystal hadn't felt well, and Brent had taken her to their cabin immediately after leaving Abby and Quince off at the house. Abby had wanted to go to her room for some privacy after the morning's ordeal, and he had respected her desire for solitude. With all the Hunter men attending the funeral, the ranch hands had scattered to work in various sections of the ranch for the day. They wouldn't be returning to the house until suppertime. All the hands were unavailable now, and a day had been lost in working with the mustangs.

Quince walked out into the yard and started toward his mount. He had dismissed the lost day as an unfortunate necessity, but he could not dismiss the memory of Glory's casual nod toward him at the funeral.

Quince mounted up and spurred his horse into motion.

Glory turned her mount onto the familiar trail back toward the ranch house. The afternoon sun had just passed the midpoint in the cloudless sky. She had gone directly from the funeral to work with the ranch hands that morning, but that decision had not worked out to her advantage. She had been tired, dispirited, and distracted upon returning—unable to keep her mind on her work. As a result, her mount had gotten cut on some barbed-wire fencing, an accident for which she blamed herself. The injury was not severe, but she had decided to return to the barn to tend to it, thereby giving herself some time to sort out her thoughts as well.

Iona Montgomery's funeral had drained her. It had galled her to see Edmund wallowing in condolences, his expression dutifully sorrowful. It seemed as if the whole town had turned out in tribute to a man who made her flesh crawl, while the poor woman who had finally escaped the misery of being his wife had gone virtually ignored.

If she had ever needed proof of Edmund's hypocrisy, it had been served to her regally by Edmund's lustful glances at Abby Hunter, who appeared to have been the only person at the funeral who was truly grieving. Those looks had far exceeded the fleeting sexual arousal she had seen in Edmund's eyes when he looked at her. She wondered if anyone other than herself had noticed his interest in Abby.

She had felt the weight of Quince's gaze as he walked at Abby's side through the morning's ordeal. Awareness of him had tingled along her spine, yet she had been somehow grateful that circumstances had contrived to keep them apart. She wasn't ready to deal with Quince. She had no resistance to him. The sight of him set her heart pounding, alerting every nerve ending to the expectation of his touch.

A touch that hadn't come.

Glory slowed her mount to a halt as they neared a familiar spot beside the trail. She looked at the quicksand bog, remembering a morning that now seemed so long ago, when another accident had caused the loss of a valuable mare, and had also introduced Quince into her life.

Frowning, she remembered other things as well: the strength of Quince's arms as he pulled her from the bog; the support of his strong chest against her back as she shared his saddle on the way back to the ranch house, and the look in his penetrating eyes as they seemed to see past her angry facade to the aching vulnerability beneath.

Glory halted the direction of her thoughts abruptly. What was wrong with her? Her every thought seemed to lead back to Quince, when she should be concentrating on more important issues affecting the fate of the Diamond C. She didn't like having her thoughts dominated by anyone, especially now, when the situation at the ranch was so uncertain.

"I thought I might find you here."

Startled, Glory turned toward the sound of Quince's voice. Annoyed at the sudden erratic pounding of her heart as he rode closer, she responded more sharply than she intended. "Did you? That's strange. I was just taking the shortest trail back to the ranch house."

When Quince did not reply but instead brought his mount to a halt beside her, she continued nervously, "Runner got himself caught up on some fencing while I was working with the mustangs. I'm on my way back to the house to tend to his cut."

When Quince still did not respond, Glory took an anxious breath. As close as he was, she could see the frown lines between his dark brows tightening as his light eyes searched her face. She saw his jaw harden and his mouth twitch into a hard line. She could feel the tension building in his powerful frame, and the emotion he held rigidly in check as his gaze dropped briefly toward her lips.

She could almost taste his mouth on hers.

No, it wasn't going to be this way!

Her chest heaving, Glory said abruptly, "I'm going."

Turning her mount, she gave a short grunt when Quince's arm curled around her waist and swept her from her saddle. Angry, somehow breathless with her face only inches from his, Glory demanded, "What are you doing? Put me down!"

She felt his grip loosen.

Oh, no.

Clinging to him, she said, "Don't drop me!"

Settling her easily across the saddle in front of him, Quince said in a voice tinged with emotion, "What *do* you want, Glory? Tell me."

Suddenly aware that she was trembling, Glory replied, "I don't have time for this. I have to get back to work."

"You don't have time for what? For this?" Turning her toward him, Quince covered her mouth with his. His kiss was deep and sweet. It paralyzed her protests as a familiar lethargy took hold. She protested unthinkingly when he drew back from her lips, but the sound was muted by the myriad emotions assaulting her as he pressed his lips to her fluttering eyelids, her cheek, the warm lobe of her ear. She heard his rasping whisper as his lips trailed her jaw, then found her mouth again. The taste of him was warm, enthralling. It heightened her senses and clipped her breathing into panting gasps. It coaxed her to separate her lips to accommodate his consuming kiss.

She felt his hands against her breasts, smoothing the hardened nipples, sending little quivers of ecstasy down her spine as his kiss deepened. She felt the mild air buffet her breasts as he opened her shirt, and gasped as he pushed away her undergarment to caress the delicate flesh with his callused hand. She shuddered under his seeking hand. She heard his groan of frustration the moment before he lowered her to the ground, then dismounted beside her to strip away her shirt with trembling hands and cover the waiting crests with his lips.

His seeking kisses devoured the delicate mounds. Clutching him against her, she encouraged him with incoherent whispers that drove him to increasing ardor. Her bliss heightening, she felt his hand fumbling at her waist. Uncertain exactly when he freed her belt, she did not resist when he stripped off her remaining garments, then knelt in front of her.

Uncertain, she looked down at him as he lowered his head to press his lips to the warm delta between her thighs. Rapture jolting her, she gasped as his tongue slipped into the moist crevice and caressed it boldly. She was shuddering when he cupped her buttocks with his palms and drew her fully to his heated assault.

Helpless against the emotions rioting within her, Glory held her breath as Quince searched her moistness more deeply, as his intimate caresses grew more intense. He was tasting her, consuming her, pressing his loving ever deeper.

Caught up in the wonder of his intimate ministrations, Glory groaned aloud. Colors whirled in her mind and sensations deepened, stealing her breath. She was quaking, her knees suddenly weak, when Quince caught her up in his arms and carried her to a grassy bower nearby. She looked up at him as he stood over her. She watched as he stripped away his clothes, exposing the impressive power of his frame and the hard proof of his passion—the same passion that flushed his features as he whispered, "I need to make you mine, Glory."

Kneeling between her thighs, Quince resumed his intimate caresses, stroking her with his tongue, exploring her more intimately. She felt it dawning then, the deep shuddering within as she abandoned herself to Quince's waiting lips, her body quaking in breathtaking, ecstatic spasms that left her finally limp and shaken in his arms.

Still breathing heavily, Glory felt Quince slip himself up over her. She felt his hard probing the moment before he entered and filled her with a groan that send a new delirium of wonder coursing through her. Enraptured, she heard Quince whisper, "Open your eyes, Glory."

No, she didn't want to.

"Open your eyes, darlin'."

Her passion-drugged eyes finally opening, Glory saw the emotion Quince held barely in check as he whispered, "Speak to me, Glory. Tell me you wanted this as much as I did."

She nodded breathlessly.

"Say it."

"Yes . . . I did want this."

"Tell me you needed this . . . tell me you felt the hunger deep inside you."

Glory took a gasping breath.

"Say it."

"It's true . . . everything you said."

"Tell me you . . ."

An emotion close to pain crossed his face, and Quince was suddenly incapable of speech. Moving inside her, he stroked her intimate warmth. His strokes grew bolder, more powerful. She was clutching him close, encouraging his thrusts, wanting, needing, knowing . . .

Quince's strong body convulsed in sudden passionate spasms. The warm heat of his fervor spilled into her, filling her with the final tribute to their lovemaking, carrying her with him to glorious fulfillment that left them suddenly breathless and complete, motionless in each other's arms.

Quince was the first to stir as they lay with their bodies still joined. She felt him cup her cheek with his callused palm, then heard him whisper, "Open your eyes and look at me, Glory."

Complying with a supreme effort, she saw Quince was intensely sober as he whispered, "This is the way it was meant to be between us. This is the way it's going to stay."

She didn't want to talk. She didn't want to think. She just wanted to feel.

Unable to speak those words, Glory slipped her arms around Quince's neck and drew his mouth down to hers.

The day had been long and tedious. Bidding the last, lingering mourner goodbye, Edmund glanced at the hall clock and saw it was mid-afternoon. He had a feeling, however, that the prolonged stay of the mourners had been more of a tribute to Hilda's good cooking and the comfort of his home than to anyone's deep sadness at Iona's death.

Edmund looked around himself, at the soiled plates left on tables around the room, at the glasses and cups lying everywhere. Hilda would clean things up eventually, but she was presently in the kitchen, making a terrible racket with the pots and pans while she blubbered on. Her crying was beginning to get on his nerves. She had had no sympathy for Iona's "problems" while Iona was alive, but she was now somehow devastated by her death.

Women were absurd—every one of them! They had not a rational bone in their bodies.

Edmund paused to rectify that thought. He had known one woman exempt from his contempt— the beautiful Beth Hunter. Yet she had made the error of refusing him. She had regretted it, he was sure of that. The driving force in his life had been to make her admit her mistake and hear her beg his forgiveness.

Edmund ground his teeth as the old wound again festered. It was Jack Hunter's fault that Beth had not lived to satisfy that desire—but he would pay. The whole Hunter clan would pay. The difficult part lay in accepting the reality that payment could come only one step at a time.

Edmund drew his watch out of his pocket to confirm the hour. The day had been wearying, but he was not too tired to move forward with his plans. He'd change into his riding clothes and be ready to leave in minutes.

And if anyone questioned his immediate departure from town—Edmund feigned a sorrowful sigh. Poor, sad widower that he was, he needed to ride out into the countryside so he could spend some time alone to grieve.

That was as good an excuse as any.

The racket in the kitchen grew louder and Edmund's expression tightened. Yes, he needed to get away.

Kane stood silently at the far end of the Lone Star bar, a glass of red-eye in front of him. He had left his cabin a short time earlier when the silence gave him too much time to think—always a problem when his thoughts involved Edmund Montgomery. He had forced himself to remember that despite his dislike of the man, his money was too good to give up. He had then come to town with the thought of occupying his mind with some of the diversions that the Lone Star had to offer. Minutes through the swinging doors, however, the situation had changed.

Paying little attention to the sporadic laughter and steady rumble of conversations progressing around him, he looked at Jack Hunter where he sat alone at a corner table. The bottle in front of him was almost empty. As Kane watched, the old man filled his glass to overflowing, raised it to his mouth with an unsteady hand, and emptied it in a gulp. He had trouble finding the rim of the glass when he attempted to refill it.

Hunter had been sitting there when he arrived. In the time since, Kane hadn't seen anyone approach the old man—not even one of the girls. The whole town was talking about Iona Montgomery's unexpected demise. Old Man Hunter had apparently known her quite well and had come to the Lone Star straight from the funeral instead of going back to Montgomery's house like most of the respectable people in town had done. It had been hours since then. He wondered if Hunter was going to sit there until he fell off the chair, or if one of his sons would come in to drag him home.

Scowling, Kane considered that thought. If one of Old Man Hunter's sons did come, it would most likely be Quince, who had stirred up a hornet's nest at the Half-Moon since returning. Kane knew from personal experience that Quince Hunter wasn't an easy man to handle. He remembered seeing Hunter riding wildly through the stampeding herd, dodging this way and that, anticipating the mustangs' moves and directing his men as they gradually regained control of the panicked horses. He recalled most clearly, however, the quick flash of Hunter's gun when he brought down one of his men. No, it wouldn't do for Hunter to see him here, especially since he expected that Montgomery would be finding more "work" for him to do at the Half-Moon sooner or later.

Tossing back his drink, Kane slapped a coin down on the bar and headed for the door. Yeah, he had better things to do right now than to wonder whether Old Man Hunter would still be sitting upright when that bottle was emptied. There was a whore in a house not too far from Diablo who liked doing things his way. It was time he paid her another visit.

Outside on the street, Kane was mounting his horse when he saw Montgomery turning out of view on the road leading out of town. He was wearing riding clothes, a rare occurrence that meant he had a familiar destination in mind.

Kane nudged his horse into motion.

Following a discreet distance behind Montgomery as Diablo faded into the distance, Kane was tempted to laugh. The bastard wasn't as smart as he thought he was. Riding as if he owned the world, Montgomery had no idea that he was being followed. It occurred to Kane that if he wanted to, he could bring Montgomery down with one shot and take whatever cash he was carrying—all before the arrogant jackass knew what hit him.

Kane considered that thought. It was tempting. He didn't like the way Montgomery talked to him. He liked even less being threatened. It would make him feel real good right now to shoot him dead.

Kane's hand slid to the handle of his gun. His finger itched on the trigger.

But if Montgomery was dead, the money that had kept Kane in comfort would come to an end. No, he wasn't the kind of fool who'd cut off his nose to spite his face.

Kane's hand fell away from his gun.

Abruptly tired of the game he was playing, Kane scrutinized the terrain around him, then spurred his mount to a faster pace. Montgomery turned toward him as he neared. He saw annoyance flash in Montgomery's gaze before he urged his mount off the road into a clump of trees and waited for him to follow.

Not one to waste time on pleasantries, Kane pulled his horse up alongside Montgomery's and said, "I figured you was heading out to see me."

Equally brusque, Montgomery replied, "As a matter of fact, I was."

Kane eyed him coldly. "You must've done some fast thinking to come up with another plan so soon, especially since you buried your wife this morning."

"It wasn't difficult. I had plenty of time to think during Reverend Crawford's extended eulogy."

At Kane's raised brow, Montgomery shrugged. "Everything Crawford said about my dear wife was nonsense. There wasn't a person in that church who believed she had any of the sterling qualities he described. As far as they were concerned, Iona was an embarrassing drunk who was better off dead."

Kane gave a caustic snort. "I can see you feel real bad about losing your wife."

"She's dead, and I'm relieved. That much said, let's get to the business at hand. I do have a job for you—another accident for you to manage." Edmund frowned. "With the emphasis on *accident*, if you understand what I mean."

"I told you before, I ain't stupid."

Ignoring his response, Montgomery continued, "It's a good time to strike. I read the notice Fort Griffin posted. The Half-Moon and the Diamond C don't have much time to get the first batch of mustangs saddle broken and delivered to the fort. An accident now will look as if someone got careless in the rush."

"And everybody will figure that hard luck's just making its way around."

"Exactly."

Kane nodded.

"No slip-ups this time, Kane."

Annoyed, Kane grated, "There won't be no slip-ups as long as you don't expect me to try playing catch-up like you did last time."

"And no excuses!"

"They ain't excuses."

Choosing to ignore his reply, Edmund began, "This is what I want you to do."

"Oh, no, you ain't getting away with that," Kane sneered. "I don't do no listening unless there's something in it for me."

His lips tight, Montgomery reached into his pocket and withdrew a roll of bills, then said, "Let me remind you, you'll get the other half of this payment only if you carry through successfully."

Snatching the money from his hand, Kane snapped, "Just tell me what you want me to do."

Montgomery assessed him for a silent moment, then said, "It's simple enough. You should have no trouble with it."

Kane listened as Montgomery outlined his plan. He smiled when Montgomery was done. Like he said, it would be real easy.

Sober and thoughtful, Glory neared the ranchhouse yard. The afternoon was fading, but the wonder of the moments she had spent in Quince's arms was with her still—as was her growing confusion. She remembered her lingering departure from Quince a short time earlier and the ache inside her when she rode away. She couldn't understand herself. No matter how strong her determination to put all else aside to concentrate on the Diamond C's pressing problems, she was helpless the moment he touched her. Being in his arms had felt so good that she was even now able to think of nothing else.

Turning a corner of the trail, Glory glimpsed her father where he sat in his chair on the porch, and she was filled with a familiar discomfort. She had no time for Quince and the distractions he represented! She had only to look at her father to see how short his time was. He had had so many disappointments in life, yet had given her so much. She needed to make sure he got something back before it was too late.

Drawing up in the ranch-house yard, her thoughts still rioting, Glory approached her father. "You're back early," he said. "I thought you were going straight from the funeral to work with the hands."

"I did, but I had to come back to get some salve for Runner's cut."

"What happened?"

"I got careless."

Hesitating, Byron said, "That's not hard to understand, considering the way the day started out." He frowned. "How did Iona's funeral go?"

"All right, I guess."

"All right?"

"Sure. Edmund was enjoying himself."

"Glory!"

"Well, he was, Pa."

"I expect the whole town turned out."

"Of course. Nobody would dare rouse Edmund's displeasure by not coming—not even me."

"Whatever her faults, Iona Montgomery was a good woman. It was only right that you paid her the respect she deserved."

"With all the rest of the hypocrites, you mean?"

Preferring to change the subject, Byron responded, "What about the mustangs? Did you and Jan have a chance to look them over more closely?"

"Jan was already sorting them out when I got there. We finished grading them. We know which ones look like they'll have the most stamina and make the best saddle horses. I figure on breaking them first if Major Tremain is going to use them when he rides out after Victorio."

"That makes sense."

"It'll be tight, but we should be able to get them to Fort Griffin on time."

"What's the matter, Glory?" Byron asked abruptly, his assessing gaze keen.

"What do you mean?"

"You're frowning."

"I'm tired."

"Hard work doesn't usually make you frown."

"Watching the town fawn over Edmund does."

"Don't worry about him. Once we're out from underneath his thumb, he'll be out of our lives for good."

Glory attempted a smile. "You're right. It's just that things don't move as fast as I'd like sometimes."

"Things have been moving a little too fast to suit me of late," Byron responded unexpectedly.

Glory was taken aback by his comment. Was he reading her mind? No . . . she was being foolish.

"I'd better take care of Runner's cut before it gets infected."

"Yes, do that, and don't bother going back out to meet the hands. It's too late, and you look tired. Take a rest before supper. I'll call you when Pete has it ready."

"All right, anything you say."

"Oh, well!" His smile softening his comment, Byron continued, "You *must* be tired to be so agreeable."

"Pa . . ."

"I'm going inside to work on the books anyway. And don't look at me like that. Things are looking better financially now that Quince Hunter has gotten involved here."

Unwilling to react to his comment, Glory watched as Byron rolled his chair back into the house. She drew her mount behind her as he walked toward the barn. If her father only knew.

Chapter Twelve

The morning sun was rising as Quince and the Half-Moon wranglers reined up their mounts near the west pasture. He knew that Glory and the Diamond C wranglers would probably be meeting on Diamond C land for the same reason that morning. He had not slept much the previous night as memories of the afternoon with Glory had played over and over in his mind. Despite the beauty of the moments they had spent in each other's arms, despite the instinctive response to his lovemaking that Glory had been unable to deny, he had sensed that uncertainty had begun making inroads into her mind before they had even said their goodbyes.

She was committed to the success of the Diamond C that her father had always dreamed of. He knew that despite the femininity she sought to ignore, she was capable and strong-willed enough not to allow anyone or anything to get in the way of her commitment—no matter the self-sacrifice involved.

Quince frowned at that thought, realizing that aside from her fiery beauty, those same qualities— her toughness and resolve—had drawn him to Glory that first day, as well as his perception that behind the shield she had so carefully constructed lay a vulnerability that somehow touched his heart. As annoyed as he often was by her determination to deny her feelings, he knew that her denial only made him want her more.

But the truth was, with his body responding to the very thought of Glory, he could not possibly want her more. As for her strong-willed determination—she didn't realize it yet, but *she had met her match in him.*

Turning his mind back to the work at hand, Quince assessed the ranch hands assembled. Buck, Red, Curly, and Hank. The funeral the previous day had put them a day behind in working with the mustangs, and they were short-handed. Abby hadn't been up to riding out that morning. Iona's death had hit her hard. Sleeping in the bedroom next to hers, he had been aware of her restlessness during the night. She had come to the breakfast table dressed and ready to ride, but one look at her face and he had sent her back to bed. Her silent acquiescence had been revealing. Losing Iona had been like losing their mother all over again. He wasn't sure how long it would take her to adjust to the loss.

It wasn't until Pa failed to appear for breakfast

that he realized their father hadn't come home from town last night. Not that Quince should have been surprised. His father had too many bad memories and too much guilt, and the bottle was a forgiving friend.

Quince scanned the wranglers' faces. Without Abby or Pa's help, getting the mustangs ready to be delivered to Fort Griffin on time would be difficult to manage. He had hoped—

The sound of hoofbeats interrupted Quince's thoughts. Turning, he saw Brent approaching. Unable to read his brother's expression as he neared, Quince felt a familiar tension stir. Aware that the hands shared that feeling, he remained silent as Brent drew up and asked, "Where is everybody?"

"Abby wasn't up to riding out today."

"And Pa?"

"He didn't come home last night."

"That figures." Brent paused, then said, "Getting those mustangs to Fort Griffin on time might turn out to be a problem with you being short a couple of wranglers. I figure you could use another hand."

Hardly aware that the ranch hands had ridden back toward the fenced pasture to allow them privacy, Quince remained silent as his brother continued soberly, "Look, Quince, we both know that Pa is what he is; but that fact aside, what he said the other day has been running through my mind. He was right. I don't know whether or not you'll have trouble getting paid for those mustangs when you deliver them, but you signed that contract in good faith, and it doesn't make sense for me or anybody else in this family to make it hard for you to deliver. I figure we've got enough problems on the Half-Moon without my adding to them out of pure mulishness and pride."

Emotion further deepening his tone, Brent added, "The truth is, we both want the same thing, Quince—to put the Half-Moon back on its feet like Ma would've wanted. Somehow that fact got lost along the way, but I figure it's time to put the past behind us and stand together . . . like brothers should. What do you say?"

Quince looked at the conciliatory hand Brent extended toward him. It seemed he had waited most of his life to hear his brother say the words he had just spoken.

Quince accepted Brent's hand and shook it firmly. The strength and commitment of their handclasp reverberated inside him. Somehow at a loss for a more adequate response, he said simply, "Right . . . like brothers should. Let's get going."

Riding side by side, they nudged their horses into motion toward the pasture.

"I really appreciate your help, Edmund."

Jack was disheveled, bleary-eyed, and humble as he stood opposite Edmund in the foyer of his home. Were he not so revolted at the sight of the man, Edmund knew he would be enjoying the moment—but he was not.

Jack had staggered to his front door shortly after Edmund had returned from his encounter with Kane the previous evening. So drunk that he was incoherent and hardly able to stand, Jack had mumbled about the past while imploring him to "understand" before collapsing into a living room chair. Disgusted, Edmund would have thrown him out onto the street had Hilda not come into the hallway at that moment. Forced to feign beneficence, he had told her to cover Jack with a blanket so he could spend the night in relative comfort, and had then retired to his own room.

Jack had awakened repentant and ashamed. His repeated apologies sickened Edmund. "Of course I let you stay the night!" he snapped, losing control. "Did I have a choice?"

Immediately regretting his lapse but realizing from Jack's pathetic smile that the fool had understood him to mean their friendship had allowed him no recourse, Edmund took a firmer grip on his patience. He added with a soft note of hypocrisy, "You know Iona wouldn't have wanted it any other way."

Silently amused when his statement reduced Jack to even further humility, Edmund urged, "Go home, Jack. Your family is probably worried about you."

Jack shook his head. "No, I don't think they are."

"Abby is, I'm sure."

Jack did not respond.

"I'm going to the bank now." At Jack's surprised reaction, Edmund forced himself to add with a masterful hint of distress, "This house is too filled with memories of Iona. I wouldn't be able to bear it today. I need to occupy my mind."

Jack's rheumy eyes held his. "I understand. I

can't stop thinking about Beth when I'm alone, even after all these years."

Beth's name on Jack's lips brought to life a familiar, latent rage. Striking back with a benevolent smile that masked his true intent, Edmund said, "I'm leaving now, but I can see you aren't feeling as well as you should, Jack. I have a bottle of brandy in the living room that I opened yesterday. A sip might steady you. Why don't you sit down and relax with it until you're feeling better. Take as much time as you want. Hilda won't be in until later, so she won't bother you."

"That's mighty kind of you, Edmund."

Jack was already headed toward the bottle when Edmund walked out through the front door.

Edmund took a deep breath and started down the street. The stupid fool would be drunk again within the hour.

Turning onto the main thoroughfare, Edmund indulged the memory of the beautiful Beth and wondered how she had ever been able to stand the man.

"Pa hasn't come back yet?"

Frances shook her head in response to Quince's question as she placed a sliced ham on the table and began cutting the bread. The men had herded some of the mustangs closer to the house and had come in for an afternoon meal. Pressed to feed them quickly as the ranch hands took their places around the table, Frances said with characteristic frankness, "I haven't seen hide nor hair of your pa. He's usually back by this time, too, no matter how drunk he gets the night before."

Frowning, Quince looked at Brent, who said, "He's probably lying in an alleyway somewhere, still sobering up."

Silently concurring, Quince turned toward Abby when she appeared in the doorway. Her eyes red-rimmed and her face blotchy, she surprised him by saying, "Somebody should go out after Papa to make sure he's all right."

Quince stood up and slipped his arm around her. "How are you feeling, darlin'?"

"I'm all right." She did not smile when she moved away from him and walked into the hall-way.

At her side in a few long strides, Quince turned her toward him to see tears streaking her cheeks as she whispered, "I keep thinking I shouldn't have listened to Iona when she told me she was well enough to get along without me. I should've stayed with her a little longer no matter what she said. I knew she wasn't really well yet. Maybe if I hadn't left her alone—"

"You couldn't have changed anything, Abby. Iona died in her sleep. That would've happened whether you were there or not."

Abby leaned against his chest, silent for long moments before she stepped back from his comforting embrace. Appearing suddenly embarrassed by her tears, she wiped them away with the back of her hand and said, "I don't suppose I'll ever be sure. I don't want anything like that to happen again, Quince."

"What are you saying?"

"Somebody has to go after Papa. Maybe he's still drunk and maybe he isn't. He could be lying somewhere, hurt and unable to help himself."

"I don't think so, Abby."

Abby briefly averted her gaze. "You're probably right."

"Rest a little longer, darlin'. I heard you walking the floor last night. I know you're tired. We'll be back at suppertime, and we can talk some more then."

"All right."

Something about the tilt of her head rang a note of caution in Quince's mind. He questioned, "Abby . . . ?"

"I'm going out after him, Quince."

"I don't want you to do that."

The look in Abby's eyes was revealing. She'd be saddling up the moment they left.

Unwilling to put her through the pain of dealing with their father's drunkenness, Quince said, "All right, I'll find him. You go back to your room."

"No, I'm fine."

"Go to your room, darlin'. Do it for me, please. I'll take care of it."

Abby searched his face with a gaze so like their mother's that Quince was momentarily unable to respond when she whispered, "Promise?"

He forced a smile. "Yes, ma'am."

He waited only until Abby's bedroom door closed before turning back toward the dining room. Grabbing his hat off the rack, he said, "I'll see you all later."

He had reached the front door when Brent halted him. "You're going out to find Pa because Abby asked you to, aren't you?" To Quince's sober nod, he responded, "All right. Don't worry about anything here. I'll keep things moving until you get back."

What went unsaid was *like a brother should*.

That thought was a consolation as Quince mounted and turned his horse toward town.

"Where is she?"

Lobo stared at O'Malley. He had boldly entered the Lone Star minutes earlier. After scanning the room, he had just as boldly approached the bar with his question, and he had no intention of leaving until he was ready.

Lobo stiffened his stance as he stared at O'Malley coldly. He was tired of being run out of the Lone Star. He was tired of asking questions that received no answer. He was sure of one thing: If somebody didn't start talking soon, there was going to be trouble.

When O'Malley didn't respond, Lobo grated, "I'll ask you again. Where's Blanche? I've been looking for her, but nobody's seen her for more than a week. I'm worried about her."

O'Malley's full, black mustache twitched. "I bet you are."

"Talk is she wasn't feeling too good after somebody sneaked up on her in an alleyway near here. Talk is she didn't see who did it."

"That's right."

Lobo almost smiled. "She ain't living at the

boardinghouse no more. I checked. I know she didn't leave town."

O'Malley wasn't talking.

"I asked you a question."

"That don't mean I have to answer."

When Lobo went for his gun, O'Malley raised his shotgun from behind the bar. Lobo heard the scrambling at the tables behind him as O'Malley pointed it straight at his stomach and said, "You wore out your welcome here, Lobo. I told you that once before. I ain't going to tell you again."

"I want to know where Blanche is."

"If she wanted you to know where she was, she would've told you."

"That ain't no answer!"

"It's all you're going to get. Now, git!"

O'Malley's finger twitched on the trigger, and Lobo took a backward step. He wouldn't put it past the fat bastard to pull the trigger just for fun.

Taking another backward step, Lobo smiled tightly. "All right, have it your way. But if you see Blanche, tell her I was asking about her. Tell her I'm worrying about her. Tell her I'll catch up with her one of these days so she can set you all straight about me."

"Get going!"

Lobo had pushed his way through the swinging doors when he heard O'Malley break the silence that followed by saying, "Step up to the bar, fellas. The next drink's on me."

Seething, Lobo crossed the street, then slipped into the restaurant doorway where he could watch the Lone Star unseen. He didn't know what was going on, but he didn't like it. Blanche had only gotten what she had coming, but he wasn't through with her. He liked the arrangement they had, and he was almost out of money. He had been thinking about her in other ways, too—about the private times they had spent together. He was pretty sure Blanche would never forget them. Yeah, he could feel it. She was probably wishing he was with her right now. She'd made a mistake when she turned him down in the alleyway, but she wouldn't do that no more.

Lobo nodded to himself, then made himself comfortable in the shadows. He'd watch and wait. He had nothing else to do. He'd find out what was going on sooner or later.

Scanning the alleyways as he rode, Quince moved slowly down Diablo's main street. He glanced up briefly at the sun as it began a downward arc in the afternoon sky. He had searched every ditch and gully along the road on the way to Diablo, looking for his father. He wasn't sure if he was relieved or not that he hadn't found him. All he did know was that he was becoming more frustrated with every minute that passed.

Another wasted day! The schedule for delivery of the mustangs had been tight, and was growing tighter. He was needed at the ranch, but his frustration didn't end there. He wanted to see Glory. He needed to talk to her.

His body reacted predictably to that thought, and he frowned. Who was he trying to fool? He wanted to be with her, to hold her so close that she'd forget everything except being in his arms. Yet Abby had still been so distressed over Iona's death that he'd been unable to let her go out looking for their father when he knew what the old man would probably be like when she found him.

Poor Iona. Abby was truly the only person grieving for her. Her daughter, Juliana, most likely didn't even know her mother had died, and he doubted that Edmund had ever loved her. He remembered thinking even as a child that Edmund never looked at Iona the way he'd sometimes seen Pa looking at his mother.

Because Pa had loved his mother. Quince had always known that. He supposed that was the reason Pa hadn't been able to forgive himself for what he'd done, even after all the years in between. But that was fine with Quince. No one else in the family had been able to forgive Pa for what he'd done, either. He didn't suppose they ever would.

Quince paused at that thought. But Pa was still their father, and he needed to find him, especially since Abby was in such an emotional state. She wouldn't be able to live with herself if anything happened to Pa.

Satisfied that his father wasn't lying in one of the alleyways along the main street, Quince headed reluctantly for the Lone Star. If Pa was there, it wouldn't be easy getting him out; and if he wasn't, there was no telling where he'd find him. He would have no chance of seeing Glory that night.

Glory of the dark eyes that burned him.

Glory of the pale, sweet-tasting skin.

Glory of the slender, welcoming body that took him in.

Glory of the searing heat that had branded his heart.

Forcing those thoughts from his mind when he reached the Lone Star, Quince dismounted and walked inside. He scanned the crowded room briefly, then walked up to the bar. He motioned to O'Malley, and asked as he approached, "Has my pa been around here today?"

"I ain't seen him."

"What about yesterday? Did he leave here under his own power?"

"Look . . ." O'Malley's full face reddened. "I ain't no information depot. If you want to know where your pa is, keep track of him yourself."

Quince stared after O'Malley as he walked to the other end of the bar to pour a drink. He didn't like the answer O'Malley had given him, but he knew the portly bartender was right. Pa was a Hunter. He was their responsibility and nobody else's.

Turning, Quince looked around the room again. Most of the women employed there would tell a man only what did her the most good, but he knew he could depend on one of them for a straight answer.

Grasping the arm of a saloon girl as she passed, he asked, "Where's Blanche? Isn't she working today?"

"Blanche?" Caution flashed in the sultry blonde's eyes before she responded with a smile,

"You don't need Blanche when I'm around, honey."

Short on patience, Quince said, "Ma'am, I'm looking for Blanche. Is she in today?"

"I don't know nothing about Blanche."

The woman walked away abruptly, leaving Quince staring after her. Something was wrong here. He had noticed the woman's reaction when he first said Blanche's name, and he didn't like it.

"Hi there, fella. Looking for some company?"

Quince looked down at the fading brunette who had pushed her way up to the bar next to him. He was about to respond when the woman continued, "My name's Madge. I've been around here longer than most, and I can answer almost any question a fella can ask if he buys me a drink."

Quince assessed Madge's heavily painted face. Her smile was professional, but there was a serious look in her eyes that belied it. Motioning to O'Malley, he tapped the bar and waited until filled glasses were placed in front of them. Immediately picking up her glass, Madge drank it half down, then turned to him and asked, "Did I hear you say you're looking for Blanche?"

Quince nodded.

"She ain't been working down here for a while."

"Why not?"

Madge shrugged. "I guess you didn't hear about her trouble, then."

Quince went still. He remembered Blanche's simple honesty. It had touched him. She had done the best she could to help herself, but he'd somehow known that trouble would find her in a place like the Lone Star.

"What trouble?" Quince demanded.

"She got beat up a week or so ago."

"Beat up!"

"Yeah. She was unconscious in an alleyway when somebody found her."

Anger filled Quince. Blanche didn't deserve that. Innocent in ways that had nothing to do with her profession, she was a target for the kind of man who'd take advantage of her. The thought of that innocence being beaten from her body sent the blood rushing to his face as he said, "Where is she?"

"She don't need no more trouble."

"I don't intend to make trouble for her."

"What she needs right now is a friend."

Quince met Madge's gaze directly. "She has one. Just tell me where she is."

Madge scrutinized him a moment longer before saying, "She's upstairs. O'Malley let her have the room at the end of the hall until she's back on her feet."

Back on her feet.

Quince strode toward the rear staircase, unaware of the glances that followed him as he took the steps two at a time. Arriving at the room at the end of the hall, he paused, then knocked.

He frowned at the hesitant response, "Who's there?"

"It's Quince Hunter, Blanche."

The key turned in the lock. He heard Blanche whisper as the door opened, "Come in . . . quick."

Blanche pushed the door closed behind him when he entered. He was stunned into silence when she turned to face him. Her bruises were beginning to fade, but it was obvious that both her eyes had been blackened. Her face and jaw were still somewhat swollen, and her lips were badly cut. Her arms were marred by black-and-blue marks, but what struck him most powerfully was her obvious pain when she attempted to pull herself erect. He knew the signs. She had broken ribs.

"Who did this to you, Blanche?"

Her soft brown eyes suddenly brimming with tears, she shook her head. "I . . . I don't know."

She knew.

"Are you afraid to tell me?"

"No . . . no, I just . . ." She trembled as she whispered, "I don't want no more trouble."

"Are you afraid he'll come back?"

Blanche's trembling increased.

Attempting to console her, Quince took her gently into his arms and whispered against her light hair, "Don't worry. The girls downstairs aren't telling anybody you're up here, and O'Malley isn't the talkative kind. If it wasn't for Madge—"

"Madge knows you're my friend."

Quince said sincerely, "I *am* your friend. You can tell me who hit you."

"No."

"If he tries to bother you—"

She drew back from him and shook her head again.

"Blanche . . ."

"I'll be all right."

271

Realizing he was only upsetting her, Quince said, "Do you need anything, then? Money to hold you over until you can work again?"

"No . . . no, I'm fine."

She didn't look fine.

"Everybody here has been treating me real kind—kind of like a family. Even O'Malley."

Even O'Malley. That was saying something.

Earnestly, Quince said, "I want to help you, Blanche. Let me help you."

"I'm fine, really."

Helpless against her determined denials, he said, "All right, whatever you say, but if you need me for anything while I'm gone—anything at all—tell Joey Weatherby, the blacksmith's son, to come and get me. I'll make sure he knows to ride out right away."

Blanche nodded. She winced with pain when she attempted a deep breath, and Quince's frustration mounted.

"Blanche . . ."

A tear spilled down her cheek as she looked up at him.

Filled with a deep sadness, Quince wiped the tear away with the palm of his hand. He said regretfully, "I have to go. There's something I have to do."

Kissing her lightly on the forehead, he said, "Remember what I said."

Hoping she would, Quince looked toward the blacksmith's shop at the far end of town as he stepped out onto the street. He'd stop there first to tell Joey Weatherby to expect Blanche. The young fellow would be glad to oblige him, and he'd make it worth his while.

Then he'd find his father—one way or another.

Watching from the shadows of the restaurant doorway, Lobo sneered. He didn't need anybody to tell him what was going on now. He had seen Quince Hunter run up those steps in the Lone Star, then come back down a few minutes later, looking madder than a hornet. That's where Blanche was staying. He was sure of it.

Seething, he remembered how Hunter had stood up for Blanche that day in the Lone Star. He knew now that Hunter was the reason she had turned him down in the alleyway. It wasn't hard to figure out what that blond witch was trying to pull, but she wasn't going to get away with it. He'd get her back under his thumb again. It was just a matter of time.

Regretting every step he took, Quince walked boldly across the outer office of the Diablo State Bank. He stopped at the doorway to Edmund's office, his expression cold when Edmund looked up from his desk.

Strangely, Quince hadn't considered for a moment that Edmund wouldn't come to the office the day after his wife's funeral. He was sure the devious bastard had an excellent excuse for being there, but he knew the truth was that he didn't care enough to spend another day mourning his wife.

Quince did not bother to smile as Edmund said,

"Well, Quince, I didn't expect to see you so soon."

"I could say I didn't expect to find you in the office so soon after Iona's funeral, but that wouldn't be the truth."

"I couldn't stay home with memories of Iona all around me."

Choosing to ignore his reply, Quince said, "I'm looking for my father. He didn't come home last night. I figured you'd know where he was."

"I'm not your father's keeper, Quince."

"No, you're my father's 'friend.' "

Edmund stood up abruptly and walked around his desk to stand opposite Quince. "It's because I'm your father's friend that I let him sleep off his excessive drinking in my house last night." At Quince's raised brow, Edmund continued tightly, "I can't say that I know where he is right now, but he was sitting in my living room when I left. Unfortunately, it's my feeling that he had an eye on my liquor cabinet. I didn't have the heart to lock it in front of him. It would have hurt his feelings to think I didn't trust him."

"You are too kind."

His fair skin flushing, Edmund raised his chin. "Your sarcasm isn't wise, Quince. Your father has too few friends in this town for you to dismiss my efforts to help him."

Again refusing to comment, Quince replied, "He was at your house when you left this morning. You haven't been back since?"

"No . . . the memories."

Unable to bear any more of Edmund's hypocrisy, Quince replied, "You can go home now without worrying. I'll make sure my father's gone when you get there."

Dismissing Edmund without a backward look, Quince strode out of the bank. He was approaching the Montgomery house when the front door opened unexpectedly. Jack swayed uncertainly in the entrance. Unkempt, unshaven, reeking of liquor, he stood motionless as Quince approached and said, "Are you ready to go home now?"

Nodding, not bothering to voice a reply, Jack walked out onto the street and followed Quince to his horse.

Chapter Thirteen

Quince rode silently toward the west pasture as the new day dawned. He glanced beside him where Brent rode as silent as he. Abby still hadn't recuperated from the funeral, and Pa had been too sick to make it out of bed that morning.

Brent had been at the house when he'd brought Pa home. His older brother's furious reaction had been predictable and obvious to all—especially to Pa. But Quince could not blame Brent. He felt the same way; and from the look of the ranch hands, even they were beginning to give up on the old man.

Abby had been relieved to see Pa home. Not that relief had constituted approval or even sympathy over his deplorable condition. That was apparent when she took one look at him and went to her room without speaking a word.

Abby had knocked on Quince's bedroom door later to thank him for going after Pa, and her expression had said it all.

Blanche returned briefly to mind, and Quince felt a rush of anger. In a way, he was glad he had been forced to go to Diablo to find his father. If he hadn't, he might not have heard what had happened to Blanche. O'Malley and the women at the Lone Star had been kind to her, but she was afraid. He couldn't allow that to continue; he couldn't stand the thought that the man who had hurt her had gotten away with it. She was presently too scared to tell him who had done it, but he'd find out. When he did, he'd make sure Blanche didn't have to be afraid anymore.

But most of all, he wanted to see Glory. He needed to talk to her, to reassure her that . . .

Quince's thoughts halted abruptly when the west pasture came into view. They had decided to move the mustangs closer to the house—but they were too late.

The mustangs were gone.

Spurring his mount toward the break in the fencing where the mustangs had obviously escaped, Quince dismounted. He heard Brent curse softly as he also dismounted, then said, "Something must've scared those mustangs real bad to make them crazy enough to knock down the fencing and run off."

"They couldn't have gotten too far." Turning to Buck, Quince directed, "Ride back to the ranch house and tell them we're going after the mustangs. Then hotfoot it to the Diamond C and let them know what happened. Tell them to post a guard on their mustangs to make sure the same thing doesn't happen there. When you come back, bring enough supplies for a couple of days. It might take us that long to round the mustangs up again."

Hesitating, Quince looked at his brother. "Maybe you should go back with him, Brent. There's no way of telling how long this is going to take, and Crystal's alone at the cabin."

"No, that won't be necessary. I don't have to worry about Crystal. Abby will see to it that she stays at the ranch house while I'm gone." Lowering his voice, Brent continued, "Besides, I don't like this. It's a little too coincidental that every time we start to take a step forward at the Half-Moon, something happens to set us back again."

Quince's jaw hardened to stone. "We'll get the mustangs back first. Then we'll find out what's really going on."

With a last look at Buck as he rode back toward the ranch house at a gallop, Quince mounted and waved the men forward.

His demeanor surly despite the bright sunlight that had started the day, Edmund entered the bank. He ignored the cautious morning greetings of his tellers as he walked directly to his office and closed the door behind him. It was only the second day after Iona's funeral and he was already tired of playing the grieving widower. The need for continued pretense annoyed him.

The hypocrisy of a few fellow citizens of Diablo

was his only present source of amusement. He had
not missed the fact that Iona wasn't yet cold in her
grave before Matilda Wilson, for all her pretended
piety, found time to stand close enough to him so
that her full breasts would brush his arm when her
husband was looking the other way. Then there
was Sally Pringle, who had been so solicitous when
her stiff-backed parents weren't watching her at
the wake, that she had actually moved him off into
a corner and kissed him "to relieve his sadness."
Nor had he missed the sultry glance he had gotten
from Jim Pierce's young wife as she had passed
him on the street that morning.

Edmund gave a caustic snort. He'd get around
to all of them in time.

Too agitated to sit, Edmund walked to the window and stared blindly out at the street. The only
problem was, he had little interest in women who
fluttered their lashes in his direction. Iona had been
one of those simpering females, and he had grown
tired of her even before he left their marriage bed.
That thought had sent him to the house of his favorite whore the previous evening, where his visits
were a well-kept secret and his "grieving" wasn't
discussed. He had given her a run for her money,
too.

Thinking of her now, Edmund felt a pang of
disgust. She was a fleshy witch with pendulous
breasts and an ample backside. Her main appeal
was that she refused him nothing when the price
was right. He had depended on her greed last night
more than ever before. It had given him pleasure
to taunt her with ever increasing sums until she

reached extremes of which even he had not believed her capable.

Galling him, however, was his realization that the satisfaction she granted him was neither complete nor lasting.

Haunted by the image of Beth Hunter, he knew there was only one woman alive who could possibly sate the carnal need that gnawed at him.

Abby's image came to mind, and his body reacted predictably. Yes, he'd bring her around to his way of thinking. It was just a matter of time.

Still standing at the window, Edmund saw Kane move into sight on the side street facing him. Concealed from general view, Kane leaned back against the wall of the telegraph office and looked at Edmund with a half smile he had come to know well.

Anxious to hear his report, Edmund beckoned Kane toward him. Prepared and waiting when Kane appeared at his office door, he said in an elevated tone that he knew was overheard in the outer office, "Mr. Kane, come in. I have your paperwork ready."

Waiting until Kane closed the door behind him, he asked, "It's done, then?"

"I scattered them mustangs so far that it'll take a month of Sundays to round them up again."

"Good." His smile sincere for the first time that morning, Edmund continued, "Just make sure you stay close by for a while. I'll tell you when it's time to follow up with that 'accident' we discussed."

Kane's gaze narrowed. "Seems to me we need

to take care of a little business matter first, before we talk about the future."

"Payment, of course." Edmund opened his desk drawer and removed a sheaf of papers. "I've decided, however, that we need to establish a reason for your recent visits to this office. You'll be happy to know that you'll be opening an account with the Diablo State Bank."

"An account!" Kane laughed aloud. "I ain't the kind who deposits money in banks. I only make *withdrawals*."

"Just sign the papers! I'll take care of the rest."

"Is that right?" A new light of interest entered Kane's eyes. "Are you going to make me a rich man, Montgomery?"

Holding Kane's gaze steadily, Edmund replied, "You'll get as much as your work's worth, especially if Quince Hunter's mustangs never make it to Fort Griffin."

Kane's reply was succinct. "Just show me where to sign."

Obviously mystified, Madge asked, "What's the matter with you, Blanche?"

Dressed in a plain street dress, Madge stood opposite Blanche in the early morning silence of her upstairs room at the Lone Star. Without the heavy makeup of her trade, Madge looked older and more worn than her twenty-odd years. It saddened Blanche to see her friend that way; and she saw herself in Madge—aging rapidly as the life she led grew harder with each passing year.

When she did not reply, Madge pressed, "You

should be happy as a lark after Quince Hunter came running up the stairs to see you yesterday. Ain't you glad he came?"

"Of course I'm glad."

"You don't look it."

Blanche was somehow unable to smile. Madge didn't understand. Her heart had pounded like a drum when she'd heard Quince's voice in the hallway yesterday. Her hands had shaken as she pulled the door open, and seeing him standing there had been like a dream come true. But the dream had been short-lived. Instead of the love she had envisioned shining in his eyes, she had seen only pity.

And a determination to make her ills right.

Quince had wanted to know who had hurt her, but she had known instinctively that she couldn't tell him. Lobo was dangerous. He wouldn't flinch at putting a bullet in anybody's back. She couldn't let Quince risk his life for her.

Nor was there any way to explain to Madge how she had ached when Quince took her into his arms to console her. She had wished those brief minutes would last forever. His brief, chaste kiss had been almost more than she could bear. She had always known he didn't love her the way she wanted him to—that he never would—but the truth had been so clear in that moment that it had been like a knife in her heart.

"He cares about you, Blanche." Madge was frowning. "You should've seen his face when I told him you were hurt."

"I saw his face."

"He cares about you, I tell you! If you play your cards right, you can get him, just like Crystal got his brother."

"Brent loves Crystal. That's why he married her."

"So? With just a little effort, you could hook that big fella, too."

"Quince doesn't love me that way. He thinks of me like . . . like a sister."

"Yeah?" Madge took an aggressive step. Grasping her by the arms, she said, "Listen to me, will you? I ain't never had a fella look at me the way Quince looks at you. Sister love or not, he cares about you. If you let him get away, the odds of something like that happening for you again are pretty steep." When Blanche did not reply, Madge said, "Look at yourself! You're bruised and battered, but you're young and you're healing. You got that much going for you right now." She added coldly, "Now look at me. This is what you got in your future if you don't grab the chance to get out when you can."

Pain jolted in her ribs and Blanche gasped. Madge released her abruptly. Remorse was apparent in her gaze when she said, "I didn't mean to hurt you."

"You didn't. It's just hard for me to breathe sometimes."

"Blanche, honey . . ." Madge tried to smile. "Think about what I said. That Quince Hunter is all man, from the top of his head to the tips of his boots. No matter how bad you got hurt in that alleyway, there ain't a girl in this place who wouldn't trade places with you now, just as long as Quince Hunter came along with the deal."

"But—"

"Just think about it. Will you do that?"

Blanche did not respond.

"Blanche?"

"All right. I'll think about it."

"Attagirl." Madge nodded approvingly. "I'd better go back to the boardinghouse now. I need to pay the rent today or Anne might let my room out from under me."

Blanche smiled.

"That's it, honey. Smile. You'll be looking like your old self soon, and the next time Quince Hunter comes back, he'll start singing a different tune."

The door closed behind Madge, and Blanche's smile lingered. For a while she'd let herself believe it.

Standing on the Diamond C ranch-house porch, Glory faced Buck sober and tight-jawed. She and her wranglers had started breaking the mustangs that morning. The work had been going smoothly until she'd spotted Buck's horse pounding into the yard. Buck had drawn up in front of the porch where her father sat, and she had reached them just as Buck began relating Quince's message.

"Where is Quince now?" she asked anxiously.

"Quince, Brent, and the rest of the boys went out after the mustangs. It ain't going to be easy to round them all up again."

Panic nudged Glory's senses. Quince had given

his word he'd meet the army contact. She knew how much that meant to him. He'd push himself to the limit to get those mustangs back, no matter the risk involved.

Her reply was spontaneous. "We have to help him."

Buck responded, "Begging your pardon, ma'am, but Quince didn't send me here to get help. He just wanted me to tell you all to put a guard on the mustangs in your corral so the same thing wouldn't happen here."

Frowning, Byron interjected, "No, Glory's right. Quince needs help before those mustangs scatter too far. Where are you going from here?"

"Back to join up with Quince and the rest of the men as soon as I put some supplies together."

"Did you already stop at the Half-Moon to tell them what happened?"

"Yes, sir, but Miss Abby had gone off to visit Miss Crystal because she wasn't feeling too good the last time she saw her, and old Jack was under the weather, so I left the message with Frances."

"Good. We'll give you the supplies you need and you can go straight out from here. Shorty and Miles will stay behind to guard our mustangs, and Glory and the rest of the hands will go with you."

"Quince said—"

"My wranglers are going with you." Unyielding, Byron turned toward Glory and instructed, "Tell the men to get ready. I'll have Pete put the supplies together."

At her hesitation, Byron asked, "What's the matter, Glory?"

"I think we should leave more than two men here, just in case."

"In case of what?" Byron paused to scrutinize his daughter's expression, then added more softly, "You don't have to worry about me, if that's the problem. Pete's here. The two of us did just fine while you were gone the last time, and Shorty and Miles will be coming back and forth to alternate shifts at the mustang corral. Just get those men moving. You don't have time to waste."

Glory hesitated a moment longer, then nodded. She needed to help Quince, and Pa was right. They didn't have time to waste.

They'd be on their way within the hour.

A tight smile on his lips, Lobo crept up the Lone Star's rear staircase as the sun began a slow descent in the afternoon sky. He had tried the back door several times since he had seen Quince Hunter run up the staircase to the second floor the previous day. Furious when he tried the rear door and found it locked, he had waited, hiding behind the building for the opportunity which had presented itself when Chester Weed came out to dump garbage a few minutes earlier and left the door unlocked. Judging from the way Hunter had strode past the doors on the landing, Blanche was staying in the last room at the end of the hall.

Lobo frowned at that thought, knowing it would be hard to reach that doorway unnoticed from below. He could only hope O'Malley was distracted at the bar and wouldn't see him. He'd only need a few minutes to slip past, and once he got to Blanche's door, she'd let him in. She'd be too scared not to.

Hesitating when he reached the top of the staircase, Lobo peered down into the saloon below. O'Malley was busy at the bar, the card tables were crowded and the saloon girls all appeared to be occupied. He'd never have a better chance.

Lobo walked swiftly down the hallway. He reached the last doorway at the end of the hall and waited. Not a sound. No one had seen him.

A hard smile on his lips, Lobo tried the door. Locked.

No longer smiling, Lobo knocked lightly. When there was no immediate response, he knocked again. His smile returned when he heard Blanche's voice ask, "Who's there?"

"It's me, Blanche." His smile broadening as he sensed Blanche's panic, he repeated, "It's me, Blanche. Open up. I want to talk to you."

"I don't want to talk to you."

"Come on, sweetheart. You know we got things to discuss. I've been missing you."

"Go away."

"Open up. You'll be sorry if you don't."

"Go away!"

Lobo's voice hardened. "You didn't learn nothin' about turning me down, did you, Blanche? I'll say it just one more time. Open up now, and I'll make it easy on you. If you don't . . ."

Lobo chose not to finish his warning. He knew Blanche. She was scared. She'd open the door, and when she did, he'd make sure she never locked him out again.

He waited.

*   *   *

Trembling, Blanche stared at the door key where it rested in the lock. Her nightmare had come true. Lobo was back and he was at her door. He wanted to come in, and he wouldn't take no for an answer.

What should she do? She could call for help and hope somebody heard her over the noise below, but even if somebody came, it would only put off the inevitable. She couldn't hide in this room forever.

Or she could let Lobo in now and beg him not to hurt her again.

Blanche took a shuddering breath. But he *would* hurt her. She could hear it in his voice.

And even if he didn't, he'd make sure she paid somehow for making him wait. He'd never let her go while she was still of some use to him.

"Blanche—"

Blanche closed her eyes. She couldn't live this way. She couldn't stand waiting for the moment when Lobo would catch up with her to make good on his threats. Nor could she tell Quince, knowing she'd hear sooner or later that Quince had been found lying dead somewhere with a bullet in his back.

Her hands shaking badly, Blanche gripped the key. Just a single turn—

"What are you doing here, Lobo?"

Blanche froze at the sound of O'Malley's voice in the hallway.

"What do you think I'm doing?" His tone took

on a friendly note. "I'm trying to get in to see how my girlfriend is doing."

"I told you, you ain't wanted in the Lone Star."

"I ain't in your saloon. I'm up here to see Blanche."

"She doesn't want to see you."

"Sure she does." Blanche could almost see Lobo's confident expression as he addressed her though the door, "Tell him, Blanche, honey. Tell him you was just going to let me in."

Blanche could not respond.

"Blanche . . ."

Her teeth chattering with fear, Blanche rasped, "No."

Lobo's voice deepened in unspoken warning as he said, "I ain't sure I heard you right, Blanche. What did you say?"

"I said no . . . I don't want to see you. Go away."

"You heard her, Lobo. Get moving."

"She didn't mean what she said."

"I said, get moving!"

His voice drifting away as he moved down the hallway, Lobo called back, "I'll be back to see you, Blanche. You can depend on it."

She was still standing at the locked door, unable to move, when she heard O'Malley say, "You don't have to worry no more, Blanche. He's gone."

Still shuddering too hard to react, Blanche managed a hoarse "Thanks," then listened to O'Malley's heavy footsteps as they moved back down the hallway.

Blanche strove for control. O'Malley had turned out to be a good friend, but he was wrong. She had to worry now more than ever, because there was one thing she was sure of. Lobo wouldn't break his promise.

He'd be back.

Glory looked up at the rapidly darkening sky with a frown, then glanced at the men riding beside her. They were also frowning. It was taking longer than they had expected to find Quince's party.

"Don't worry, Miss Glory." Jan's gaze was sober and direct as he addressed her. "Even if it don't look like we're making good time, the Half-Moon wranglers left a clear trail, and we're traveling faster than they are because of it. We'll catch up with them soon."

As if in confirmation of Jan's statement, Glory saw a campfire flickering in the distance. She heard Jan mumble, "Speak of the devil."

Riding briskly as they neared the camp, Glory saw Quince's unmistakable figure as he stood up, and her heart skipped a beat. His expression was unreadable as they drew their mounts to a halt.

He waited for her to dismount, then asked, "What are you doing here, Glory?"

Surprised by his reception, she responded, "You need help if you're going to catch those mustangs before they stray too far."

"You didn't have to come. We could've handled it."

Taken aback by his tone, Glory stated flatly,

"My father sent me. He said you could use all the help you could get."

His voice dropping a note softer, Quince said, "Brent and I are thinking there's more to this than meets the eye. We figure the mustangs breaking loose might not have been an accident. There might be trouble when we catch up with them. If there is, I'd rather you weren't here."

"My men can handle themselves."

"It's not your men I'm worrying about."

"I can handle myself, too."

"I'm not doubting your ability as a wrangler. I'd never do that again. I just—"

Halting at Brent's approach, Quince addressed his brother. "It looks like we're going to have some help finding those mustangs."

Acknowledging her presence with a polite greeting, Brent responded, "That's good. We could use the help." Turning toward Buck as the Diamond C wranglers dismounted, he asked, "What did you bring for us to eat?"

Brent walked toward the supply horse without waiting for a response.

Continuing where he had left off as the Diamond C wranglers moved toward the campfire, Quince said, "I want you to go back with Jan, Glory."

"No."

"Don't be stubborn! It's too dangerous here for you."

Glory raised her chin. "The army contract means as much to me as it does to you. The Diamond C needs it, and I don't intend—"

His expression suddenly hardening, Quince grated, "The Diamond C be damned!"

Unexpectedly pulling her a few steps into the shadows, Quince enveloped her in a crushing embrace as he covered her mouth with his. His hands tightened in her hair, and he drew her head back to plunder her mouth more deeply, hunger sounding in his soft groan as she separated her lips under his. His breathing was ragged as he moved away from her abruptly.

"I've been dreaming of doing that since the moment you left my sight." When she didn't immediately respond, Quince pressed, "Your father didn't send you here, did he?"

Breathing as heavily as he, Glory rasped, "Yes, he did."

"But you wanted to come—to be with me."

Silence.

"Glory . . ."

"Yes . . . I did."

His light eyes searched her face. "I'm tired of secrets, Glory," he whispered. "I'm not going to hide how I feel about you anymore."

Uncertain of the reason for her protest, Glory responded, "I didn't come here for this, Quince."

"But you're here now, and if you won't leave, this is what you're going to get."

Her heart pounded as Quince brushed her mouth again with his, as he trailed his lips against her fluttering eyelids, her cheek, then moved to her ear.

"Is that a threat, Quince?" she whispered.

"No," His breath was warm and sweet against her skin. "It's a promise."

A promise.

Leaving the shadows minutes later, Glory walked to the campfire beside Quince. She did not protest again when he sat close beside her to eat the bread and smoked ham Pete had packed. Intensely aware of the sweet taste of him that lingered in her mouth, of the warm press of his thigh against hers and the shivers radiating through her body as his male heat encompassed her, she did her best to ignore Brent's wink in his brother's direction and the knowing glances of the men. She strove to concentrate fully when the conversation around the campfire turned to strategy for the coming day. She did not utter a word of protest, however, when Quince laid his bedroll down beside hers and she turned toward him to see his gaze intent on her. Her throat was suddenly tight at the myriad emotions welling within her.

"I'm glad you're here, Glory," he whispered.

Unspoken went her sudden realization that there was nowhere else she'd rather be.

"You won't be gone long, Pete. I'll be all right. Don't worry about it."

His whiskers twitching with uncertainty, Pete returned Byron's stare in silence. "I still think I shouldn't go," he said. "I don't like leaving you alone here at the ranch."

"I won't be alone." Doing his best to conceal his shortness of breath, Byron smiled. "Shorty will be back from his watch soon."

"Maybe. Maybe not. Miles took him out something for breakfast because he told Miles he might not come back until later this afternoon. He plans to separate them troublesome mares from the rest of the herd and drive them off to a separate corral like Miss Glory wanted."

"I'll be fine."

"If you're fine, why do you need your medicine so bad that you can't wait until Shorty gets back here?"

"I'm not a complete invalid, Pete. I can take care of myself."

"I know, but—"

"No buts about it. Admittedly, I didn't expect to run short of my medicine and I'm not my best without it. Miss Glory will be back soon, and if I'm looking peaked when she gets here, we'll never hear the end of it."

"There's truth in that."

"There surely is. All you need to do is take a short trip to the apothecary in town and we can avoid upsetting her. Just tell Martin to mix me up a batch real fast. I'm the best customer his shop has. He won't give you a problem."

"All right, I'll go." His reluctance apparent as he started toward the door, Pete turned back to caution, "But don't you go doing anything you shouldn't while I'm gone."

"I'll be fine, Pete."

Waiting until Pete had cleared the doorway and was walking toward the horse he had saddled earlier, Byron took an unsteady breath. The pains in his chest had been getting stronger and he had been increasing the dosage as Dr. Gibbs suggested. With his mind occupied by the Diamond C's problems, he had neglected to have his prescription re-filled, and he was now paying the price.

The sound of Pete's departure relieved some of his anxiety, and Byron turned back to his ledgers. Pete would be back before noon.

Stunned, hardly able to believe her eyes, Glory looked down at the mustang herd milling at the water hole. She turned toward Quince to whisper, "It's a miracle!"

His strong features moved into an infrequent smile. "It sure as hell looks like one."

Remaining motionless as Quince signaled directions to the men, Glory stared at the mustangs. The wranglers had been up at first light and had been tracking the herd for less than an hour. Aware that they were drawing close, they had been prepared for any eventuality with guns ready. They had not expected, however, that not only would they encounter no outside interference, but they'd also find the herd intact, as if waiting for them to find it. There could be no explanation except that after having stampeded to the point of exhaustion, they had simply followed the lead mare to the natural crevice below, and had paused there to water and graze.

Not offering a protest when Quince signaled for her to ride at his side, Glory descended the slope cautiously and took her appointed position as the herd was urged into motion. She was reacting automatically, herding and swinging the stragglers into line, when the thought occurred to her that somehow this was too easy.

They'd be back at the Half-Moon before the day ended.

"What do you mean, you have to wait for the stage to get here? You ain't got none of Mr. Townsend's medicine on hand at all?"

Martin Smythe was sweating profusely. Running short of a necessary ingredient for his best customer's prescription was unprofessional. He didn't like being unprofessional. Replying cautiously to Pete's question, he said, "I expected the medicine to arrive on an earlier stage this week, but it's certain to come today. Actually, Mr. Townsend is a bit early in refilling his prescription."

"Early? What does that mean, that you got everything timed right down to the day? Hell, that don't seem right!"

"This is an unusual circumstance, but you needn't fear. The stage will be here in a few hours at most, and I'll mix the medicine up for you immediately."

"A few hours!"

"Or sooner—perhaps."

"I ain't got a few hours to waste. With most all his wranglers out chasing the Half-Moon mustangs, Mr. Townsend's alone back at the Diamond C."

"You can come back into town later tonight, then," Martin suggested, beads of perspiration appearing on his upper lip. "I'll have the prescription ready for you."

"You're telling me Mr. Townsend will have to

spend the whole day without his medicine, then?"

"I'm sorry. That's the best I can do."

Shaking his head, Pete considered his alternatives, then grated, "I'll wait here in town—but you'd better hope that medicine's on the stage when it comes."

"It will be."

Withdrawing a spotless handkerchief from his pocket, Martin wiped his forehead as Pete stomped out the doorway. Startled, Martin turned toward Edmund Montgomery as he stepped into sight in the doorway. Embarrassed at the exchange the banker had obviously overheard, he stammered, "You can be sure I'll get Mr. Townsend's medicine ready for him as soon as the stage arrives."

"Of course you will."

Smiling his thanks as Edmund Montgomery paid for his purchase and walked out onto the street, Martin shook his head. To have a leading citizen like Mr. Montgomery witness his lapse was humiliating. It did not bode well.

Struggling to conceal his jubilation, Edmund forced himself to maintain a steady pace as he walked down the street. Strangely, the headache that had sent him to the apothecary had disappeared the moment Pete had walked out the door of the shop. All he needed now was to find—

The appearance of Kane's unmistakable figure at the far end of the street halted Edmund's thoughts abruptly. He cursed silently when Kane slipped out of sight in the livery stable. He couldn't afford to let Kane ride off before he could talk to him.

Forcing a smile for the short, heavily bearded proprietor as he entered the livery stable minutes later, Edmund said, "I understand you have a buggy for sale, Barney."

Obviously delighted at his interest, the fellow responded, "Sure do, Mr. Montgomery. I got a real nice four-seater out back that Jeremy Post sold off when money got tight. You can go out and take a look while I finish up what I was doing, if you like."

"I'll do that."

Edmund walked through the stable toward the rear door. Spotting Kane in passing, he caught his eye with an indication to follow, then continued on. His patience was short when Kane finally appeared.

"Barney will be out here in a few minutes," Edmund said tensely. "I have to make this short. Do you remember that job I said might be coming up soon?"

Kane nodded.

"All the hired hands are away from the Diamond C and the old cripple is alone in the house. You'll never have a better chance than now to get the work done."

Kane nodded again and walked back into the stable without a word.

The sound of Kane's horse departing moments later was music to Edmund's ears.

They had started driving the mustangs back toward the Half-Moon soon after discovering them in early morning, and had continued a steady, rapid pace throughout the day. Looking up at the position of the sun in the cloudless sky, Glory realized that although it was only mid-afternoon, they would soon be on Half-Moon land.

Glancing toward Quince, Glory felt a familiar stirring inside. She remembered his crushing embrace when he had swept her into the shadows and taken her into his arms last night. She recalled the hunger in his voice and the longing in his gaze when he had lain beside her on his bedroll. That same longing still drummed inside her.

Somehow resentful of her body's reaction to her thoughts, Glory spurred her mount toward a straying mare. She had established strict priorities for herself that didn't include selfish contemplation of her own future when so much work lay ahead in the short time her father had left to him. She knew that—so why was she so conflicted?

Her mind occupied with that thought as she guided the stray back into line, Glory did not see Quince making his way toward her until he was riding at her side. Noting with a glance that Brent had assumed Quince's position beside the herd, she turned toward him as he said, "We'll be on Half-Moon land soon. I told Brent to take over and settle the mustangs in for me because I had something else to do."

At Glory's questioning glance, Quince said, "Come on. Let's get out of here. We need to talk."

"My men will wonder—"

"Brent will take care of your wranglers."

"I need to stay with my men."

"Glory." Quince's gaze locked with hers. She felt the power of the emotions he suppressed. They rocked inside her as he said, "We need to talk . . . now."

They rode out of sight of the herd before Quince spoke again. Indicating a stand of trees nearby, he said, "We can stop there so the horses can water in the stream while we talk."

Waiting only until they had settled the horses, Quince turned toward Glory. Slipping his arms around her, he whispered, "I meant it when I told you I wouldn't hide my feelings for you any longer, Glory. I sent your men back to the Half-Moon without you because we're going to ride back to the Diamond C together and talk to your father."

"No." Glory attempted to pull free of Quince's embrace. When he refused to release her, she protested, "I told you, this isn't the time."

"Why not? Because your father is sick? Because he doesn't have much time left?"

"That's right." Panicking as the warm press of his nearness began assuming control of her senses, Glory rasped, "I can't think of myself now. My father—the Diamond C needs all my attention."

"I can help you."

"How can you help? The Half-Moon is as unstable as the Diamond C—maybe even more so."

"That's only temporary. The army contract will put both our ranches on better financial footing. Your father knows that."

"My father needs to see something tangible—to see the result of our work register in his ledger. He needs to be certain the Diablo State Bank isn't one step from foreclosing on the Diamond C."

"Edmund Montgomery will never get either one of our ranches. I promise you that."

"The Diamond C isn't your responsibility, Quince. It's mine. I accepted that obligation a long time ago, and I intend to follow it through."

"But you don't need to follow it through alone."

"Quince, please—"

"Listen to me, Glory. Let me help you. I want to help you. I *need* to help you."

Quince was stroking her hair. He was kissing her cheek, running his lips over the line of her jaw. He was pressing his mouth to hers in light, fleeting kisses that stole her breath.

Aware that her resistance was quickly slipping away, Glory said, "I can't do this to my father, Quince. He's worked toward one goal all his life, to replace the home that was taken from us years ago. My mother died before he could realize that dream for her. I don't want to steal his moment of triumph from him now, when it's so close. Please, Quince, try to understand."

"I understand, but that doesn't change the way I feel. I love you, Glory."

Glory closed her eyes. Those words . . . those precious words. But she didn't want to hear them now.

"I want you with me, to be a part of my life."

Not now.

"Tell me you love me. Say it, Glory."

Quince was kissing her, his lips searching deep and sweet. His palms were stroking her back. They moved to cup her buttocks, to draw her tight against the hard proof of his passion, and her body moved instinctively to accommodate him. She was kissing him back, her arms wrapping around his neck, her fingers tangling in his dark hair. She was beyond protest when his kisses grew more ardent, when he stripped away her riding skirt with trembling hands. Uncertain of the moment when she first felt the cool grass pressing against her back, she gasped as he probed her moist warmth, and she reacted with responsive passion when he plunged deep and full inside her.

Giving herself up to the moment, Glory accommodated his loving thrusts as they grew stronger, penetrated deeper. The wonder of their joining robbed her of thought; she felt only the power of his loving, the intensity of the winging emotions he raised within her. Sensing the approaching moment, Glory held her breath until it burst from her in a soft cry that mingled with Quince's impassioned groan as they soared to mutual ecstasy in each other's arms.

Still entwined in a loving embrace, Quince clutched her closer still and whispered, "This is the way it's meant to be between us, Glory. This is the way it's going to be."

That thought lingered as the silence stretched long and lovingly between them.

Kane dismounted a distance from the Diamond C barn. He had scouted the area carefully. Montgomery was right. There wasn't a wrangler to be seen near the ranch house, and the cook was probably still waiting for the stage to arrive in Diablo. The only person on the ranch was the cripple, Byron Townsend, and he'd be no problem.

Kane walked boldly into the barn. A mare heavy with foal in the first stall whinnied at his approach, and he sneered. Montgomery wanted an "accident," and the mare would serve his purpose well. Nobody would believe a fire was started deliberately with that horse locked in one of the stalls.

Ignoring the mare's nervous whinnies, Kane staged the scene carefully. He needed to keep Montgomery happy.

Taking a lantern from a hook on the wall, Kane spilled the fuel out over the hay in a corner of the barn. He removed the lantern from the wall at the rear of the barn and took care to douse the stalls as he splashed out the contents. With particular satisfaction, he walked back to empty out the last of the fuel on the stall door of the noisy mare.

Content that he had done his work well, Kane took a box of matches from his pocket.

With great deliberation, he struck a match to flame.

Byron raised his head from his ledgers and listened intently as the panicked whinnies from the barn grew louder. Sheba was due to foal within a few months and was extremely agitated. He had instructed the men to keep her in the barn until she settled down, but something was frightening her.

Byron rolled his chair cautiously toward the

porch door. Having convinced Pete to go to town, he couldn't afford an incident which might reveal just how unstable he knew his health to be.

Halfway toward the doorway, Byron bolted suddenly erect in his chair. He smelled smoke!

Thrusting all caution aside, he propelled his chair out onto the porch. He stopped, his breath catching in his throat at the sight of flames visible through the barn doorway.

Panicking, Byron rolled his chair down the porch's side ramp. Barely managing to halt its forward surge in time to avoid a fall, he ignored the increasing ache in his chest as he struggled to move forward on the rutted, uneven ground.

Reaching the smoke-filled doorway of the barn at last, Byron struggled for breath as the pain increased, numbing his one arm into uselessness.

But the flames were leaping higher.

Sheba's screeching whinnies were growing louder.

Unable to ignore the mare's terrified cries a moment longer, Byron propelled his chair into the smoke-filled barn. Coughing, his vision limited and his pain intense, he inched forward through the searing heat, knowing he needed only to reach the first stall to get Sheba out.

The unbearable heat robbed him of breath, and his chest pain was fierce, but Byron reached the stall doors just as they burst into flame. Fumbling with the door, he managed to unlock it, then moved aside as it flew open and Sheba bounded out toward the yard.

Suddenly disoriented amid the swirling smoke and crackling flames, Byron realized he had not a moment to lose. Turning his chair with a supreme effort, he propelled himself in the same direction the mare had taken.

Outside in the ranch yard moments later, Byron looked back to see the barn roof explode into flames with a roar. The pain in his chest all-encompassing, he was fighting for each breath when he was startled by a figure visible through the thickening smoke.

A man was standing a safe distance behind the barn. He was watching it burn and making no effort to help!

Jolted by sudden realization, Byron recognized the fellow. His name was Kane. He was rumored to be a gun for hire.

For hire—just as he had suspected!

Fury replacing caution, Byron shouted out over the din of the crackling flames, "You . . . Kane! I see you! You won't get away with this! You won't—"

A lightning bolt of pain struck Byron's chest, stealing his breath. Helpless as excruciating spasms overwhelmed him, darkening his world with agonizing pain, he realized in a flash of clarity that he'd be unable to tell anyone what he had seen—that he'd be leaving Glory more vulnerable than she had ever been before.

Regrets . . . fear . . . loss inundated his mind, yet the most powerful of all was his sorrow at leaving her alone without bidding her a sweet goodbye.

* * *

The wooded copse was silent as Glory averted her face from Quince's scrutiny and adjusted her clothing. She looked up as he slid his arms around her and said, "We'll go back to the Diamond C together."

Aching inside, Glory whispered, "Please understand, Quince. My father needs me more than ever now. He . . ."

Glory's words trailed away as her attention was caught by dark clouds of smoke rising into the sky in the distance. Sudden fear curdled deep inside her as she gasped, "Fire! The smoke's coming from the direction of the Diamond C."

Unable to recall her headlong gallop toward the Diamond C or the moment of confirmation that the ranch was indeed ablaze, Glory reached the ranch yard at last. She leaped from the saddle at the sight of her father lying on the ground beside his chair as the last of the flaming barn timbers shuddered to the ground.

The realization that she was too late registered keenly in her mind even before she reached his side. Numbed as she took her father's limp hand, Glory shrugged off Quince's touch.

Her father was dead. She had failed him.

Motionless and dry-eyed, uncertain how long she had remained kneeling beside her father's lifeless form, Glory turned sharply toward Quince as he attempted to raise her to her feet.

"Leave me alone," she said fiercely. "This is my fault. If I had been here, he would still be alive."

"It's not your fault, Glory."

Glory stared up into Quince's sober face. She wanted so much to believe him. She wanted him to take her into his arms to console her—even now, when she knew she had been indulging in the ecstasy of his embrace when instead she should have been with her father when he needed her.

That thought more than she could bear, Glory shrank from Quince's touch when he crouched down beside her. "Please go," she said coldly.

The smoldering barn timbers crackled and popped. The fiery showers of sparks illuminated Glory's tormented gaze, expanding the ache inside Quince as he whispered, "None of this is your fault, Glory."

"Yes, it is."

"It isn't. Don't torture yourself this way."

"Go away."

Quince rasped, "Listen to me. You had no way of knowing this would happen."

"Go away . . . please."

"It's not your fault. It's not *our* fault."

"Go away! Do you hear me? I said, go away!"

The first Diamond C wranglers pounded into the yard, and Quince stood up slowly. He moved back as Glory, still dry-eyed, continued to clutch her father's hand. He watched as the wranglers stamped out the last of the smoldering flames and Jan went to Glory's side. He remained silent as Byron's body was carried into the house, with Glory following behind, leaning heavily against Jan's shoulder.

He stood immobile as a rider was dispatched to town.

Alone in the yard at last, aware there was nothing he could do, Quince mounted up and rode away.

Chapter Fourteen

His gaze fixed on Glory's slim figure as she walked behind her father's coffin, Quince followed the funeral procession toward the churchyard. A day had passed since Byron had been discovered lying near his burning barn. With Glory still refusing to talk to him, he had had no choice but to simply accompany his family as they paid their last respects to the man who had been their neighbor and friend.

His own family was well represented—Brent and Crystal walked ahead of him and Jack lingered behind—but the line of mourners was otherwise limited to wranglers who had known Byron well, and to the few who had maintained contact with a longtime invalid who seldom came to town.

Fortunately, Edmund had chosen to make only a short appearance at the wake, citing his mourning for Iona as an excuse to remove himself quickly.

Quince looked down at Abby, who walked beside him. Abby was upset. She identified closely with Glory and the difficult circumstances that had brought her father and her to Texas. She related personally with Glory's struggle to keep the Diamond C solvent and with her love of horses. A similar resolve had kept both women focused during difficult, trying years. Quince also knew that Byron's death somehow stirred vivid memories in Abby of their own mother's funeral. He knew, because those memories had stirred inside him as well.

Even now, certain similarities troubled him.

Glory refused to see or talk to him. She blamed herself for allowing the lovemaking that had brought her back to the Diamond C too late to save her father. He wanted to explain to her that there was no way she could have known a fire would break out in their barn when Byron was left alone for a few short hours, that she couldn't blame herself for a series of circumstances that no one could anticipate, and that her father wouldn't want her to blame herself, because he had loved her too much to see her weighed down with unnecessary guilt.

Guilt touched his own mind. He had blamed his brother Matt for not coming home on time the day their mother was killed, believing that if Matt hadn't been in town taking his own pleasures, he would have been home to stop his father from killing their mother in a drunken stupor. He realized now that their mother had loved Matt too much to see him suffer for something over which he'd had no control.

But realization of his own shortcomings in judging his brother did not alleviate the present agony of standing helpless as he watched Glory's distress.

He loved her. He needed to make her see that his love was strong enough to sweep away the sadness and harsh memories. He had already resolved that he would make her understand—somehow—but the present rift between them caused a painful knot inside him that would not dissipate.

Complicating the already difficult situation was the news Jan had delivered to the Half-Moon—Glory had ordered all work on the Diamond C to stop. She had given no reason for the order, perhaps because she had none that could be easily explained.

Glory needed time to heal, he knew that, but time was their enemy, and the Diamond C mustangs were needed to meet the army contract.

Quince watched as the coffin was lowered into the ground, as Glory finally turned away and allowed Jan to lead her to the buggy. His arms ached to hold and comfort her. Instead, he guided Abby back to their buggy as the mourners dispersed, and watched as Glory rode off down the street without looking back.

Blanche rooted desperately through her meager possessions. She owned so little of value that she hadn't thought to go through the things Anne had packed in a wooden crate and sent to the Lone

Star when she had rented out her room.

The memory of Lobo's promise when he came to her door two days ago still echoed in her mind, and Blanche shuddered. She had not needed to see Lobo's face when O'Malley drove him off. The image of Lobo's anger was too fresh in her mind to forget. She had refused to let him in, and he would make her pay for her refusal.

She had pondered her alternatives in the time since, hoping to avoid the only solution available to her. Two sleepless nights had followed until she had finally decided she had no choice in what she must do.

Blanche reached the bottom of the crate and touched the carved wooden handle of a six-gun. She pulled it up through the jumble of wrinkled satin and worn underclothing covering it, then wiped away the tear that rolled down her cheek. Aside from rusty tools and an old horse, the gun was the only thing her pa had left her. She had sold the horse and the tools, but she'd been unable to part with the gun he had been so proud of.

She had never expected it would possibly save her life.

Dressing carefully in her most inconspicuous clothing, Blanche bound back her blond hair and covered it with a shawl. She hid the gun in the folds of her dress, limped into the hallway, and made her way down the steps to the rear door. Her heart pounding, she scanned the twilight shadows of the rear yard, then moved quickly toward the street.

Aware that few would recognize her as she was

dressed, she headed directly toward the establishment she sought. She paused for a deep breath when she reached the doorway, then walked inside.

"You did a good job, Kane—a very good job."

Sitting opposite his swarthy henchman in the unkempt, isolated log cabin that was Kane's home base, Edmund refilled the glasses on the table in front of them from a bottle that was already half empty. He had arrived there an hour earlier with the payment Kane was expecting. He had wanted to put the money directly into Kane's hands this time, so pleased was he with the way things had worked out.

He had attended Townsend's wake briefly that morning. He had stayed just long enough to learn that the red-haired witch had ordered all work on the Diamond C to stop until further notice. The wranglers, although almost as upset as she over Byron Townsend's unexpected death, knew what that would mean.

So did he. The Diamond C was as good as his.

"Drink up, Kane." Edmund laughed loudly. "We deserve this celebration. Two for one! You not only caused a masterful delay at the Diamond C when you burned down the barn, but you eliminated a burr that had been stuck under my saddle for far too long. Byron Townsend was the financial expert in that family. Without the old man, the Diamond C is lost."

"That old man." Kane belched, then continued

with a lopsided smile, "You should've heard him yell at me."

Startled by Kane's unexpected revelation, Edmund said, "He saw you there?"

"Yeah, he saw me standing out back watching the fire and he hollered out that I wouldn't get away with what I had done, that he'd make sure—"

"Make sure of what?"

"I don't know." Kane's lopsided smile stretched wide over his crooked teeth. "He didn't get a chance to finish. He just keeled over dead."

Edmund hesitated. "You made sure he was dead before you left, of course."

Kane's smile froze. "How many times do I have to tell you I ain't no amateur?"

"You won't have to tell me again." Mellowed by the whiskey, Edmund declared, "All in all, you've been an extremely valuable employee, Kane. I'll still have use for you in other areas when the Half-Moon and the Diamond C are mine, but when my ultimate goal is reached, I'll be looking for a dependable man to oversee my empire in general."

"Forget it. I ain't no businessman. I expect to be independently rich by that time, anyway."

"You won't be able to turn down the money I'll be offering."

Interest sparked in Kane's small eyes.

"Especially when you won't be required to do much more than ride around and make sure people aren't taking advantage of their positions in my organization."

"You're talking about me being a watchdog."

"A watchdog with sharp teeth and a fast gun."

"I got them all right!"

Laughing uproariously for long moments, the two men emptied their glasses. His hand unsteady as he again refilled the glasses to the brim, Edmund indulged in a loud belch. It was time to celebrate, all right, and he was going to make a night of it. He had made a plausible excuse to Hilda for his intended absence—necessary only because he hadn't liked the change in her attitude since Iona's death. He never could stand the woman anyway. He was stuck with her for the time being, but he'd get rid of her eventually.

Edmund was struck by an amusing thought. He could turn Kane loose on her—but no, Kane's talents would be wasted. The old cow wasn't worth the trouble.

Yes, the future was looking bright. Quince would fail to meet the contract, and the loans that Jack had so carelessly signed would come due in quick succession, with no way of paying them. Edmund avidly anticipated the moment when he would inform Jack that the Diablo State Bank could no longer extend him credit.

Jack would be stunned. He'd plead. He might even cry. There was no certainty what Jack would do when he finally accepted the fact that his stupidity had driven the Half-Moon under.

His sons would desert him—they already hated him—and poor Abby would be left floundering, with no home to call her own.

Poor Abby, who would then be ripe and ready for him.

That thought heating his blood, Edmund drank long and deep.

Weary, his clothes still bearing the dust of a long day in the saddle, Quince rode into Diablo as sunset neared. Two difficult days had passed since Byron's death. He had attempted to talk to Glory, only to be informed as Pete had blocked his entrance into the house that Glory didn't want to see him.

Had it not been for his realization of Glory's fragile state, he would have forced his way past Pete and made her listen to him. He would have told her that Byron wouldn't want her to throw away the Diamond C's chance at financial independence, that what her father really wanted was to see her happy. He would have repeated that however things eventually turned out, *he* was the man who could make her happy. Yet he'd known those words would have been wasted.

Glory needed time to grieve, and time to come to her senses. He had come to Diablo hoping to gain time for both of them.

Halting in front of the telegraph office, Quince dismounted. Justin Van Clef was as dedicated a telegrapher as the company presently had. He'd still be at the key, and Jonah Tremain would receive his request for an extension of the contract delivery date within the hour. He had no doubt Jonah would give him the extension if it was at all possible. He also knew that it might *not* be pos-

sible, with the campaign against Victorio imminent.

With those uncertainties in mind, Quince entered the office and emerged later, frowning. He'd
have to wait until the next morning for a reply,
which meant spending the night in town. So ab-
sorbed was he in his thoughts, he did not see
Shorty emerging from the general store, or notice
that the wrangler watched as he glanced at the
Lone Star before starting toward the hotel. Nor
did he see Shorty walk toward the telegraph office
the second he disappeared through the hotel doorway.

Upstairs in his hotel room, Quince looked at the
lumpy bed occupying the center of the room.
Lumpy or not, it called to him. He needed to go
to the Lone Star to make sure Blanche was all
right, but he hadn't slept in days. He needed a few
minutes to close his eyes.

Quince stripped off his guns and lay down.
Within minutes, he was asleep.

Glory stood staring at the charred remains of the
Diamond C barn as twilight brought another day
to a close. She had ordered that nothing be moved
or changed since the fateful afternoon two days
earlier when she had found her father lying dead
near the burning barn. She had ordered all ranch
activity to stop. She had done that because her father deserved the respect that a period of mourning
represented, but also because she needed the still-
ness in order to get her thoughts in order.

A familiar knife of pain stabbed her sharply. She

had stepped into a nightmare when she had gone straight from Quince's arms to find her father dead in the ranch yard. The knowledge that he had died alone and helpless, with his most cherished dream going unrealized, tormented her. She had been acutely aware of his failing health, but she had always believed he'd die peacefully with her sitting at his side.

Her traitorous thoughts turned unexpectedly to Quince, and her guilt increased. She had been lost in Quince's arms while her father lay dying. Could she ever forgive herself for that?

"I'd like to talk to you, ma'am, if you have a few minutes."

Turning at the sound of Jan's voice behind her, Glory looked at the somber, ruddy-skinned foreman of the Diamond C. Her throat choked tight. Jan had been as close a friend and confidant as her father had ever had. He had proved that friendship by standing beside her, a silent, stalwart presence through the ordeal of the past few days. She could not remember thanking him for all he did. She thought it was time.

Her smile weak, Glory said, "I suppose I need to do some talking first, Jan. I never did thank you for—"

"No, don't thank me, ma'am." Interrupting her uncharacteristically, Jan frowned. "I'm thinking you shouldn't thank me when I haven't done all I should have for you."

Stunned, Glory asked, "What are you talking about?"

"I've been kind of letting things ride, but I figure

it's time to set some matters straight." Jan's lined face briefly softened. "I hope you don't think I'm assuming more than I should if I say I didn't only work for your pa, that I was his friend, too."

"No, of course not. I know Pa talked to you about things man to man, in ways he couldn't talk to me."

"That's right, he talked to me in real straight language. So now that he's gone, I feel I got a responsibility to talk to you the same way—and I have to tell you, ma'am, that your pa wouldn't want you to be acting the way you are now."

Taken aback, Glory said, "What do you mean?"

"I don't need to tell you how proud your pa was of you. He figured you was about the best thing in his life, but what he was proudest of most of all was your spirit. He was always saying there was nothing that could get his girl down for long, that she was all woman on the outside but was as tough as any man when she needed to be. He said you were putting your own life on track better than any son of his could—that he knew whatever happened to him, you'd carry on because it wasn't in you to give up."

"Jan—"

"Excuse me, ma'am, but I'm not done." The lines in his narrow face deepening with concern, Jan continued, "He told me he didn't need anybody to tell him he was a good father because you had already given him the greatest reward a man could ever get by turning out to be the woman you are."

Overcome with emotion, Glory could not reply.

Jan paused, as though he found it difficult to say his next words. "But your pa wouldn't feel right about the way you're acting now. He'd expect you to understand that what happened to him—the way he died—wasn't your fault."

"But I—"

"Please, ma'am, let me finish. You was thinking Pete would be with your pa while you were gone."

"It wasn't Pete's fault! Pa sent him into town for his medicine. Pa couldn't wait to the end of the day or for somebody to come home to get his medicine. He figured Pete would be gone only a little while, and Pete had no way of knowing what would happen while he waited for the medicine to come in on the stage."

"Like you couldn't know your Pa would be alone while you were gone, you mean?"

Glory averted her gaze. "There are things you don't know, Jan. I . . . I could have been here sooner, maybe in time to save him."

"Maybe you could've and maybe you couldn't, but that don't make no never mind now. Your pa wanted you to have a full life, and he knew you couldn't if your whole life revolved around him. He expected you to take some time for a life of your own sooner or later."

"He was alone when he died. I wasn't with him."

"If you were where you wanted to be, that would've made him happy."

"But I wanted to be there with him!"

"You were, ma'am." His eyes growing briefly

320

moist, Jan rasped, "There wasn't a moment when you weren't with your pa. I can vouch for that. And you can be sure you was with him when he closed his eyes that last time, because he wouldn't have been thinking of no one else but you."

Raising her chin, Glory brushed away the tear that streaked her cheek and said, "I wish I could be sure of that."

"Knowing your pa the way I did, I don't see as how you could doubt it even for a minute."

Jan gave Glory a moment to overcome her emotion, then continued more firmly, "That said, ma'am, there's something else I need to make clear. Your pa loved this ranch—not for himself, but for you. He wanted it to be your home. He figured the contract Quince brought here was the guarantee that the loans would be met. And he liked Quince. He told me he could see in his eyes that Quince was a man of his word—and to his mind, there was nothing better than that. He'd be expecting that you'd be true to your word, too, no matter what happened."

"But I let my father down, Jan."

"No, you didn't. Quince brought that contract here because of you, and that contract brought your pa true hope. What's left is to finish off what you started."

Jan paused again, then said, "So I figure I have to tell you now that Shorty saw Quince in Diablo today. He was sending a telegram to Fort Griffin."

"Fort Griffin?"

"Shorty didn't know what was in the telegram,

but I have a feeling you should know it was important enough that Quince is staying overnight at the hotel to wait for the reply."

Allowing a few moments for that thought to sink in, Jan said abruptly, "I said my piece, ma'am. I figure the rest is up to you. I've got some things to do in the corral, so if you'll excuse me, I'll be going."

Silent, Glory watched Jan's departing figure.

Unsmiling, she walked back to the house.

The evening streetlamps were lit on Diablo's main street when Blanche walked softly up the staircase to the second floor of the hotel. She searched out the room she was looking for and then paused in front of it, her courage momentarily deserting her. The swelling on her face had gone down and her lips were almost healed, but the bruising was still apparent. To offset those drawbacks, she had taken particular care with her hair and was wearing her best street dress, a blue cotton gingham she especially liked although it had seen better days. In her heart she knew, however, that it made little difference how she looked because Quince did not see her as a woman.

Fixing that reality firmly in her mind, Blanche knocked lightly and waited for a response that did not come. Her heart pounding, she knocked again, then heard heavy footsteps approaching the doorway. She noted Quince's surprise when he pulled the door open, and held her breath as doubts inundated her mind. Perhaps she had been wrong in coming. Quince hadn't come to see her when he entered town an hour earlier. Maybe he had forgotten all about her. If it hadn't been for Madge's watchful eye, she wouldn't even have known he was there.

"Blanche . . . what are you doing here?"

Her smile faltering, Blanche replied, "I . . . I wanted to talk to you."

"Come on in." Opening the door wider, Quince allowed her to enter, then pushed the door closed behind him and said, "I was asleep. It's been a hard few days."

"I know." Quince's thick, dark hair was ruffled as if from an impatient hand, and his shirt was open to mid chest, exposing a glimpse of firmly muscled flesh underneath. She had seen him like this many times in her daydreams, fresh from sleep when there was a special intimacy to the moment. In her daydreams, Quince would now take her into his arms. She would lay her cheek against his powerful chest as he held her close, and she'd then raise her mouth to his.

Daydreams.

Instead she said, "I heard about Mr. Townsend's unexpected death. His daughter must be very upset."

"She is." Appearing unwilling to discuss the subject, he then said, "Did you remember who hurt you? Is that why you're here?"

"No." Her throat suddenly tight, Blanche said, "I . . . I just came to say goodbye because I'm leaving Diablo on the morning stage."

"You're leaving?"

Blanche blurted out, "I can't stay here, Quince. I need to go somewhere else where it's safer."

"It would be safe for you here if you'd tell me the name of the man who hurt you."

"No, I need to leave Diablo."

His gaze direct and so sincere that Blanche ached inside, Quince said softly, "I want to help you, Blanche. Let me help you."

Blanche could not immediately reply. She wished she could tell him it was Lobo who had hurt her so she wouldn't have to leave. She wished she could make herself believe that if she stayed, Quince might even start looking at her the way he looked at Glory Townsend.

Reality returned with a sudden flush of panic. But it wouldn't be that way. Lobo would find out Quince was after him, and he wouldn't waste time trying to meet him face to face.

No, she couldn't let that happen.

Blanche responded, "I didn't come here for help. I just came to say goodbye."

"Where are you going?"

"To the next town . . . or the next."

"He'll find you if he wants to, you know."

"No, he won't. I'm sure he won't."

"Blanche . . ."

Suddenly trembling, Blanche repeated, "I just came to say goodbye. That's all—just to say goodbye."

She saw Quince's hesitation. She hoped he couldn't read her feelings in her eyes, how much she wished he would ask her to stay only because he couldn't bear to let her go.

A sad smile touching his lips, Quince said, "None of this makes any sense, you know. You don't know where you're going, yet you're sure this fellow won't follow you."

"Maybe it doesn't, but at least I'll be away from here."

"Do you think you'll be that much better off wherever you're going than you are in Diablo?"

"No . . . yes . . . I mean . . ." Blanche took a shaky breath. "All I know is that I have to leave. He'll come after me if I don't."

"If you tell me—"

"I can't tell you! I won't!"

Taking a long moment to search her flushed face, appearing to accept her resolve at last, Quince asked, "How much money do you have to travel on?"

"I have enough."

"Blanche—"

"I have enough to get where I'm going."

"You only have the price of your ticket, don't you?"

"I sold my father's gun. I got more than enough to get me to the next town."

Quince reached into his pocket.

"I didn't come here for money."

"I know you didn't."

Frowning when Blanche refused to accept the roll of bills he tried to put in her hand, he said, "You're too good for the life you're leading, Blanche. You need a chance to show some fella what you're really worth, and you can't do that while you're wondering where your next meal is coming from. I want you to take this money."

"No."

"Take it. It won't make you rich, but it'll buy you time to find the right place to settle in." His voice dropping a note lower, he whispered, "Blanche, let me do this for you. I don't want to think about you having to please a man for money when you should be finding the right man to love. I want to know that good things can happen for you. I want to be able to get a letter from you someday telling me you have a good life and you're happy."

The thickness in her throat increasing, Blanche rasped, "You want all that for me?"

"You're damned right I do."

"No matter how long it takes to happen?"

"No matter how long it takes."

Blanche searched Quince's eyes. He meant what he said—every word of it.

Opening her fist, Blanche allowed Quince to place the roll of bills in her palm. She held his gaze as he closed her fingers around the money and said, "I want you to be happy, Blanche. Will you do that . . . for me?"

Quince slipped his arms around her when she was unable to respond, and Blanche closed her eyes. Her daydream—*this very important part*—had come true.

Drawing back from Quince abruptly, she whispered, "I'll write to you. I promise."

Tears she had stringently withheld streaming

down her cheeks, Blanche ran back down the hallway minutes later.

Tears, because she loved him.

Tears, because she hadn't really wanted to say
goodbye.

Chapter Fifteen

Hurriedly dressing as the silver light of dawn shone through her bedroom window, Glory pulled on her boots. She ignored her reflection in the washstand mirror as she left her room, and with a few words to Pete strode out the front door toward the corral. She glanced at the charred remains of the barn in passing but pushed back the incapacitating ache that had numbed her.

She had spent a difficult night as images, both warm and horrific, inundated her mind. She had remembered the intensity of Quince's gaze as she had lain in his arms, as he had lowered his mouth to hers with whispered words of love. She had seen her father lying beside the burning barn, then Quince's pained expression as he had attempted to take her into his arms to share her grief. She had experienced again a guilt so intense that her only defense against it was to shut herself off from the man who hoped to console her.

She wasn't sure how her priorities had become so confused, but sometime during the middle of the night she had realized that her commitment to her father's word could not end with his death, and that to abandon it would be to dishonor everything her father stood for. To abandon it would also be to abandon Quince, whose only offense had been to love her.

Jan's words rang in Glory's mind as she mounted. She had placed the contract in danger. By doing that, she had placed the Half-Moon and the Diamond C in danger as well. Quince would not have stayed the night in town to await a telegram from Fort Griffin if the situation wasn't critical. She hoped she wasn't too late.

Glory spurred her mount into motion.

Blanche scanned the early morning street cautiously, then stepped out onto the boardwalk and started toward the stagecoach office at the far end of town. She did not truly believe Lobo would be lying in wait for her at such an early hour. He was probably lying somewhere in a numbed stupor with an empty bottle beside him.

Blanche took a firmer grip on her bag and increased her pace. Too frightened to tell anyone she was leaving for fear Lobo would find out, she had left notes for O'Malley and for Madge and the other saloon girls. She hoped they would forgive her.

The stage pulled into view as she approached,

and Blanche walked faster, her heart pounding. She couldn't afford to miss it.

She was seated inside the bulky conveyance minutes later, across from a drummer who was snoring softly, when the driver started the team forward with a crack of the whip that reverberated eerily in the early morning silence. Her throat tight, she glanced out the window as Diablo began fading into the distance, and her heart stopped at the sight of Quince standing in the shadows of the hotel doorway. Bittersweet joy twisted tightly inside her. He had been watching, on guard to ensure she would be safely on her way to her new life. He cared about her. He truly did. She would carry that truth with her wherever she went. It would make her strong.

A new life.

She had made him that promise, and she would keep it.

Blanche raised her hand to wave a last farewell. She thought she saw Quince tip his hat to her, but she couldn't be sure through the haze of her tears.

Quince read the telegram in his hand a second time. Determined that Blanche would leave Diablo safely, he had been up at dawn. He had watched as she made her way cautiously up the street. Her fear had been obvious, but knowing it had taken all her courage to make the decision to leave, he had not dared to approach her.

He had watched with mixed emotions as the stage jerked into motion and Blanche was finally on her way. He had been somehow glad when she spotted him out the window at the last moment and waved. He had tipped his hat in a fond salute, putting a stamp of finality on a brief, bittersweet friendship that he knew he would always remember.

Would she write?

He hoped so.

The sun had barely risen before he had crossed the street and walked to the telegraph office, but the telegrapher had been waiting for him with the message he now read.

"EXTENSION GRANTED."

Jonah had responded in record time. He had never been a man to waste words.

Determination tightened Quince's lips. With this message in hand, he'd talk to Glory today, and he wouldn't leave until she listened.

He'd tell her he loved her. He'd tell her that when all was said and done, they were meant to be together, whether fighting a loan deadline, running mustangs, or just loving each other. He'd tell her she'd had enough time to come to terms with her grief alone, that she needed someone to share it with. He'd make her understand he was that man, that he'd share her grief willingly and lovingly, just as they'd share the rest of their lives.

Quince mounted up and spurred his horse into motion with that thought firmly fixed in his mind.

The fury inside him building, Lobo watched as Quince Hunter left the telegraph office and mounted up. He was leaving town.

Lobo scrambled out of the alleyway beside the

boardinghouse and ran toward the shadows where he had left his horse secured. He had entered town just past dawn, making sure to avoid the main street so he would not alert anyone to his arrival, but his caution had been his downfall. He had reached the Lone Star in time to see Blanche walking rapidly up the street. Movement in the hotel doorway had alerted him to Quince Hunter's presence there, and he had known immediately it was a trap—intended for him.

He had watched with mounting rage as Blanche boarded the stage, the stage departed, and Hunter tipped his hat in Blanche's direction. He had determined at that moment that whatever their plans to meet in the future, they were in for disappointment. Hunter would have no future past the moment when he caught up with him on the trail home and ended his life with a well-placed bullet.

With Hunter out of the way, Blanche would be fair game.

Anticipation mounting, Lobo followed Quince out of town.

Edmund stood unsteadily beside the trickling stream. His head ached and his innards were lurching. Aggravating him more than his ills was the reality that Kane was back in the cabin snoring peacefully while he had spent the time since awakening purging his stomach.

Edmund attempted to take a deep breath. It stood to reason, he supposed, that a man who enjoyed his work as much as Kane did would have a stomach of iron—while he, accustomed to a more refined way of life, would discover his body rebelled at excess.

A hard smile creased Edmund's lips despite his discomfort. There was a type of intimate excess that his body tolerated quite well, however. He would make sure his celebrations in the future were turned in that direction. At present, it was time to go home to Diablo, where his temporary discomfort would be alleviated by the bright future at hand.

Resolved despite his uncertain step, Edmund turned toward his horse.

Quince rode at a carefully calculated pace. He turned a bend, then urged his mount up a gradual slope that gave him a vantage point over the trail behind him. Concealed in a stand of trees when he reached the apex, he frowned when his suspicions were confirmed. He was being followed.

He squinted into the distance to identify the horseman. The rider's long, sandy-colored hair and broad, powerfully built frame were as easily identifiable as the markings on the bay he rode. He had thought he had discouraged Lobo's attentions to Blanche that first day in the Lone Star, but it appeared he had just made matters worse for her.

Accepting that accountability, he also acknowledged the reality that he had made himself an enemy whose intentions were deadly.

His attention was caught by a rider advancing toward town from the opposite direction, and Quince felt his stomach lurch. The brilliant color of the rider's hair blazed gloriously in the light of the morning sun.

It couldn't be!

But it was.

Taking a moment to glance back at Lobo's steadily advancing figure, aware that Lobo would realize he had been seen when Quince wasn't visible on the trail ahead, that he'd react with violence when he discovered the tables had been turned on him, Quince spurred his horse down the incline. He had to get Glory out of the line of fire before Lobo rounded the bend and all hell broke loose.

Reaching level ground again, Quince rode at a gallop toward Glory as she drew nearer. He was unaware of the moment when Lobo turned the bend and saw him riding furiously toward her. He did not see Lobo pull his rifle from its sheath and aim it in his direction.

His gaze was fixed on Glory. Quince did not even hear the bark of gunfire that sounded simultaneously with the shattering burst of pain that exploded in his back, knocking him from his horse into a spiraling darkness that abruptly consumed him.

Glory had drawn her mount up short when Quince appeared unexpectedly on the trail ahead. She'd gasped with shock as a shot rang out, abruptly halting his frenzied race toward her. As if in slow motion, she saw his powerful frame shudder with the impact of the bullet that struck him, then saw him tumble from the saddle to strike

the ground and disappear from sight in the brush
beside the trail.

Spurring her mount toward Quince, Glory saw
a rider advancing from the opposite direction. He
raised his rifle toward her. She turned her horse
off the trail just as the bark of gunfire sounded
almost simultaneously with the snap of a bullet
striking a shrub beside her.

Plunging headlong into the brush, Glory remained pinned there as bullets continued striking
the ground around her. She reached for the gun at
her hip, then realized that the gunman had disappeared from view.

Helpless against the assault of the unknown
gunman and horrified that she was unable to go
to Quince, Glory realized with a stunning jolt of
regret that in taking so long to come to her senses,
she might have lost forever the chance to tell
Quince she loved him.

Dismounting, Lobo moved steadily through the
heavy brush alongside the trail where Quince Hunter had fallen. Cautious, he realized that Hunter
had been aware he was being followed and had
been waiting for him to turn the bend in the trail.
Had it not been for the unexpected appearance of
the Townsend woman, it could have been he instead of Hunter who was now lying somewhere in
the brush. He also knew that if he did not find
Hunter and finish him off now, Hunter could one
day finish him off instead.

Satisfied that the Townsend woman had been
terrified into immobility by his gunfire, that he

need only send a few sporadic bullets in her direction to keep her pinned until he was ready to take care of her as well, Lobo continued moving warily forward.

He was momentarily amused at the way things had turned out. Blanche was riding toward an unknown destination where she probably expected Hunter to join her—but he'd be the one to join her instead. She wouldn't be hard to find. A woman like her, traveling alone, would be easily remembered. He could almost see her shock turning to terror when he caught up with her. He hadn't decided exactly what he would do when he did. There were so many uses for a woman like Blanche.

Dismissing that thought as he drew closer to the place where Hunter had fallen, Lobo moved more carefully than before. Hunter was smart, and if he wasn't already dead—

Lobo halted abruptly as Hunter's motionless body came into view. He was lying on his side, the circular bloodstain on his back clearly visible, as was a gash on his forehead where he had obviously struck a rock when he fell. His eyes were closed and his breathing was shallow. He wasn't dead yet—but he soon would be.

Enjoying his moment of victory, Lobo stood over Hunter and eyed him contemptuously. He wasn't so big and quick with his gun now.

Lobo prodded Hunter with his foot. Leveling his rifle at him when he did not react, Lobo was somehow disappointed. He would so much rather have seen a moment of fear in Hunter's eyes before he fired the last bullet, but he supposed he'd have to be satisfied that—

"Drop your rifle!"

Lobo's head twisted in the direction of a woman's shouted command from somewhere in the nearby brush.

"You heard me! Drop it!"

His lips pulled into a sneer. He had underestimated that Townsend woman . . . and now she had him.

Lobo's rifle dropped to the ground, and Glory stepped out into the open. She glanced at Quince, noting the bloodstain on his back and his shallow breathing. She needed to get him to town, to Charlie Herbert, who had probably removed more bullets than Doc Gibbs ever had, and who had probably saved as many lives as well. She needed to know that Quince would survive so she could say all the things she had been too confused and uncertain to say before—that she loved him, that she'd spend the rest of her life working beside him, proving that with her declaration of love came the promise to be his lover, his wife, the mother of his children, and a partner who would share equally everything that accompanied a lifelong love. She wanted to tell him—

Glory did not see Lobo's hand move to the gun belt at his hip until she heard the slap of leather and saw the gun in his hand.

A shot rang out, and she gasped.

Numbed, momentarily motionless, Glory felt nothing as Lobo stared at her blankly for long seconds before slumping slowly to the ground with a bloodstain rapidly widening on his chest. She looked back at Quince in time to see a smoking gun slipping from his grip.

At Quince's side in a moment, Glory slid her arms around him. Deaf to all but the pounding of her heart, she pressed her lips lightly to his with whispered words of love. She did not hear the approach of the Diamond C wranglers who slid their horses to a halt beside her. Unaware of them as they dismounted and checked Lobo's lifeless figure, then moved toward her, she felt only a surge of love when Quince's weak gaze met hers.

Holding him tightly, Glory whispered from the bottom of her heart that she was with him now, where she would always be.

Chapter Sixteen

"You're sure you should do this?"

"Glory, we both know what the best medicine is for what ails me."

"No, I mean . . ." A smile broke across Glory's lips as she lay beside Quince in the wide bed that was now their own. As naked as he underneath the light coverlet, she turned toward him, her warm breast brushing his chest as she scrutinized his face. He had grown thinner during his recuperation. Strangely enough, the weight loss had had little effect on the relentless power he exuded as they professed their vows in Diablo's small church—which, at Quince's insistence, had come about as soon as he had been able to stand.

The Hunter clan had been present at the nuptials: Brent and Crystal smiling, Abby tearfully joyous, and Jack silent and sober. Only Matt had been missing, an absence Glory knew Quince felt keenly. The Half-Moon and Diamond C wranglers had attended proudly in their Sunday best, with a few townsfolk making up the rest of the invited.

She remembered the moment shortly afterward when Jack, solemn and sober, drew her aside and thanked her for saving Quince's life. With all sincerity, he wished them both true happiness. She wondered if she would ever be able to convince Quince that his father wasn't really as cold-hearted as his sons believed him to be.

At Jack's insistence, Edmund had been present at the wedding. He had stood apart from the general festivities with the excuse of extended mourning, but Glory knew better. Although he would be the first to deny it, she guessed that the banker had not been pleased that Quince's near escape from death had spurred the Half-Moon and Diamond C wranglers to new effort—the first delivery of mustangs to Fort Griffin had been made with a week to spare.

However, she had a far greater reason to be thankful to Jan and the other Diamond C wranglers. Concerned when she left the Diamond C with only a few words to Pete on the morning Quince was shot, they had ridden out after her. Without them, she was certain she would not have been able to get Quince into town in time to save his life.

As for Quince and herself, they had taken up residence together on the Diamond C immediately after their wedding. Jan and the men had accepted Quince easily. They understood as well as she that his deep commitment to the Half-Moon would never end, even though the Diamond C had become his home.

Then there was the effect the shooting had had on Quince himself. Glory closed her eyes as his lips trailed her jaw, her neck, the line of her shoulder. She gasped softly as he kissed her breasts, then suckled them gently. She sighed as he stroked her flesh with his callused hands, sending a quiver down her spine. She accommodated his muscular weight as he shifted it full upon her, then gazed down soberly into her face and probed her briefly before entering her in a quick, efficient thrust.

He murmured erotically, "The best medicine a man can have."

As he began a subtle movement inside her, she rasped, "But you're still recuperating, and in light of last night—"

"Hummm . . . last night."

They had made love for hours. She had given as freely as she had received, experiencing limitless satisfaction in giving pleasure that had left him softly groaning.

She responded, "I just thought—"

"You just thought it was your turn now?"

His smile fading, Quince whispered against her lips, "I was beginning to believe this time would never come for us."

Not of a mind to hold anything back from him, Glory responded, "I know now, Quince, that I somehow sensed I would love you that first day."

"When you were so angry with me."

"Yes."

"When you chased me away."

"Yes."

"When you were horrified to see me again at the Half-Moon."

"I wasn't horrified."

"The truth, Glory."

"I didn't want to surrender to my feelings."

"Why?"

Glory said sincerely, "I didn't know it was possible to love anyone the way I love you. I didn't think it was possible for someone to share my thoughts and dreams and want to make them come true just because he loved me." Pausing, she whispered, "I resented your strength because I thought it made me appear weak, and because I thought I'd end up standing in your shadow if I stood beside you. I didn't know then that the reverse would be true, that only by accepting your love and loving you back would I be all I could be."

"There was never any doubt for me." Quince's response was spontaneous and earnest. "You planted yourself deep inside me the first moment I saw you. You dominated my thoughts until I knew the only way forward for us was to be together." He hesitated, then said, "But it's not over yet, darlin'. There are hard times still ahead of us here and at the Half-Moon, and a lot of questions that still need to be answered."

"We'll face them together."

Quince's voice dropped to a passionate rasp. "I love you, Glory."

He found the intimate nub of her pleasure and stroked it sensuously. She grew breathless under his touch, soaring high in clouds of ecstasy. She was teetering at the edge of culmination with myriad breathtaking colors rioting in her mind. She clutched him close as he moved swiftly inside her, and mutual gratification came in a quick, ecstatic rush, stealing their breath and leaving them wordless, limp and satiated in each other's arms.

Waiting until her breathing was normal, Quince whispered, "We were meant for each other, Glory."

She nodded.

"Fire and ice. A stubborn redhead and a hard-eyed renegade."

He was right. She knew that now.

So very right.

Epilogue

Edmund paced through the shifting shadows of his parlor in the dark hours before dawn. The shadows suited him. They had helped him formulate plans that were equally dark.

Frustrated by the events of the past few months, he had not been sleeping well. Strangely, he had believed that with Iona's death, his life would take a turn for the better, but her dying had somehow been the catalyst for a reversal of fortune he hadn't anticipated.

He had been elated when he'd heard Quince Hunter had been shot, believing one of the greatest deterrents to the success of his grand plan had been eliminated—*but the bastard had survived.* Not only had he survived, he had married the red-haired witch from the Diamond C, thereby strengthening both his position and hers.

He consoled himself, however, that the situation was temporary. He had plans for the loving couple that they didn't anticipate.

Then there was Abby. Deprived of the opportunity for contact with her since Iona's death, he had felt her slipping further and further away, while his carnal desire for her grew deeper and hotter with each passing day. But he'd have her yet. It was merely a matter of time before the surprises he had in store for the Hunter clan brought her begging.

Only Jack had remained a slave to his machinations. Jack still confided in him . . . trusted him. He would use the drunken fool well.

Edmund halted his pacing and pulled himself erect. Enough time had elapsed for a sense of complacency to have settled over the Half-Moon, and Kane was waiting in the wings to do his bidding. He would now put his plans into action.

Edmund looked out the window at the ragged shards of dawn slicing across the night sky. His plans were like those shards. They'd cut fast and deep into the Hunter clan, consuming it as efficiently as daylight devoured the night.

He would be victorious in the end.

Yes, it was just a matter of time.

Prologue

Texas, 1870

The wind was cold and damp as it whipped Abigail Hunter's tangled hair across her face. Her body was still and her small hands were twisted into tight knots at her sides until her brother Brent took them and held them firmly in his strong grip.

For eight-year-old Abby the last two days had been confusing and devastating. Tragedy had struck their family at its very heart, and she wondered how it was possible to hurt so badly and still live.

Through blinding tears she stared at the simple pine box that held her mother's remains. Since there were no flowers to be had this time of year, Abby had woven her pink hair ribbons through a branch of live oak, and Quince had placed it on the coffin for her—a pitiful tribute to a woman who had so dearly loved flowers.

The men who worked for the Half-Moon Ranch were gathered near the family, their hats removed, their heads bowed. The foreman, Buck, met Abby's eyes sadly and nodded slightly. Charley Herbert, the barber and undertaker, was there, standing off to the side, but still a grim reminder to the young girl that he was the one who had brought the coffin to the ranch.

Reverend Crawford was praising Beth Hunter's virtues. Although the preacher was sincere, his words meant nothing to Abby. He didn't know how gentle their mother's touch had been, or how it had comforted Abby through so many illnesses— he couldn't tell the mourners how soothing her mother's voice had been, or the patience she had used when Abby had needed guidance—and Abby was always needing guidance. All that was her mother was gone forever, stilled by death's hateful hand.

The reverend was assuring Abby and her brothers that their mother had gone to a better place. But wouldn't it have been better for all of them if she had remained with the family on the Half Moon Ranch? So many dilemmas tore at her mind, and questions nagged at her that only her mother could answer.

The young girl glanced, in turn, at each of her three older brothers and saw the same grief she felt reflected in their eyes. Brent was now gripping her hand so tightly it hurt, but the discomfort helped her think about something other than the anguish that tore at her heart. She watched her brother Quince's hand tremble from the effort he was making not to cry. Her brother Matt stood alone, stoic and silent, solitary in his grief. She knew he had cut himself off from the rest of them so he could better control his sorrow.

Conspicuously absent from the grieving family grouped around the grave site was Abby's father, Jack Hunter. Abby glanced slowly up at Brent to find him watching her with concern. At twenty, he was the eldest, and it would probably fall to him to keep the family together. A sob escaped her throat, and Quince touched her on the shoulder and patted it several times. She suddenly felt her stomach churn; she was sickened and shaken to the very core of her being.

It was difficult to understand the horror of what her father had done. How could he shoot and kill her mother, when to Abby's knowledge he had never even raised his hand to her in anger? Brent said it was because he was drunk, but Abby couldn't imagine that drinking would make a man want to kill someone he loved.

Reluctantly her eyes strayed back to the coffin. Then she glanced at the crowd of people that stretched all the way to the road. Matt had earlier declared that they had come only to stare at a murderer's family, but Abby was sure they were there to pay their respects to her mother.

She met Iona Montgomery's gaze and saw the sadness and compassion in the older woman's eyes. Mrs. Montgomery had been her mother's best friend, and it was comforting to have her there. Her daughter, Juliana, gave Abby a sympathetic smile, and Abby managed to smile slightly in return. Then her attention was drawn to Edmund Montgomery, Juliana's stepfather, who owned the only bank in Diablo. He nodded at Abby and held her gaze for a moment. She stepped closer to Brent and lowered her head. She always felt uneasy around Mr. Montgomery, even though she didn't understand why.

The reverend had finished the eulogy and was talking in a quiet voice with Brent, but Abby wasn't listening. She was watching their friends and neighbors walking to their buggies, some of them already leaving without speaking to the family. The wind kicked up more, and Abby shivered.

Matt knelt down beside her and wrapped his coat about her shoulders, then held her close to his body to get her warm. Finally he took one of Abby's hands, and Quince took the other.

Abby was unaware that people were whispering and gossiping about her family, their heads nodding, their mouths pursed in disapproval. She was too young to realize that, in the years to come, the cruelty of those same people would surround her and exclude her from their inner circles. She saw only the three men with shovels standing off to the side, and she shuddered with dread as Charley Herbert gave them instructions. She shook her head in horror—those men were going to lower her mother's body into the ground and cover it with dirt!

She felt desperate. Jerking free of her brothers, she ran toward her mother's coffin, determined to stop the men. It was Quince who caught up with her and went down on his knees, holding her close.

"You have to let her go, darlin'." There were tears in his green eyes, eyes that looked so much like their mother's. "We all have to let her go."

Quince held her, speaking comforting words until she stopped trembling. Finally she wiped her tears on the back of her hand, and he led her back to the others.

Matt pulled her aside and bent down to her. "Abby, I won't be going back to the house with you. I've already told Brent and Quince, and I wanted you to know, too—I'm leaving. It'll be a long time before I come back."

Her eyes filled with fresh tears. "Mama's gone, and now you're leaving, too? Please don't go away!"

There was incredible sadness in his eyes. "You are so young and may not understand this, but if I stay, I'll probably do something I'll regret."

She touched his face, then slid her arms around his neck. "I understand better than you think— you're afraid you'd do something to hurt Papa for what he did to Mama, aren't you?"

He hesitated for a moment, then nodded.

"Will you write me?"

He eased her arms from around his neck and stood. "I'm not much for letters, Abby."

When she would have given him back his coat, he shook his head and buttoned it at her throat. "Take care of yourself, sweetheart. I know it seems like your world has turned upside down. Time passes, and wounds heal. Trust me."

She watched Matt walk away and mount his horse; she didn't take her gaze off him until he disappeared from sight. She already missed him, and she wondered if she would ever see him again.

Brent put his arm around Abby while Quince walked beside them toward the ranch house, their grief too deep, their hurt too new to put into words. The day was gray, and her heart was empty . . . cold . . . broken.

Her attention was drawn to the ranch hands ambling toward the house. The Montgomerys and a few other friends walked behind them. She wiped her eyes and closed them, but tears still seeped between her lids and ran down her cheeks. She wanted the comfort that only her mother could give her.

Matt had told her to give it time, but time would not bring her mother back, and time would never wash the blood off her father's hands.

HAWK

ELAINE BARBIERI

"How can you stand to let him touch you, Eden? He's an *injun!*" Young and idealistic, Eden believes passion will overcome the obstacle of her lover's Kiowa heritage; instead, the hatred and prejudice of two cultures at war force them apart. "Her arms cling to you and your heart answers, but the woman will never by yours." Such is the shaman's prediction about the beautiful girl he once adored, but Iron Hawk refuses to believe it. Eden's betrayal might have sent him to the white man's jail, but her smooth, pale body will still be his. A hardened warrior now, he believes her capture will satisfy his need for revenge; instead, her love will heal their hearts and bring a lasting peace to their people.

___4646-6 $5.99 US/$6.99 CAN

EAGLE
Elaine Barbieri

Cheyenne leader Gold Eagle's chiseled face and powerfully muscled body belie his wounded heart. Yet in an ambitious newspaperwoman named Mallory Tompkins, he finds the one thing that can soothe his tormented soul. But where fate has united them, deceit will destroy their bliss, unless they can forever join their love, their souls, their destinies.

___4469-2 $5.99 US/$6.99 CAN

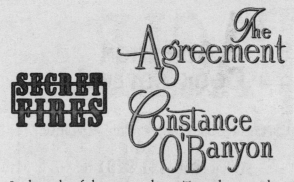

The Agreement

SECRET FIRES

Constance O'Banyon

In the midst of the vast, windswept Texas plains stands a ranch wrested from the wilderness with blood, sweat and tears. It is the shining legacy of Thomas McBride to his five living heirs. But along with the fertile acres and herds of cattle, each will inherit a history of scandal, lies and hidden lust that threatens to burn out of control.

Lauren McBride left the Circle M as a confused, lonely girl of fifteen. She returns a woman—beautiful, confident, certain of her own mind. And the last thing she will tolerate is a marriage of convenience, arranged by her pa to right past wrongs. Garret Lassiter broke her heart once before. Now only a declaration of everlasting love will convince her to become his bride.

___4878-7 $5.99 US/$6.99 CAN

Dorchester Publishing Co., Inc.
P.O. Box 6640
Wayne, PA 19087-8640

Please add $2.50 for shipping and handling for the first book and $.75 for each book thereafter. NY, NYC, and PA residents, please add appropriate sales tax. No cash, stamps, or C.O.D.s. All orders shipped within 6 weeks via postal service book rate. Canadian orders require $2.50 extra postage and must be paid in U.S. dollars through a U.S. banking facility.

Name_____
Address_____
City_____ State_____ Zip_____
I have enclosed $_____ in payment for the checked book(s).
Payment __must__ accompany all orders. ❏ Please send a free catalog.
CHECK OUT OUR WEBSITE! www.dorchesterpub.com